Pride Publishing books by T. Strange

Bound to the Spirits
Rattling Chains
Cold Blood
Laid to Rest

Bound to the Spirit

LAID TO REST

T. STRANGE

Laid to Rest
ISBN # 978-1-80250-502-3
©Copyright T. Strange 2022
Cover Art by Erin Dameron-Hill ©Copyright December 2022
Interior text design by Claire Siemaszkiewicz
Pride Publishing

LAID TO REST

Dedication

As always, for M.

Chapter One

"Where do you want this box?" Morgan asked.

"Um, anywhere over there is fine." Harlan gestured vaguely in the direction of the kitchen. He had no idea what was in the particular box they were holding, but he was feeling too flustered to check. He knew his 'system' — or, rather, complete *lack* of one — would bite him on the ass later when he was actually trying to unpack and organize, but putting it off felt better than dealing with it at the moment.

"You know you don't have to help with this part, right?" he told them. "Moving *my* stuff, not the business stuff? I mean, you didn't really have to help with that, either. It's not part of your job description — "

"Please. The 'business stuff' was like three boxes. And I write my own damn job description — unless you've come up with a written statement of what my duties entail?"

Wide-eyed, Harlan shook his head.

"Yeah, I didn't think so," they laughed, setting the box down on a pile.

Charles swooped in and glanced at it. "Mm-m, that's a bathroom one."

Morgan frowned at him.

"I'll take it," he assured them.

Harlan sighed. Of course Charles could keep track of everything.

Harlan knew it was stupid to move his business out of his apartment — all three boxes of it, as Morgan had just pointed out — immediately followed by moving in with Charles. But that was how the timing had worked out with renting an office and Charles' lease on his old apartment running out. Technically there was no hurry on his end — Harlan's apartment was his as long as he wanted it — but it had seemed silly for Charles to move all his things and get them all unpacked, only for Harlan to dump a fresh pile of boxes on some nebulous future date. Not that Harlan had that many personal possessions... At least he'd *thought* he didn't, but there had been a surprising amount to pack up and load into the truck Charles had borrowed from a friend.

"Hey, does that mean I didn't have to help, either?" Hamilton — now Harlan's business partner at Laid to Rest Investigations — laughed.

Shit. Harlan swallowed hard. "Of course not. I'm sorry —"

"Hey." Hamilton clapped him on the shoulder. "Sorry... I was just kidding. I'm happy to help you two out. Matthew would have been here, too, but he had to work." He hurried back outside, probably to grab more boxes.

"Are you okay?" Charles asked, setting down the plastic tote he was holding.

Harlan noticed that Morgan was also giving him a concerned look. "Yeah. Sorry. I'm fine. It's just—a lot."

Charles nodded, giving Harlan a quick hug. "I know. But the end is in sight!" He turned in a slow circle, taking in the boxes covering every horizontal surface. "Well, the end of *moving*. Then it'll just be unpacking—and we can go at our own pace."

Yeah. As long as we don't want to sit on the couch or find anything, Harlan thought.

He just nodded at Charles, doing his best to smile.

"I think it's just a few more, then we can go for beer and pizza."

Harlan nodded again. He turned to leave the apartment to at least get some air and pretend to be useful by carrying something back inside, but his path was blocked by Hamilton, who was carrying a stack of boxes.

"Did I hear beer and pizza?"

"You did," Charles agreed. "As soon as the truck is empty."

Hamilton set the stack haphazardly by the door. "Then it's beer and pizza o'clock. These are the last boxes."

Charles whooped, grinning at the room. "Good work, team! I thought it would take us at least a few more hours."

Morgan snorted. "It would have gone a lot more quickly if you didn't have *so many* BDSM toys."

"Ha. Just be glad Harlan hasn't really started collecting his own yet or there'd be twice as many."

Harlan found that difficult to imagine. Charles already had one of every kind of whip, flogger, paddle and cane imaginable—if not multiples.

Charles mimed dusting his hands together. "All right, if that's it, let's get out of here. Why don't you just take one car?"

Harlan's stomach sank. He was already feeling really peopled out — which was sad, because these were the people he was closest to in the world — and there would only be *more* people at the restaurant. He'd been looking forward to at least driving over with just Charles.

"You guys go ahead. I'm gonna drop the truck off. Phil can give me a ride, and I'll meet you there. Harlan, you can order for me, okay?" Charles gave his shoulder a gentle squeeze.

Great. Now he wouldn't even have Charles in the car with him? And he would have to order not only for himself but also for Charles as well? Usually, it was the other way around. It made him feel like an immature jerk and a hot mess, but their system worked for them.

"Don't worry." Charles leaned over to kiss his cheek. "I wrote my order down for you."

Well, that's something, anyway.

Charles did that magical thing Harlan still couldn't figure out how to do that sent something directly from his phone to Harlan's.

"We can take my car," Morgan offered. "Hamilton's smells like thirty-year-old Tim Hortons."

Harlan wrinkled his nose. They weren't wrong.

Hamilton laughed. "Hey, I've spilled lots of *other* kinds of coffee in there! I don't think the stuff at the precinct is even 'no name'. It's…somehow even sketchier than that. It's probably not even real coffee."

"Yeah, you probably shouldn't be drinking that." Morgan shook their head, laughing.

Harlan found himself swept out the door and into Morgan's car. He barely had a chance to wave goodbye to Charles before he was gone.

* * * *

Morgan and Hamilton put in their beer and pizza orders almost as soon as they sat down at the restaurant, leaving Harlan frantically flipping through the menu. He chose the first thing that sounded edible and didn't have too many weird specialty ingredients. He ordered Charles' pizza, and he was about to tell the waiter what beer Charles wanted, but Hamilton shook his head.

"Nah, wait till he gets here so it'll still be cold."

Harlan nodded, feeling his cheeks flush a little. He was relieved when their drinks came. It meant that he had something to do with his hands, and he didn't have to talk.

He'd ordered Pepsi. He didn't drink alcohol — or only rarely. It tended to mess up his mood the next day.

He downed his first drink quickly and accepted a refill when the waiter came around again. Having that much caffeine so late in the day would probably fuck with his sleep, but he didn't want to switch to Sprite or something else. With a dark-coloured drink, he could at least pretend he was drinking beer like the others.

For the most part, Morgan and Hamilton were happy just talking to each other and leaving Harlan alone, which Harlan appreciated. Even knowing that they *knew* him and wouldn't expect him to carry the conversation, he still worked himself up sometimes.

He slowly relaxed. Luckily their booth was in a quiet corner, away from other groups, so he didn't feel *completely* overwhelmed.

The pizza arrived before Charles did. Harlan wondered if they should wait for him, but the other two started eating right away. Of course, they'd been helping move boxes for hours, whereas Harlan felt like he'd just sort of drifted around getting in the way.

He was starting to worry that Charles' food would get cold when Charles slid into the booth beside him, giving him a quick peck on the cheek before grabbing a slice and inhaling it.

Of course Charles' mouth was full when the waiter came around for his drink order.

Harlan fumbled in his pocket for his phone, which he'd put away because he knew it was rude to have it out while socializing. Though, again, he didn't think Hamilton and Morgan would really care.

Hamilton waved a hand at him. "It's okay. I've got this." He ordered for Charles, glancing at him for confirmation.

Harlan wasn't sure if it was even the right thing, but he gave up trying to get his phone.

Charles nodded, his lips slightly parted as he tried to swallow the too-hot sauce and cheese.

Harlan groaned inwardly. Hamilton could remember what his boyfriend liked to drink, and he couldn't?

Everyone else wolfed down their food while Harlan picked at his pizza and drank soda after soda.

"Oof, I'm stuffed." Charles leaned back with a groan, his hands folded on his stomach. Making sure Harlan was looking at him, he cocked his head in the direction of the door—his silent way of asking if Harlan wanted to leave.

Harlan nodded, moving his head as little as possible and hoping the others wouldn't pick up on their little exchange. That would have felt rude. He appreciated that Charles had come up with this little system for them. Again, he was pretty sure Hamilton and Morgan wouldn't actually mind, but this way he didn't have to say it himself. And he really did want to go home. Well, back to the box-choked apartment. *Ugh.*

At least he didn't have to work the next day. Laid to Rest didn't have any open cases, which was great for having time to move and unpack but not so great for his wallet or peace of mind.

What was I thinking, trying to start my own business?

* * * *

"Knock knock!" Benjamin Xun, one of the two remaining Toronto police mediums, stepped into the tiny Laid to Rest office, his hand raised as though he were about to knock. The door was open. The office got really hot and stuffy with both Harlan and Hamilton inside, and the solitary window didn't open.

Hamilton grinned at him. "Hey, Benjamin. It's been a while." Benjamin had visited them when they had first opened a few weeks earlier, but they hadn't seen him since — though Harlan had called him once for advice about dealing with a ghost. No. Not 'dealing with'. That wasn't what Laid to Rest was about. *Helping* a ghost. "Oh, *please* tell me you have a case for us."

Harlan leaned forward. He was glad Hamilton had said it, because he'd sure as fuck been thinking it.

Benjamin shook his head. "No, sorry, guys. I just wanted to drop off some 'congratulations on starting your new business' presents. I know it's a little late, but they were on back-order and… Anyway…here." He set four gift bags down on Hamilton's desk, which was closest to the door. "They're for you two, Morgan and Charles. Charles told me what kind of phones you all have." He cleared his throat, looking away from Harlan. "They're, uh, from Beth, too, but she wasn't sure if you'd want to see her."

She was right, but Harlan didn't say it out loud. "You'll have to, um, thank her for us."

Hamilton pounced on the pile of presents and started rooting around in one of them. He frowned as he held up its contents. "Oh, great. A weird-looking phone case and a flashlight. Thanks."

Harlan got up to take a closer look. "Really? Thank you!" He picked up the bag with his name on it and held it against his chest.

Hamilton snorted. "Jeez, kid, if I'd known you were that hard-up for a phone case, I would've gotten you one."

Harlan shook his head. "No, these are special."

Nodding, Benjamin pulled out his phone, which was already in a similar case. "The mesh on the back keeps ghosts from draining the battery, and" — he plucked the package out of Hamilton's hands — "it also comes with a warded screen protector so they can't get in that way, either. The flashlight is protected by the same mesh."

Hamilton whistled, leaning back in his chair with his hands laced behind his head. "Wow. Those must've cost you a pretty penny."

Harlan gulped. He hadn't realized that a warded screen protector was part of the case. Warding was expensive. "You really shouldn't have." He put the bag back on Hamilton's desk.

"Hey, don't worry about it. I was there when you learned how much it sucks for a ghost to drain your phone and light. I — *we're* — happy to help."

"Thank you so much." Realizing he should probably say something more and that he actually knew very little about Benjamin outside of their shared mediumship work, Harlan asked, "How are things going for you two?"

Benjamin let out a soft huff of laughter. "Well, I won't lie. It has been busy without you and Leo." Leo had been the Toronto Police Service's fourth medium until she'd lost her abilities six months earlier. "But we're managing." He smiled at Harlan. "It *has* helped that you guys are handling the less serious cases and we can just concentrate on murders."

Harlan shuddered. He definitely did *not* miss that part of being a police medium. Most of the ghosts he'd dealt with through Laid to Rest had died of natural causes or accidents. They tended to look more intact than murder victims, even if their deaths had been fairly gruesome.

"Anyway"—Benjamin patted the top of a gift bag with one hand—"I'll let you get back to it. Keep up the good work!"

Harlan and Hamilton glanced at each other. Harlan could see that Hamilton's computer screen only had a game of Solitaire on it. Harlan had been looking at Tumblr before Benjamin had come in.

"Thanks, we will!" Hamilton assured him, already trying to work open the plastic clamshell package on his new phone case.

"Say...say hi to Beth from us," Harlan added. He wasn't sure that he really meant it, but it seemed like the polite thing to do.

"I will." Benjamin waved at them and left.

"You're going to cut your finger off!" Harlan laughed, watching Hamilton saw at the packaging with his pocketknife.

"Mm-m, that sounds like someone who doesn't want his new flashlight and phone case," Hamilton said airily. "Besides, I'm just the muscle. I don't need all my fingers. In *fact*, I'm probably scarier *without* all my fingers!" He held up his left hand, his ring finger tucked against his palm so Harlan couldn't see it and wiggled his others.

"Yes, very scary." Harlan rolled his eyes. "You won't be able to marry Matthew without that particular finger, though," he pointed out.

"Oh, true." Hamilton let his finger pop up again. "I'll just have to make sure to cut off a different one, then."

Hamilton and his boyfriend weren't officially engaged yet, but Hamilton had confessed that he thought it was going to happen soon.

"And you're more than just the muscle," Harlan assured him, even though he knew Hamilton wasn't completely wrong. Hamilton had lost his small mediumship ability at the same time Leo had.

Harlan cleared his throat and quickly changed the subject. "We should have some scissors around here somewhere... Maybe..." Harlan went back to his own desk and dug through the drawers. "I don't. Do you?" *Great.* Another thing he'd have to buy for the business.

"Don't need 'em," Hamilton said without looking up from tearing the package open. He pulled out his phone, transferred it to the new case and applied the screen protector, which was completely transparent. Once they'd been painted, warding runes were invisible unless a medium was looking for them. "Eh.

Not the most stylish thing, is it? Does this actually work?"

Harlan nodded. "They kept Benjamin and Beth's phones from getting drained when mine did, and their flashlights still performed."

Hamilton wrinkled his nose, tossing his phone down on his desk and beginning to attack the flashlight's package. "Well, hopefully we won't ever have to put that to the test."

"Agreed." Since it was unlikely that a rampaging ghost would appear in the office, Harlan decided he'd open his with Charles when he got home.

He and Hamilton had debated having the tiny office ghost warded but decided against it—in large part because of the cost, but also because they wanted *friendly* spirits to be able to come in. That was one of the main reasons they'd started Laid to Rest, after all. Harlan—and Hamilton and Morgan—wanted to work *with* ghosts as much as possible, rather than seeing them as a nuisance to the living and just getting rid of them.

Of course, it was unlikely that a ghost of any kind would show up. Most spirits were bound to the place they'd died, where they'd been buried or somewhere that had been important to them in life. Once they began haunting a place, it was very difficult for them to leave it.

Hamilton took out his new flashlight, loaded the batteries and clicked it on and off a few times…then a few more.

He groaned. "Would you mind if I take off early?"

Harlan shook his head. "No. I'm sure I can handle—"

"Don't say that! You'll jinx it!"

"I don't think anyone's coming in today. Better?"

Hamilton nodded.

"Besides, I told you that you don't have to be here at your desk all day. I can just call you if — *when* — I need you."

"Nope. This old workhorse needs to be in harness." He rapped the desk with both hands in fists, presumably as hooves. "Besides...Matthew's at work all day, and otherwise I'd just be kicking around the condo by myself."

"Oh, yeahhhh. Because sitting around *here* with me all day in an empty office is *so* much less sad!" Harlan teased him.

"Shut up. It is. I'm leaving now, but that doesn't change what I just said."

"Uh-huh. Say hi to Matthew for me."

"Will do. You say hi to Charles for me."

Harlan nodded and waved Hamilton out of the office.

He sighed, seriously considering following Hamilton out the door. But where would he go except home, which was cluttered with all Charles' and his junk, and if he wanted to sit down or find anything, he'd have to unpack. He didn't want to do that.

Besides...he kinda wanted to be alone after spending the day with Hamilton and Benjamin's unexpected visit, and Charles would be there until he left for work, probably six at the earliest.

It wasn't that he didn't want to see Charles! He just wasn't used to having someone else around *all* the time, and he hadn't realized how much he'd gotten used to having his own space.

It was fine. He'd adjusted to living alone. But he'd adjusted to working with Hamilton every day too, so he'd adjust to living with Charles.

It was fine.

He looked at the clock on the wall. It had come with the office, but it made him feel more legit, somehow, so he'd kept it. It was only three-thirty, and they were officially open until five — later by appointment — but there hadn't been a single phone call or anything all day. A few other occupants of the office building had stopped by, curious about the new agency. Harlan made a mental note to return the plate that someone had brought them 'welcome' cookies on. Hopefully Hamilton would remember who they'd said they were and where they worked.

He shook his head. *Return a plate.*

When had he become such an adult?

Chapter Two

Harlan glanced at his phone and groaned. Michael again. He sighed. He'd already put this off long enough, and he had promised Michael he'd let him take him out for a thank-you coffee.

He fixed a bright smile in place as he answered, hoping that the act of smiling would make him sound more friendly and less annoyed. Hopefully he'd find a way to work his preference for texting into the conversation. Oh, yeah, that was bound to come up naturally.

"Michael! Hey!" he said with forced cheer, and as if the call was a surprise rather than the latest in a long series that he'd been ignoring.

"Hey!" Michael sounded *genuinely* pleased, or at least he was better at faking it. "Harlan, I've actually got you! How are you?"

"Good!" This fake-enthusiasm thing actually seemed to be working. Maybe he should try it more often. "Sorry I haven't gotten back to you. I've just, uh, been really busy with work."

Michael laughed, a low, rumbling chuckle that seemed to go straight to Harlan's groin. *Whoa. What the fuck?* He pulled the phone away from his ear for a second and frowned at it.

"No worries. I know you're getting a new business up and running."

"Uh, yeah." *Weird.* He hadn't told Michael about his agency. He was discreetly putting out ads, but he was surprised someone like Michael had seen them. Unless... "Wait. You're not having more ghost problems, are you?"

That laugh again. Was Michael trying to be seductive, or was Harlan just horny or something? Now that he thought about it, between moving, unpacking and work, he *had* been busy—and so had Charles. It had been a while since they'd both been home at the same time and had the energy to do anything but literal Netflix and chill.

He was trying to decide if he should schedule his coffee with Michael really soon to get it over with, or— his specialty—keep putting it off indefinitely, preferably until Michael gave up or forgot about it— when Michael said, "But one of my friends is."

"Sorry, what?" Fuck, he'd gotten caught up in his thoughts and lost track of what they were talking about.

"A ghost problem. One of my friends is having a ghost problem."

"Oh! That's great!" Harlan cleared his throat. "But, uh, probably not for your friend." He realized he was saying 'uh' a lot during this conversation, even more than usual. Why was talking to Michael making him so nervous?

"Yeah, not so much." This time Michael's laugh was too dry to be sexy — or maybe Harlan was just getting used to it. "He's really freaked out."

"Of course." That was how most people felt about ghosts.

"Yeah. And he can pay you, if it works out."

"Oh." Even though Morgan had managed to secure them some funding, he definitely wasn't in a position to turn down the offer of money — and possibly word of mouth to a wealthier demographic than he and the others had access to. All their clients so far had been pro bono. A few had offered to pay, but Harlan had turned them down, knowing they couldn't really afford it. He was living off his savings, but his personal expenses were pretty low, especially since he'd moved in with Charles. At least he was managing to pay Hamilton. Morgan, so far, had declined to draw a salary — though they hadn't actually been involved in any cases yet. They'd been doing some admin work, but they still had their day job to rely on. Harlan suspected they'd been doing more work than they'd admitted.

A paying client would allow him to at least give them *some* money.

"I can definitely look into it, see if I can help." He dug around in his end-table drawer for something to write on. He came up with one of the notebooks and a pencil that Hamilton had gotten so excited about and ordered as mock-ups for the agency. Harlan and Morgan still weren't convinced enough to order real versions to give out. Harlan suspected Hamilton just wanted to feed his notebook addiction.

He wasn't sure how they'd gotten away from the office and into his home, actually. "Can you tell me more about the situation?" he asked, pencil poised.

"Sure I can. Over coffee?" Michael suggested. "Two birds? One mug? *Ah*?"

Harlan managed to suppress a sigh. "Sure."

"Perfect. Are you free tomorrow?"

"It's a date." *Fuck, why did I put it that way?*

* * * *

Harlan had thought about bringing Charles—not that this was a *date* date, it was just a…business meeting—but it was Monday, and Charles liked to sleep in. He'd been extra busy at the club lately, even going in on his days off a lot of the time. It was kinda nice to get out of the apartment and see someone besides Charles, Hamilton or Morgan—not that he saw Morgan much in person.

He'd expected that Michael's friend would be there, too, and he was surprised to see Michael sitting alone at a table in Starbucks, one ankle crossed over the other knee with his foot bouncing in midair. He was elegantly sipping from one of those tiny coffee cups. Had he brought the mug himself or did Starbucks secretly have actual dishes?

He considered just turning around and walking away before Michael saw him, coming up with some excuse—even though they really could use the money—but before he could duck his head and turn away, Michael waved vigorously at him.

"Hey! Harlan! Over here!" he called, making a bunch of other people in the coffee shop turn and look at him.

Harlan wanted to crawl into a hole and disappear, but he forced himself to stand in line, order, then cross the cafe and sit across the table from Michael.

He was more handsome than Harlan remembered — not that it would take much, since the last time Harlan had seen him, Michael had been pale and covered in sweat as he recovered from being possessed, his suit soaked with filth from the alley Harlan had found him in. The suit he was *currently* wearing was pristine, every crease razor sharp. Harlan didn't know much about high-end men's clothing, but he could tell this one had probably cost more than a month's rent for his old apartment. It fit Michael perfectly, showing off his lean body to perfection.

"Oh, you've already paid! Shoot, it was gonna be my treat. Oh well. Next time." He winked at Harlan, sounding completely certain that there would be a next time.

Harlan was beginning to agree with him. There was just something about Michael, something captivating that made Harlan want to impress him, and Harlan didn't usually notice or feel that kind of thing.

"Next time," he found himself repeating.

"So! This is kinda awkward, huh? How do we do this?"

Harlan was relieved that it wasn't just him, but he also had a suspicion that Michael's definition of 'awkward' was miles away from his own.

"Thank you for saving my life, I guess!" For a moment he looked like he was going to try to take Harlan's hand, but at the last moment he changed direction and gave Harlan a friendly punch on the arm. "I owe you. Big time. You ever need anything, you call, and I'll make it happen."

He was starting to sound like the Godfather or something, and Harlan was starting to regret telling Hamilton not to run a background check on the man they'd saved before meeting with him. "I'll, uh, yeah. Definitely. Thanks."

"I mean it. Anytime. Whatever you need. Help getting rid of a body? Done." He laughed as he said it, but Harlan got the feeling he meant it.

Turning his coffee cup around and around between his palms, Harlan nodded, trying to find a way out of the thorny conversational trap he was tangled in. Finally he settled on, "Uh, can I ask you something?"

Michael took a deep sip of his coffee and locked eyes with Harlan. "Fire away. Like I said, anything you need."

"What was it like?" Harlan wasn't sure he should be asking that of a recent trauma victim, *definitely* wasn't sure if he wanted to know the answer, but he was dying to find out.

"Oh? Oh." Michael visibly deflated, shoulders drooping and hunching forward, head lowering. "That. It was, uh—"

"I'm sorry! You don't— I'm sure you don't want to talk about this."

To Harlan's surprise, Michael shook his head. "No. It would...actually be really great to talk about it." He scoffed. "I love my family, and I have great, supportive friends, but this whole thing..." He shook his head again. "They wouldn't know what to say, and maybe I don't want them to know. Y'know?"

It was Harlan's turn to nod. "Of course. I completely understand. If you'd like, I can recommend a few therapists who specialize in psychic trauma. I go to one of them, and I highly recommend her. My partner, Hamilton, goes to another, and I know it's really helping him. But I'd also be happy to listen if you'd rather just talk to me for now." He was surprised to realize he meant it. "Wait. You haven't talked to *anyone* about what happened?"

"What can I say? I've still got that old 'pull yourself up by your bootstraps' mentality lurking around in there. But I'm trying to get rid of it, so I will tell you. Actually, how about this? I'll tell you about it if you tell me about you and your team. Sound fair?"

Harlan nodded, definitely feeling like he was getting the better end of the deal.

Michael took a deep, steadying breath, then another gulp of coffee.

"Being possessed is like..." He laughed. "I might not have told anyone about it, but God knows it's all I *think* about. Hopefully I can make this make sense.

"It's like being in a dream. You see what happens. You feel it. You know it's your body that you're watching move and speak, but you can't change it. You're not in control. You're there, present, but helpless. It's like being in the front car of a roller coaster, feeling the forces crashing over you, and you can't get away from them. You just have to surrender, or you'll break. I'm sorry." He pulled out a Kleenex and dabbed at his eyes.

"I'm so sorry. We can... We can stop now, right now, if you'd like." He managed a weak grin. "I feel like we need a safeword."

"Oh?"

Harlan felt his cheeks heat up. "Oh! Sorry! It's just...my boyfriend owns Rattling Chains. It's a—"

"I've heard of it," Michael practically purred.

"And he's always saying we need to normalize safewords in all kinds of situations, not just... Yeah."

"Sounds like a smart guy. Lucky you."

"He is," Harlan assured him.

"I wouldn't have pegged you as the kinky type," Michael said, looking him up and down, grinning. "But now that you mention it... Yeah, I could see that. You're a top, aren't you?"

Harlan's eyes widened. No one *ever* guessed he was the Dom in his relationship with Charles.

Michael's grin widened. "I'll take that as a yes. Do you boys ever...invite anyone else to play?"

Wow, is he for real? That wasn't the kind of thing that happened to Harlan, where a hot guy asked to join a threesome with him and his boyfriend. That was something straight out of porn. "I...um. Well, we..."

Michael's booming laugh filled the room, attracting attention.

Everyone turned to look at them — at Michael — and Harlan ducked down in his seat a little.

Michael waved a hand. "You don't have to give me an answer now. Fuck, you never have to give me an answer. Just, ah, know that I'm interested. Something to think about."

Harlan nodded.

Michael chuckled. "Right. What were we talking about before we got so pleasantly sidetracked? Right. Possession. It's like..." He took a long, shaky breath. "Well, let's just say I don't recommend it." He lifted his coffee mug, held it out and said, voice a little too loud, "Never again!"

Harlan clinked his cup against it. Well, not that it made a noise, because his was only paper.

He wasn't sure what to say, so he just repeated, "Never again."

They both drank in silence for a while. Harlan's drink was getting dangerously low to use as a distraction. He'd either have to get a refill or hope he was a good enough actor to use an empty cup.

"Your turn."

Harlan looked up, alarmed.

"Now you have to tell me about your agency!"

"Ah. Well. There's me? Do you have any questions for me?"

"Soooo many," Michael purred, "but I'd rather learn about you in a more…private setting."

Oh God. Was Michael hitting on him? After he'd told him he had a boyfriend? Sure, he'd had lots of fantasies about being with more than one guy, but he and Charles had never even discussed it.

"Uh, then there's Hamilton, of course. He used to be a cop before he joined. We worked together."

"I see." All Michael's focus was on Harlan, which was intimidating. Faced with that intense stare, Harlan found himself shuffling his feet beneath the table

"And what does Hamilton — is that his first name? — add to the table? Besides, I'm guessing, muscle."

Harlan smiled. "Yeah, he's definitely the muscle. Not that there's much competition from the rest of us." He hesitated a moment before adding, "He used to have a little mediumship, but it got drained a while ago."

Michael snapped his fingers. "Right! The whole evil Centre director, right?"

Harlan nodded. "But even without his power — not that there was much to take — he's still one of our best guys." Why had he said that? He was one of their *only* guys. The only other *guy*, actually.

"Who else?"

"Well, there's Morgan. They handle admin, money, accounting, that sort of thing — all the stuff Hamilton and I don't know how to do."

He glanced around suspiciously, trying to decide if he should keep talking. Michael was a surprisingly good listener, and he found himself *wanting* to tell him more. "Can you keep a secret?"

Michael mimed zipping his lips shut and throwing away the key. "In my line of work, it's essential."

Harlan frowned. "And what is your line of work? I never quite caught—"

"What would you like to tell me?"

"Morgan's talent is very…unusual," Harlan began slowly. It wasn't something he would normally share, but, again, he found himself wanting to impress Michael. "They're a shapeshifter, but it's much more unusual than turning into a…" He looked around for inspiration and his eyes landed on a corkboard. One of the posters pinned to it had a picture of a deer. Michael followed his gaze and Harlan quickly looked away. "I don't know, a deer. Morgan turns into…" How had they put it? "Anyone's ideal romantic or sexual partner."

He couldn't help a little blush, remembering how them turning into Charles had made Harlan realize he was in love.

Michael leaned back in his chair, whistling. "Yep, I'd say that's pretty 'unusual'. I've never heard of anyone else like that—not that I know all that many psychics or that much about psychic abilities." He gestured at Harlan. "Have you?"

Harlan shook his head.

"And what about this boyfriend of yours? What can he do besides whips and chains?"

"Charles—" He opened his mouth to say Charles didn't *have* an ability, but that wasn't what wanted to come out. "Charles keeps ghosts away."

"Wow!" Michael shook his head. "That's some serious talent! You've got quite the collection, don't you?"

Harlan shrugged self-consciously. "I guess. I've just been really, really lucky."

Well, now that he'd said that much, he might as well tell the whole thing.

"Morgan and I can also combine our powers — but we try not to, for their sake."

"Oh, that sounds intriguing!"

He hadn't really meant to bring up Morgan in the first place, never mind explaining more about them, but Michael was just...shockingly easy to talk to.

"We've only done it a few times, but their ability allows them to turn into someone's loved one. If the person Morgan turns into is dead and I touch Morgan, the loved one's ghost will appear."

"Holy shit!" Michael's eyes were enormous.

Harlan shrugged modestly. "We've used it to find a few people — well, bodies, I guess." He drained the last sip of his coffee. *Damn.* "Please tell me about you. I've been talking so much." Not only was he being a total conversation hog, but Harlan was also beginning to feel exhausted.

Michael waved a dismissive hand. "Nah. My life's *way* more boring than all this!" he insisted. "I'd much rather hear about what you do."

"There's not much more to say, really." He'd finished his coffee and his biggest talking point. Earlier, he would've been happy that he'd fulfilled his obligation — though it was the other way around, wasn't it, since he'd saved Michael? — and could politely make his escape, but he didn't want to leave yet. Or, at least, he wanted an excuse to see Michael again. Harlan wasn't sure what made him do it, but he found himself opening his mouth and saying, "Um… My boyfriend and I are having a kind of birthday-slash-housewarming party…"

Michael grinning at him. "Are you inviting me, or just trying to make me jealous that I can't come?"

"What?" Harlan blinked. "Oh! No! Sorry. That was me inviting you."

Michael reached across the table and patted Harlan's hand. Harlan felt a spark leap between them, a hot rush of *something*.

"It's okay," he assured Harlan. "In that case, I'm happy to accept."

"I'll text you the address and stuff." Fuck, had he screwed up? He hadn't run this by Charles, and he wasn't sure how Charles would feel about him inviting someone who was essentially a stranger — though Charles had seen Michael's unconscious body at the Centre — to an event that he'd kept small and intimate for *Harlan's* sake. Why had he invited him? It had just…slipped out, and now it was too late to take it back.

There was a moment of silence while Michael read the text, and Harlan felt the need to add, "I don't usually have birthday parties. I haven't had one since I got out—" Fuck! That was *way* more than Michael needed to know at the moment. Maybe ever.

Michael raised a perfectly sculpted eyebrow. "'Out'?" he repeated.

"It's not what you… Or maybe it is. It's not prison — not that there's anything wrong with having been to prison! Our justice system has some deep… Uh… What I mean is, I grew up at the Centre. This is my first birthday out on my own, and Charles and I just moved in together, so we thought it might be neat to have a party." *'Neat'? Yuck.* Something about Michael seemed to make Harlan even more awkward and anxious than usual, but strangely it didn't make Harlan want to get out of the situation ASAP, the way it normally would. He wanted to keep talking to Michael. He wanted Michael to keep talking to *him.*

Michael just smiled instead of running away from Harlan's babbling. "I know."

"You...do?"

Michael shrugged one shoulder. "I'm something of a paranormal buff. Word gets around."

"Oh." Harlan laughed awkwardly. "Well, that's it! That's my big secret."

Michael rested his chin in his hand, smiling. "Oh, come now. I'm sure you have more interesting secrets than that. I know *I* do."

Not sure how to reply to that, Harlan tried to take a big gulp of coffee, forgetting that it was empty. He pretended to swallow so he wouldn't look like a total idiot, nodding vaguely. "Well, I'll see you at the party, then."

Michael stood, giving Harlan finger guns. "Lookin' forward to it."

He left his dirty mug on the table. Harlan frowned at it, carrying it back to the counter when he threw out his empty cup so the employees wouldn't have to.

* * * *

Even though nothing had happened — even though he hadn't done anything — Harlan felt tense and squirmy and guilty. It didn't help that there were boxes everywhere, and so much of the stuff wasn't his own, so he didn't know where to put it, and he felt like he *should*, because he lived with Charles and they were in love, so shouldn't he know where everything went? It was their stuff now, not just Charles'. *Fuck*. At least if it were in a box, he didn't have to look at it piece by piece. He could tune out a box. He could live like this for the rest of his life if he had to, even though it made way more sense for *him*, with his flexible — and very light — schedule to unpack than Charles, who was so busy. Charles hadn't said anything about it, and Harlan didn't think he *would*, but he still couldn't help feeling guilty, even as he just flopped on the couch, turned on some music and ignored the mess until Charles got home.

He usually liked to give Charles a few minutes to get in the door and at least take his boots off and breathe before jumping him, but he couldn't wait any longer.

"I did something kind of... You might think it's stupid," he blurted.

Halfway through unlacing one boot, Charles looked over his shoulder at Harlan. "Oh?"

"You remember that I had my coffee with Michael — the guy Hamilton and I saved — today?"

"Yeah." Charles kicked off one shoe and started on the other.

Harlan felt a strange rush of pleasure at the sight. Charles was home. In *their* home. Together. "He actually has a case for me."

"Hey, that's great! What's dumb about—?"

"That's not the dumb part. I kinda...sorta...invited him to the party."

Charles toed off the second boot and straightened with a groan. "Why would that be dumb?"

Harlan scuffed the floor with his socked foot. "I dunno. I just... I didn't run it by you first? It was kind of an impulse thing."

"Harlan, that's fine! It's *our* party. You can invite people to it. You know I'm inviting a few of my friends and staff."

"But I've met most of your friends at boardgame night, right?"

"Most of them."

"And I've probably at least seen most of your co-workers around." Harlan didn't add that he probably knew none of their names, but he knew he didn't have to.

"Yeah."

"But you don't know Michael at all."

"So this is the perfect opportunity to meet him." Charles gave his hand a little squeeze.

"You don't think it's weird?"

Charles headed for the couch and sank into it with a contented groan. "Do *you* think it's weird?"

"Maybe. A little. I mean, we don't really know anything about this guy. You've never even met him while he was awake."

"Ah, but he doesn't really know anything about *us*, either." Charles blinked. "Did that make sense? I was going for 'wise', but I think I'm too tired."

"Of course! Sorry. I should have waited..."

Charles patted the couch beside him, and Harlan sat. It was Charles' old couch, and Harlan loved the way the saggy cushions tipped him toward Charles for snuggles.

"It's okay," Charles assured him, draping an arm over Harlan's shoulders. "It'll be nice to meet the guy when he's conscious. And if we hate him, we never have to see him again. Deal?"

"Deal." *It's* our *party,* Harlan repeated to himself.

"As much as I'd like to cuddle, I stink. I'm gonna hit the shower before I get too comfortable and fall asleep on the couch."

"Yeah. Of course." Harlan found himself missing Charles, even though he was just in the bathroom. He couldn't sit still on the couch, and when he realized he'd been pacing the living room, he gave in and followed Charles.

Charles smiled when he saw him and opened the shower door.

Harlan knew Charles was too tired to get up to anything sexy—which seemed to be happening more and more lately, as Rattling Chains got more popular— but he was happy to just stand in the warm water with Charles, their fingers trailing together, sliding their hands over each other's bodies in a loving but not sexual way. He soaped Charles' back, massaging some of the stubborn knots he knew Charles always carried.

"Mmm," Charles purred, bracing himself against one of the shower's tile walls. "You always take such good care of me."

Harlan's hands froze mid motion. "*I* take care of *you*?" he asked so softly that he wasn't sure Charles would even be able to hear him over the water.

Charles looked over his shoulder, straightening and turning completely around when he saw Harlan's expression. He reached over and turned off the water. "Of course! You don't think so?"

Harlan shook his head, wishing Charles had left the shower running in case he started crying.

"Of course you do," Charles repeated, wrapping Harlan in a warm, wet hug. "We take care of each other."

"I don't know. I just feel like I don't do anything. You deal with food stuff, and you do most of the cleaning and unpacking, and…"

Charles reached up to cup Harlan's face in one broad hand. "Sweetheart, I do that because I love you. I get to come home and do those things with you, and that's amazing!" He cleared his throat and sniffed suspiciously.

Harlan was glad it wasn't just him.

"I was beginning to think I wouldn't find someone like that in my life. But every day I get to come home to you. Even if you just sat around all day and didn't do anything, you'd still be taking care of me. Just being around you lights up my day. You know that, right?"

Harlan shrugged one shoulder, looking down and away so he wouldn't have to make eye contact.

"Well, it's true. And I'm going to prove it to you over and over until you believe it." He punctuated each word with a kiss, starting at Harlan's collarbone and ending with a lingering kiss on the lips. "Should we get out of the shower?" he asked, pulling away just a fraction.

Harlan nodded. "I am getting chilly," he realized.

"Let's dry off and get into bed, then."

Harlan nodded. He had to get up for work in a few hours, so he wouldn't be able to sleep with Charles, but they could at least hold each other for a while.

They took turns toweling each other dry, then got into bed. It didn't take long for Charles to fall asleep.

"I love you," Harlan whispered, and he could have sworn Charles smiled in his sleep.

Chapter Three

"You made it!" Even though Michael had said he would come, some part of Harlan had thought he was just being polite or whatever and that he wouldn't show. He found himself strangely touched that Michael *had* turned up. "Uh, come and meet my…Charles." For some reason he didn't want to say 'boyfriend'.

"All right," Michael laughed. "Can I put this down first?" He held up a present wrapped in shiny red prismatic paper, turning it from side to side almost hypnotically.

"Oh! You didn't have to…" Harlan said, suddenly embarrassed.

Michael scoffed. "Of course I did. It's not every day that the man who saved my…life? My soul? The man who saved me invites me to his birthday-slash-housewarming. It's the least I can do."

"It's, um… People have been putting presents over here." Head down, Harlan led the way to the sideboard—a word he hadn't even known until he'd moved in with Charles, at least not well enough to picture the piece of furniture it described — which was already piled high with presents. Harlan let out a long, slow breath through his mouth. *Great.* He hated opening presents in front of people. Hopefully most of them were slash-housewarming gifts and he could make Charles open them.

Charles caught his eye, silently checking in.

Harlan plastered on a fake smile and nodded.

No. That wouldn't work, not with Charles. He didn't *want* it to work. It was an old, automatic reaction, one he wanted to leave at the Centre — or at least in the office. He hadn't needed to use it there yet, but it might come in handy one day. He'd always thought it was super obvious when he was faking it, but no one had ever called him on it…except Charles.

Fuck. He'd taken too long to respond. He closed his eyes, just for a second, and did an extremely rapid version of his calming breathing exercise — *inslowoutslowinsloweroutslower.* He was a little surprised it worked, but his smile was genuine by the time he opened his eyes. He nodded at Charles in return. This wasn't an awkward birthday at the Centre, where everyone else was only there for the cake and because they had to be. These were people who knew him — for more than just his ability track — and cared about him. Or at least about Charles, and Charles cared about him, so it was basically the same thing.

He waved at Skye, who had just arrived.

She waved back, signing, *"I'm just here for a second. I have to get back to work, but I wanted to drop this off and say happy birthday and—"* She held up a small purple present.

He wasn't familiar with the last sign, but he assumed it meant 'housewarming'.

"Thank you! I'm so glad you could make it. We have to have that coffee soon!" he signed back. He was glad he didn't have to raise his voice to be heard, but he wanted to go see her anyway. He hurried across the room, Michael trailing behind him. No, that wasn't right. Michael wasn't a trailer. More like a trail*blazer*. Leading from behind? Did that make sense? Herding him?

"I know the perfect place." She was smirking as she signed it.

Unsettling, but he was too keyed up to worry about that at the moment.

He took the present from Skye, and they exchanged a quick hug. Were they on hugging terms now? Apparently.

Skye waved to him and Michael, then left.

Harlan realized he hadn't introduced her to Charles. She'd never met him. *Well, apparently she still hasn't.*

He turned to Michael with an apologetic smile. "Sorry about —" No, he had nothing to apologize for — Canadian to a fault — so he shouldn't say he was sorry. "Right. Present." He led Michael — or Michael drove him — over to the sideboard.

Michael carefully set his present down, and Harlan found himself checking out his ass as he bent over. *Fuck, what is wrong with me?* That wasn't like him at all.

He had a really great ass, though. Tight, but not flat.

"Here... Why don't I get you something to drink?" he quickly offered. That was what you were supposed to do with guests, right? He hurried over to the dining-room table and the bowl of non-alcoholic punch Charles had made. He couldn't seem to get anything but the lemon slices floating on the surface. He finally managed to shove them all to one side and scoop out some liquid.

Michael touched his shoulder — he wasn't sure how he knew it was Michael, but somehow he did — and he sloshed most of the ladleful onto the tablecloth.

"Shit!" He had a sudden, crazy urge to dab at the spill with his brand-new white dress shirt. He'd only owned T-shirts. Charles had insisted that he would be fine just wearing one of those, but Harlan had wanted to make a good impression, so he and Charles had gone clothes shopping together for the party. Yeah, he was so pathetic that he couldn't even do that on his own.

Had he wanted to make a good impression on *Michael*?

He recoiled from the thought and the table.

"Here." Michael closed his hand around Harlan's, guiding the ladle back into the punch and up to the cup he was holding in one trembling hand. He dipped it again, filling a second plastic cup for himself.

Shit. Harlan hadn't even been able to get him a drink properly. He was a terrible host. What business did he have host...ing? *Is that a word?*

Cohost, he remembered. He looked over his shoulder and there was Charles, as if he'd summoned him. He felt a wave of welcome calmness wash over him, and his tight smile softened.

It returned a moment later when he realized this was it, the moment Charles met Michael. He wanted — needed — them to have a good first impression of each other.

He downed his punch in one swallow without tasting it, then managed to pour himself another while trying to watch them out of the corner of his eye. Luckily there weren't any ice cubes in his cup, or he probably would have choked to death.

Charles grinned at Michael and offered him his hand. "Hi. Charles Moore. We met really briefly at the— No, I guess you were unconscious the whole time."

"Michael Clark."

They shook hands, and Harlan hoped he wasn't imagining the way their fingers brushed, tangling together and lingering there for a moment longer than necessary. He was probably reading too much into it, but he hoped not.

"Oh, I see someone spilled." Charles frowned at the damp tablecloth.

"It was—"

"Me," Michael interjected before Harlan could finish. "I can be a bit of a klutz. Just get me a tea towel, and I'll take care of it." It sounded almost like an order coming from him.

Harlan didn't like lying to Charles, not even about something as small and stupid as that, but it was too late to take Michael's words back.

"No. Please. You're a guest," Charles laughed. "I'll take care of it. You and Harlan can catch up." He touched Michael's wrist, briefly, before pulling his hand away again.

Harlan thought it was going well. *Is it going well?*

"Well, I can at least go to the kitchen with you," Michael said, making it sound like a long, dangerous trek instead of a few feet away.

"All right. I guess I can allow it." Charles grinned.

Was he imagining Michael winking at him as they left?

At that moment, Morgan swept in—late, as usual, but somehow that was just part of their charm. They wore a long, flowing, dark-coloured skirt, and they turned heads as they passed. They hurried over to Harlan, air-kissing both his cheeks, something they'd never done before. Well, this was just a day for strange greetings, wasn't it?

"I didn't bring you a present," they whispered.

"Thank you," he whispered back. He didn't think it was them being…frugal or something. Maybe they remembered how uncomfortable he'd been at Centre-mandated birthday parties. Or — more likely — they'd just hated them as much as he had.

They went over to talk to Hamilton just as Michael returned from the kitchen, leaving Harlan alone with him again.

"Shall we?" Michael gestured to the couch, which was miraculously wide open.

Harlan nodded. Luckily Charles didn't expect him to mingle. He could just sit and talk to Michael. How hard could that be?

He didn't remember what they talked about, but time flew by, then everyone was leaving, and he was alone with Charles…finally.

* * * *

Harlan absolutely wasn't imagining it was Michael's hand stroking him instead of Charles'. He wasn't.

But maybe he was imagining that Michael was there as well.

"Are you okay?" Charles asked afterwards, when they were snuggled in their afterglow. "You seem kind of distracted."

"Yeah."

Charles raised an eyebrow at him, and Harlan knew he'd gotten off easy. If Charles had given him such a curt, obvious brush-off, he would've been upset. "Sorry. I'm just…"

"Distracted? Michael seems interesting." Charles laughed. "Now that I'm meeting him while he's conscious. You seemed to think so, too." His voice held no trace of judgement, only amusement.

Oh, fuck. Was Charles secretly a mind reader? He floundered for an answer.

"It's okay if you are," Charles assured him, squeezed his hand. "It's normal to find people attractive, even while you're dating someone. I know a lot of this is new for you, but I want you to know that."

Was it, though? Was it normal to imagine him in their bed with him?

"And...I can't say that I'm entirely uninterested," Charles rumbled.

Harlan sat up and spun to face Charles so quickly that it felt like someone had electrocuted his spine. "Really?" *Oh thank fuck it's not just me!*

"Really." Charles caught Harlan's hand, brought it to his lips, and kissed it. "I know we haven't really talked about it — well, it hasn't really come up — but I'm not...against the idea of being poly. I haven't done it before, personally. I'm not in that high demand."

Harlan frowned at him but didn't say anything.

"But I have friends who are. Well, you've met Steve, Jim and Alejandro at game night." He rubbed Harlan's hand in small, slow circles. "And I know everything is still kinda new with us just moving in together, and I'm not saying I *want* something to happen — or that you do — buuut...maybe the three of us should get together for coffee."

Was Charles actually blushing? That was usually Harlan's arena.

* * * *

He texted Michael the next day about getting together, and he agreed to have a Skype conversation with the two of them to set up a time and place.

Harlan hated video calls, but he could admit it was the easiest and most practical way for the three of them to talk, and he couldn't deny that he was excited.

"Hi!" Michael greeted them brightly, waving from Charles' laptop screen.

Charles smiled at him. "Hi, Michael. It's good to see you again."

"You, too."

Harlan just gave an awkward little half wave — not quite, but close to, the 'queen wave'.

"So, I was thinking the three of us could get together for drinks to get to know each other better? I know this new place I haven't been to yet..." Michael suggested.

Charles glanced at Harlan.

Knowing where this was going, Harlan looked away and concentrated on not blushing.

"Harlan doesn't drink," Charles told him.

"Oh! Oh, sorry. I didn't realize. Is it...?"

Harlan didn't know what, exactly, he was trying to ask, but he decided to just be honest. "Alcohol fucks with my medications."

Michael blinked. "Oh." He laughed, shaking his head. "Well, that makes sense. You crack me up, Harlan."

Frowning slightly, Harlan glanced at Charles.

Charles shrugged. "I think you're funny," he replied quietly to Harlan's silent question.

"Well, coffee then. I know Harlan likes coffee — or at least sugar masquerading as coffee," Michael laughed. "How 'bout you, Charles?"

"I like coffee. Coffee-coffee."

"Coffee-coffee it is. Same place work for you guys?"

They agreed and set up a date and time.

Harlan found himself both nervous and excited for their first joint date with Michael. *Oh, God.* It sounded so scary and dramatic when he thought of it that way. Coffee. It was just coffee. He'd gone out for coffee with Michael already, and it hadn't been a big deal. He just really wanted Charles to like Michael. Not that they hadn't already met, but meeting someone at a party — even a small one — was different than talking one-on-one. Well, two-on-one. *Whatever.*

He didn't want to discover that he'd made a mistake bringing Michael into their lives. Or was it 'life', now that they were living together? He wasn't sure how he felt about that. Part of him liked it — it made his heart flutter — but it also made him...nervous? Something not good that he couldn't quite identify, anyway.

No. Just because they were living together and shared a life in their new home, it didn't mean they weren't still separate people with separate lives. *Fuck.* He was *way* overthinking this.

* * * *

Once again, Michael was already at the coffee shop. He stood and waved at them from the table he'd chosen. He gestured at the line of people and his cup of coffee, then sat again.

Harlan assumed he didn't want the table stolen if he came over to them, and he nodded.

It took a long time to get to the head of the line and order, which Harlan found super awkward with Michael sitting there looking at them the whole time. Harlan glanced over at him a few times, giving him a little smile, and he was pretty sure he saw Charles do the same thing.

Finally, they had their drinks — a large black coffee for Charles and a frappe for Harlan — and joined Michael.

Michael got up again. He gave Harlan a hug without hesitation, which Harlan happily accepted, then turned to Charles. He waited until Charles gave a little nod, which Harlan appreciated.

He watched the hug carefully — without making it obvious that he was analyzing their interaction, he hoped. It was somewhere between the friendly, manly hugs Charles and Hamilton exchanged and the sweeter, more intimate one Michael had just given Harlan — at least Harlan thought so. Not that he was very good at this.

The three of them sat, Charles and Harlan facing Michael.

Michael asked Charles about his work, and Charles was happy to tell him. It was one of the first things people asked him about when they found out what he did, and Harlan was used to this conversation. It was nice, because he could just sit and watch and listen and sip his drink without having to contribute much or do anything.

Unfortunately, they eventually finished with that subject and Michael turned to Harlan. "So, how's the detective agency?"

Harlan frowned. "Well, it's not really — "

"I know. I'm just joshing you."

Harlan grinned, a little stiffly. He didn't think he'd ever heard anyone actually say that in real life.

Charles patted Harlan's thigh, giving it a gentle squeeze. Harlan was pretty sure it meant that Charles was ready to keep talking and distract Michael if Harlan didn't want to answer right then — or at all, even though that kinda defeated the whole purpose of them having coffee, didn't it? Although Harlan and Michael had already talked a fair bit. Yeah, maybe this was more for Charles and Michael to get to know each other.

Right. He could keep telling himself that.

He shook his head. He could at least talk a little. Michael was easy to talk to, and a very engaged listener—maybe *too* engaged for Harlan sometimes, but he was sure that was his problem, not Michael's—and probably not a problem at all for Charles.

He told Michael about their last few cases—not that there had *been* more than a few. *Fuck.* It was a good thing he wasn't tight on money and Charles didn't mind…helping while he took on his crazy side project. He must have included a few details he hadn't told Charles, because he laughed and shook his head a few times along with Michael.

"How about you, Michael?"

"Mmm?"

"What do *you* do?" Charles asked.

"Oh, fuck, you don't want to hear about that!" Michael protested. "It's really boring—not like both of yours. Holy shit!" He asked Charles a question, which got Charles started on another story—one Harlan hadn't heard, actually—that had all three of them laughing.

It was Charles, of course, who brought them around to the real topic at hand—though Harlan wouldn't actually have been surprised if Michael had done it, either.

"So," Charles chuckled, "am I correct in thinking you're interested in Harlan?"

The look Michael shot his way was pure lust, and Harlan knew he didn't deserve to be looked at like that—except by Charles, but he already had that, and it had sorta just crept up on him. Fuck. He already had Charles! How much more was the universe or whatever going to throw his way?

"You are," Michael purred, turning that look on Charles, and Harlan was gratified to see that Charles blushed in return. At least he wasn't the only one affected that way.

Charles smiled back at him, his expression soft. "And maybe not *just* Harlan?" he suggested, and holy *shit* Charles was brave, so much braver than Harlan could ever even imagine being.

"Not just Harlan, especially now that I've gotten to know you better, Charles."

Holy shit, this was actually happening! Harlan forced himself to take a deep breath, but it came out as more of a gasp, and the other two turned to look at him. He quickly shook his head, taking a sip of his drink.

"Well. I can't say that I'm...unmoved." Charles walked his fingers across the table, bringing his hand to rest close to but not quite touching Michael's.

It was weird watching Charles obviously flirt with someone besides him, but jealousy was the furthest thing from Harlan's mind. He shifted in his seat, hoping the other two wouldn't notice. They seemed pretty distracted, and he was content to just sit and watch them both.

"There are a few things you should know about us, maybe things Harlan hasn't mentioned." There was no judgement behind that, which Harlan appreciated.

Michael nodded, stretching out his fingers to brush the ball of Charles' thumb. After a moment, he put his other hand on the table, reaching out for Harlan.

Harlan took it, feeling a little silly—it was like a weird Mexican standoff, especially when Charles reached over and put his other hand on Harlan's thigh and Harlan closed his fingers around it. This felt good. Right. Like closing a circuit, and oh God, he couldn't help imagining how it would feel to do it with *more* skin touching, all three of them bare...

"Go on," Michael said, snapping him out of his fantasy — which was a good thing.

"Well, you know what I do for work." He gave Harlan's leg a little squeeze, and Harlan jiggled it in return.

Michael grinned. "Yeah."

"Let's just say I take my work home with me, if you get my drift."

"I do. And Harlan already told me."

"Really?" Charles raised an eyebrow, looking pleasantly surprised. "Huh. How about that?" He shrugged. "Which isn't to say that neither of us enjoys vanilla sex, if that's more in your wheelhouse."

Fuck, Harlan was glad he had Charles to do the talking for him. He probably would have spontaneously combusted, starting with his face, if he had to say those things out loud. It was a good thing the café was busy and noisy and no one was paying attention to them.

Michael smiled, moving his hand away from Charles' to trace little circles and spirals on the wooden tabletop. They were hypnotic, drawing Harlan's gaze in and keeping it there. "It certainly *has* been," he acknowledged, "but that doesn't mean it's not something I wouldn't be...interested in exploring, with the right people."

"I think that could be arranged," Charles said slowly after glancing at Harlan and getting an enthusiastic nod from him.

All three of them grinned at each other like idiots, and Harlan was once again glad it wasn't just him.

"But there's no rush," Charles added.

Harlan hoped his disappointment didn't show on his face—but really, what had he expected, that the three of them would just...get up, run out of the Starbucks and jump into bed together? That was ridiculous.

Wasn't it?

Yeah.

Michael nodded. "Of course not."

"We can take this slow. Get to know each other."

"I'd like that," Michael agreed, stroking a thumb across Harlan's knuckles and setting the fingers of his free hand across the back of Charles'.

"In the meantime, I'd like to give you a few things to think about, if that's all right."

Michael shot Charles a confused frown but nodded. "All right," he agreed, but a little cautiously, Harlan thought. Not that he could blame him—even Harlan wasn't entirely sure where Charles was going with that.

Charles laughed, shaking his head. "Don't worry. It's nothing serious. Just a little homework."

"Ooh, will teacher cane me if I don't do it?" Michael smirked. He was looking at Charles rather than Harlan. "Sorry...too much?" he asked after neither of them reacted.

"Maybe a little," Charles said dryly, shaking his head—but he was grinning even as he said it.

"Sorry," Michael repeated. "Go on."

"Well, a few basic rules and safety things first— though I'm personally of the opinion that things like safewords should be used more, even outside of a BDSM context or even the bedroom at all."

Michael snorted. "Yeah, Harlan might've mentioned that."

"Really?" Charles raised an eyebrow.

Harlan shrugged. "It came up." Of course now he couldn't remember how, for the life of him. Hopefully he hadn't made it too awkward.

"Anyway, yeah. Safewords are a big thing, obviously."

Harlan suddenly found himself reluctant to share the private safeword he and Charles used, and he was relieved when Charles said, "With you, just starting out—" He lifted his hand off Harlan's leg and raised it in a cautionary gesture. "If we get that far—we'd just use the basic traffic-light system, until we got to know each other better. So we'd check in with each other— any and all of us, not just whoever's topping. Well, and any of us could say them at any time. It doesn't have to be during a check-in. 'Green' means everything is all good, keep going. 'Yellow' means we might need to pause and change position or something like that, that we're close to but not at a limit. And 'red' means—"

"Stop right now," Michael interjected.

"That's right. All that sound good so far?"

Even now, Harlan realized, *Charles is checking in.* He just couldn't turn it off or stop, and it was adorable.

"Green," Michael agreed, grinning.

Charles grinned back at him. "Very good. Another big one for the two of us is alcohol. Not that Harlan drinks, as you know, but we don't mix alcohol with BDSM. We're a little more flexible when it comes to vanilla sex, but I know I generally prefer it sober."

Harlan nodded, though he didn't really have any strong thoughts on the matter either way. It had never really come up.

"That all makes sense."

Charles outlined a few more things, including what they tended to be into—mostly spanking and bondage, at least for Harlan, who still wasn't that advanced.

Even though all three of them had just agreed to take things slowly, Harlan found himself strangely reluctant to part with Michael after they'd finished their drinks and the conversation had started winding down.

"Do you want a ride home?" Charles offered.

"Well... All right."

They didn't make it to Michael's place. They didn't even get his address. Harlan had offered up the passenger seat to Michael, and he and Charles made eye contact in the rear-view mirror.

"Want to come back to our place?" Charles asked, which Harlan knew he *never* could have done.

"I do," Michael purred.

Harlan barely remembered the rest of the drive, just the intensity and longing to put his hands all over Michael — all over both of them. Then, somehow they — all three — were in his and Charles' bedroom.

Harlan wanted to pull them both down onto the bed with him at once, but luckily it didn't look like he was the only one.

Michael, apparently shameless, had already tossed his suit jacket over their dresser and was unbuttoning his shirt, revealing an honest-to-God undershirt beneath it. Harlan couldn't help wondering if that was something all businessmen still wore, even outside of the fifties, or if it was just a quirk of Michael's. Well. He doubted he'd get to see many more businessmen undress.

Michael peeled off the thin white shirt, too, leaving his chest bare. He was so pale and thin compared to Charles. He looked a lot more like Harlan, actually, except he had a tan and some muscle definition that strongly suggested that he spent some time at the gym, which didn't surprise Harlan.

Harlan wanted to lick him all over, to suck one of his nipples into his mouth, to —

"Well?" Michael asked, looking at the other two expectantly, slowly, slowly popping open the button of his slacks. Was that the right word? Harlan wasn't sure. They weren't jeans, and he didn't think they were dress pants.

Harlan and Charles grinned at each other sheepishly, realizing they were both still fully dressed.

Luckily, Charles made the first move — Harlan knew he, for one, was definitely feeling a little self-conscious now that he'd seen that Michael was just as yummy beneath his clothes — and they hadn't even seen his cock or ass yet.

Swaying his hips a little, Charles pulled off his T-shirt. He wasn't wearing anything underneath, and his thick hair and round stomach were immediately on display.

Harlan looked from one to the other. *Yep.* He definitely liked both — or maybe it was just that he really, *really* liked men.

They both turned to look expectantly at Harlan, but luckily Charles quickly refocused on Michael, taking the pressure off Harlan again.

Harlan watched Charles reach up and put a hand on each of Michael's shoulders, slowly trailing his fingers down to his collarbones and fanning out. His middle fingers lightly brushed Michael's nipples before he gave Harlan a gentle prompting look.

Right. He wasn't supposed to just be watching — or at least he didn't *have* to be. He could join in the fun.

He stepped in behind Charles, grinding just a little against Charles' ass and feeling Charles rut against Michael in turn. He smirked, and Michael smiled down at him over Charles' shoulder, taking away all his doubt and insecurity. He wanted this, and Michael wanted this — wanted *both* of them. All Harlan had to do was listen to his body and give in to what it knew it wanted.

He reached around to the button on Charles' jeans, only to find Michael's slim fingers already there. They both laughed, and between the two of them they opened Charles' fly completely.

"Fuck," Charles moaned, his head falling back against Harlan's chest as he surrendered himself.

Michael shimmied Charles' pants down until they fell in a puddle around his ankles, stroking Charles' nicely padded hips. He caught Harlan's hands, bringing them with him, and it was like touching Charles for the first time as Michael explored him. Now Charles was only wearing his briefs, and they were straining to hold him in.

Charles' breathing was quick and shallow already, and looking down at him, Harlan could see his eyelids fluttering as the two of them started taking him apart.

"Fuck, you're lovely," Michael told him admiringly, hooking a thumb beneath the waistband of his briefs and giving them a gentle, encouraging tug.

"Mm…" Charles made a soft sound of protest, looking away — but he did pull them down.

Harlan, molded to Charles' back, nodded. "You are," he told Charles, his lips right against Charles' ear.

Charles squirmed but didn't protest again.

Feeling his covered erection between Charles' naked cheeks was good, at least for now, and there was something really hot about being fully dressed while Charles was naked.

He hooked an arm beneath each of Charles' armpits, pinning him against his chest and not *quite* lifting him off his feet.

Charles moaned, arching his spine and resting all his weight against Harlan.

"Mm, what a pretty picture," Michael purred, sliding a hand onto each of Charles' shoulders, bending down to kiss him roughly while Harlan held him fast.

Charles alternated between rutting against Michael and grinding his ass on Harlan's covered erection.

"Come here, Harlan," Michael called.

Harlan wasn't a sub or a bottom, by any means, but that voice... It made him want to obey. And it seemed like all Michael wanted was a kiss. Harlan wanted to kiss him.

He kept the pressure, the strain, on Charles' shoulders — and, by extension, his back — while leaning forward to meet Michael's lips with Charles pressed between them. His lips were soft and tasted of some trendy botanical ChapStick addition, like...jojoba or...kale. *No, probably not the second one.* He also tasted slightly of Charles, which only heightened it for Harlan.

"Wanna keep holding him like that while I suck him?" Michael suggested.

Charles shivered eagerly between them, his soft cry muffled.

"Sounds perfect." Truthfully, Harlan was surprised that Michael would offer to be the suck-er rather than the suck-ee, but it was a pleasant surprise. "Charles?"

"Green."

"Do I have your permission, Harlan? He is yours, after all."

Harlan laughed. "You do, but we — the two of us... We're not really like that. All you need is Charles' permission."

"Ah, okay. I think that might be something fun to play with eventually, though, don't you?"

"Maybe." Harlan grinned. He settled his grip on Charles again, giving him a good yank to pull him flat against his chest — maybe a little too forcefully, considering how much Charles outweighed him — and knock him slightly off balance for Michael.

After looking around for a moment, Michael grabbed his suit jacket and folded it into a little cushion before kneeling on it between Charles' thighs.

"Oh, fuck," Charles groaned as Harlan told Michael, "We could get you an actual pillow." Even though this was one of the hottest things he'd ever seen — buttoned-down Michael kneeling on his business suit in front of Charles, naked in all his round, muscular, hairy glory.

It was like two very different gay porn genres being mashed together — *Businessman Goes Down on Bear* — and Harlan was right in the mash. *Fuck.*

"This is fine," Michael assured him. He put a hand on each of Charles' hips, his fingers fanning out across them, sliding back briefly to grab his ass — Harlan bumped them with his thighs — before returning to the front. He grinned up at Charles. "Ready?"

Charles made a strangled sound, struggling against Harlan's grip on him for a moment.

"I didn't hear a 'yes,' did you?" Michael teased. "Consent is very important, y'know."

Harlan snorted. "No, I didn't, actually." He gave Charles a little shake.

"Yes! *Please*, yes!" Charles gasped, throwing himself against Harlan's restraining arms so he could look down at Michael.

"Better. Should we make him tell us what he's asking for?"

Fuck, Michael was *really* good at this. Much better than Harlan was. He felt like normally the thought would have filled him with fear and doubt and insecurity, but right now it just...didn't. "Nah," he said aloud, having mercy on Charles.

Harlan was tall enough that he could see over Charles' shoulder and look down the length of his body to watch as Michael leaned forward and let Charles' cockhead slip between his lips. He could definitely feel the way Charles tensed then relaxed, his breath going out in a hiss.

"...Fuck," Charles groaned again.

Michael laughed. "Oh, Charlie, I'm just getting started."

Harlan blinked. It had never — would never have — occurred to him to call Charles by that nickname, and he realized he had no idea how his partner felt about it. He couldn't see Charles' face from this angle, but he didn't say anything or seem to be reacting to it, so either he didn't mind, he hadn't noticed or he was too distracted to care at the moment. Harlan would have to try and remember to ask him later...if he remembered. If Charles hadn't said anything, it probably wasn't important.

Michael leaned forward, drawing Charles deeper.

Charles moaned, his hips arching out and away from Harlan's.

Harlan tightened his grip, reminding Charles that he wasn't going anywhere — not that he really wanted to.

Michael reached up and put a hand on Charles' hip, pushing him back against Harlan and reminding him he wasn't in control. He waited a long moment, his lips wrapped just past Charles' cockhead, until Charles was steady and still again, before sliding deeper.

"Fuck!" Charles gasped, his head flying back against Harlan's collarbone.

Harlan put a few fingers under Charles' jaw, forcing his head back even farther, and kissed his temple. He didn't let go. Somehow, just being around Michael, his energy, seemed to make him feel more confident and...Dom-y than usual. Or maybe he was just trying to make a good impression and even show off a little. "That's it," he murmured against Charles' ear. "You're doing so well."

Charles shivered, a wordless cry breaking from his lips, getting louder at the end as Michael took him even deeper.

Harlan and Michael's eyes met down the length of Charles' body, and Harlan smiled down at him.

In response, Michael leaned forward, his lips meeting his hand where it was wrapped around the base of Charles' shaft.

Charles keened, struggling in Harlan's grasp.

Harlan let go of his neck, just to make sure he wouldn't hurt him by accident, but he kept his tight grip around Charles' arms and shoulders.

Michael and Charles began to fall into a natural rhythm, Charles pushing forward as Michael drew back along him, then Charles molding himself against Harlan's front when Michael pressed deeper again. Harlan was sure Charles could feel him pressing against his ass each time he came back. Fuck, he was hard. He wondered if he could fuck Charles like this while Michael sucked him. It might absolutely blow Charles apart.

As though he'd read his mind, Michael pulled all the way off Charles — ignoring Charles' desperate little cry of protest — and grinned up at Harlan. "Wanna fuck him?"

Harlan grinned back. "Yeah. Charles?"

"Oh, fuck," Charles said in a very small voice. "Yeah. Fuck, yeah." He laughed, a little shakily. "Be careful letting me go, though. My legs are pretty unsteady right now."

Before either of them could move, Michael hummed thoughtfully. "Where do you guys keep your lube?"

"Top drawer of my nightstand," Charles said breathlessly. "The side we're on," he clarified.

Michael was back a moment later with the bottle, and he squeezed some onto his hand. He knelt on his suit jacket again, reaching up between Charles' legs to slick Harlan's cock.

"Oh, fuck," Charles gasped, his head resting heavily on Harlan's chest.

Fuck, Harlan agreed silently, distracted by the feeling of Michael's unfamiliar hands on him.

It didn't take Michael long to finish, trailing one finger down the underside of Harlan's shaft, then — from the way Charles jumped and shivered — he must have done the same thing to him.

Then Michael was grinning cheekily up at Harlan again. "Ready to take him apart?" he asked, his voice almost deep enough to call a growl.

"Fuck, fuck...!" Charles gasped, struggling in Harlan's grip — but not for real.

"Ready," Harlan agreed. He reluctantly let go of Charles just long enough to squirm out of his jeans and underwear. He grabbed Charles again with his left hand, keeping his right free to give himself a few quick strokes and line himself up. "Ready?" he asked Charles directly, right against his ear.

"Fucking...! Yes, please, Harlan, *now!*"

It was the closest Harlan had ever heard Charles' voice come to a whine. He was more than happy to oblige. He pressed the head of his cock against Charles' opening, just slicking him up with some of the lube dripping off Harlan's dick, enjoying the hot, wet sensation of their sensitive skin sliding together without resistance.

Charles moaned, his head flying back and hitting Harlan in the collarbone. "Sorry!"

"It's all right," Harlan assured him, kissing the top of his head. To prove there were no hard feelings, he lined himself up again and pressed forward and slightly down. Charles' entrance was slick enough and he was relaxed enough for Harlan's cockhead to slide in without too much resistance.

"Ohhh," Charles gasped, or maybe it was him. It felt like all three of them inhaled together.

Harlan saw Michael lean forward, preparing to take Charles in again just as Harlan took Charles, but Charles shook his head sharply, pressing back against Harlan and driving him a little deeper before Harlan put his free hand on his hip to stop him.

"N-No," Charles protested. "Not yet. Not until he's all the way in."

"All right," Michael agreed, grinning up at both of them. He leaned back, stroking himself in long, leisurely motions.

Not wanting to make either of them wait any longer, Harlan let go of Charles' hip and wrapped his arm around Charles' again, matching his left side. He gave Charles an extra little yank once he was back in position and properly pinned again.

"Fuck, oh, fuck," Charles gasped, and Harlan could feel him fighting himself to keep still and let Harlan be in charge.

"Good boy," Harlan murmured, and had he ever called Charles that before? He wasn't sure, but it felt right in the moment. And it was too late to take it back.

The way Charles shivered against him made him think Charles didn't mind.

He pressed deeper, slowly spreading Charles wider and opening him up, holding fast to Charles' arms both to keep him from moving and to support himself. "Fuck, you feel good," he murmured against Charles' ear, feeling Charles tremble in response.

He filled Charles slowly, carefully, taking his time and enjoying every inch of progress he made — every inch they made *together* — until he was fully sheathed.

They hung there for a moment, Charles impaled on him, practically suspended by his ass and armpits, Harlan adjusting to the tight heat around him, before Michael's voice broke the silence. "Can I?"

Harlan looked down, feeling his cheeks heat with embarrassment. He'd gotten so distracted by Charles' body he'd almost forgotten Michael was even there. Michael was still kneeling, stroking himself and looking up with quiet expectation.

Harlan nodded, then realized that, whatever they might try in the future, this time it wasn't really his call. "Charles?" he asked softly, reaching up to pet Charles' shoulder, his fingers splayed across it.

Charles nodded, over and over, but without saying anything, and Harlan got the sense that was what Michael was waiting for.

"Yes," Harlan said aloud on Charles' behalf.

Michael grinned up at him and nodded, rocking forward again and wrapping his lips around Charles' cockhead.

"Oh fuck, oh *fuck*," Charles gasped, the back of his head mashed against Harlan's collarbone.

That was all right. Harlan didn't think he'd even really noticed.

"You two really are gonna take me apart, huh?" Charles laughed unsteadily.

Michael couldn't say anything, obviously, but his eyes flashed with wicked mischief—though Harlan was pretty sure Charles couldn't see that.

Harlan nodded, tightening his grip on Charles' arms and leaning forward to whisper, "Yes," in his ear.

He began to move, and it didn't take long for him and Michael, with Charles caught between them, to find a rhythm.

Harlan had never done anything like that, had barely let himself *imagine* doing anything like that. He'd slowly gotten used to the idea that Charles liked him—loved him—and wanted him around, wanted to be with him and have sex with him, but he wasn't the kind of guy who had spur-of-the-moment threeways—or even, like, carefully planned threeways. But here he was. Here they were, all three of them.

"I'm... I'm... *Fuck*," Charles gasped, digging his nails into Harlan's hands a little. "Not gonna last."

"That's okay," Harlan assured him, his voice coming out surprisingly steady. "I'm close, too."

Michael started stroking himself again, faster this time, as he took Charles deep.

Charles came with a yell, pumping furiously into Michael's mouth.

Harlan followed a second later, the force of his orgasm practically ripped out of him by the white-hot tightness enveloping him.

Michael was slightly behind, but he caught up quickly, coming on the floor between them with his lips still wrapped around Charles' shaft.

As Harlan slowly came down, he found himself wondering if Michael had gotten any cum on his suit jacket, or if he'd even care under the circumstances.

Charles hissed softly, squirming a little in Harlan's arms.

"Too much?" Harlan asked.

Charles nodded, and Harlan slowly, carefully pulled out as Michael slid off, too, releasing Charles' head with a wet popping sound.

Charles staggered a little, but even though he was heavier, Harlan still had a good grip on him and was expecting it. He helped Charles over to the bed and sat him down, then turned around. Michael was still kneeling, so Harlan offered him a hand up.

Michael took it, hauling himself to his feet, grinning at Harlan.

Harlan grinned back, but now that his head was clear again, he couldn't help worrying that Michael might feel ripped off. As much as he'd seemed to enjoy it, he'd really only given a blowjob and jerked himself off. Not nearly as exciting as what *they* had done, at least in Harlan's opinion.

Michael stumbled over to the bed and sat beside Charles, then threw an arm across his shoulders. "Charlie? Harlan? We have *got* to do that again." He laughed. "But not for at least a few hours."

Chapter Four

Harlan's personal cell rang, and he groaned. It was Michael. Did he want to talk to Michael right now? He was at work, but there was nothing going on. He watched Hamilton roll himself on his desk chair to the coffee machine and back. Yeah. Not a lot happening. He answered.

"Hey, Mi—"

"Harlan! I'm so glad you answered!" Michael sounded slightly out of breath.

Harlan frowned at the phone. "Is everything okay? What hap—?"

"My friend's in trouble."

Harlan didn't like the way Michael had just interrupted him twice in a row, but Michael did sound worried. Scared, even. "Your friend... The one with the ghost problem?" he guessed.

"Yeah. Can you come now? Like *right* now?"

Harlan glanced at Hamilton, who now had his head tipped back and was balancing a pencil on his upper lip. "Uh..."

Michael must have misinterpreted his hesitation, because he quickly added, "I — he'll pay you more, since it's a rush job. Double."

Harlan whistled silently to himself. That would be a *big* help. "That won't be nec — "

"You'll come?"

Harlan frowned at the phone. Again with the interrupting. Still, like he'd already thought, Michael sounded really freaked out. "I'll come. What's the address?"

"Oh thank God," Michael sighed, and gave it to him. "I'll give you the details when you get here."

"Hey, Hamilton, wanna go on a field trip?" Harlan asked after he hung up.

Now Hamilton was trying to balance the pencil with just the eraser end on his scrunched-up lip. "Oh, please, teacher!"

Harlan laughed. "Don't call me that. We've got a case." He frowned. "Well, it's a case we already had, but it's been bumped up."

Hamilton shrugged, already setting down the pencil and standing. "Whatever. I'll get my coat."

* * * *

Michael frowned when he saw Hamilton get out of the car after Harlan. "When you said 'us', I thought you meant you'd be bringing Charles."

Harlan shot him a confused look. "Why?"

Michael seemed a little nervous. "Just, you know, in case things get out of hand."

Hamilton snorted. "Trust me. The kid here has dealt with *way* worse ghosties than whatever's in an office building." He snorted again. "What? Are the spreadsheets haunted?"

Harlan made a face at him, having to force down a grin so he wouldn't encourage him. And did Hamilton have to call him that in front of his...boyfriend? "I'm sure it'll be fine," he assured Michael.

Michael looked skeptical but nodded.

"What happened?" Hamilton asked, automatically kicking into cop mode.

Harlan raised an eyebrow.

Hamilton grinned sheepishly and took a half step back.

"Earlier, you said we could do this one any time," Harlan reminded Michael, "but you made it sound really urgent on the phone just now."

"One of my friend's co-workers brought in a priest to sanctify the building or whatever. My friend told me it was a ghost—I thought it was a ghost—but apparently it went nuts right after the priest started doing his thing. The priest collapsed. He said it was a demon." Michael shook his head. "He died on the way to the hospital."

"Holy shit," Hamilton grunted, exchanging glances with Harlan.

Harlan shivered. He'd never come across a demon before. Hell, he wasn't even sure he believed in them. He could only hope that the priest was wrong—had been wrong, he reminded himself. *Yikes*— and that this was just another ghost. An unusual ghost, darker than most, maybe, but a ghost, nonetheless.

Michael laughed awkwardly—the first time Harlan had really seen him *look* awkward—rubbing the back of his neck with one hand. "Yeah. That's kinda why I figured you'd bring Charles."

Hamilton raised an eyebrow. "Did you tell Harlan about this before he got here?"

"Well…" Michael shook his head.

Hamilton shrugged.

"The priest was still alive when I talked to him on the phone," Michael said quietly. "Do you want to call Charles now?"

Harlan glanced at Hamilton. Hamilton shrugged again. Harlan sighed. Okay, apparently the decision was up to him. *Great. My favourite thing.* "No. I'll go in and scope it out first."

Hamilton grinned at him, and Harlan made a face at him in return. He hadn't gotten that phrase from his time as a quote-unquote police officer, just from watching movies and TV.

"If it looks like more than I can handle, I'll absolutely bring in Charles," Harlan promised Michael.

"Okay." Michael reached out and gave his hand a squeeze, which wasn't how Harlan would have *preferred* for Hamilton to find out they were in a relationship, but it was too late now.

Hamilton coughed pointedly but looked away without saying anything.

"Are there still people in there?"

"Yeah. My friend wanted to evacuate the building, but the higher-ups told him no."

Harlan groaned. No wonder Michael had sounded so frantic. "Okay. I'll get started right away." He started walking towards the building's entrance with Hamilton right behind him. It took him a moment to realize that Michael was also following them.

Harlan turned. "Uh, it's probably best if you wait out here."

Michael shook his head. "Uh-uh. No way. I'm coming with you. I gotta see this." He crossed his arms over his chest.

Harlan gritted his teeth, letting his breath out in a hiss. He didn't have time for this. The people inside the building didn't have time for this. "Fine," he said, keeping himself from snapping, but only just. "But you will do *exactly* what me and Hamilton tell you to do, immediately, without question, all right?"

Michael grinned, giving him a jaunty little salute. "Yes, sir."

Harlan groaned silently and kept walking, pointedly *not* looking at Hamilton.

As it turned out, it was a good thing Michael had come with them, because Harlan had no idea where he was going. Hamilton could have—and would have— asked for him, but Michael led them directly to a room on the seventh floor. "This is where the priest did the 'exorcism'."

It would've been obvious, even without Michael telling him. The lights were off, and the air in the room was heavy with incense. Hamilton sneezed. There were several tipped-over candles littering the room. They were lucky none of them had started a fire. There was also an open Bible lying on the middle of the floor, its pages crumpled beneath it. Harlan wasn't religious, but it still seemed disrespectful. He picked it up, dusted it off and set it on a nearby desk.

Harlan closed his eyes.

"Now—?" Michael started asking.

"Shh," Hamilton told him.

Harlan smiled without opening them. *That* was why he brought Hamilton with him on these field trips, even after he'd lost his minimal powers.

Harlan could feel the spirit nearby, not quite in the room but close. Watching them. *Observing* them. It didn't *feel* like a demon — not that Harlan would know what a demon felt like. It felt like a ghost. Fuck, he was freaked out now. He was *afraid*, but he didn't think it was entirely his own fear. He was pretty sure the ghost — or whatever — was pumping out some of its own to influence him. Hopefully he was taking the brunt of it, as the only medium in the room. *Great.* He wanted to turn and run, but he forced himself to do the opposite and begin to draw it out. "My name is Harlan Brand. I'm a medium. I'm here to..." Negotiate a truce? No, that was way too dramatic. "I'm here to help."

Cold laughter shook the walls. Michael let out a squeak, and Hamilton reached for a gun he was no longer permitted to carry. *Very helpful, Curt.*

Harlan did his best to look unimpressed by the display.

"Help...them!" an utterly inhuman voice rasped, the sound like a thousand fingernails scratching at Harlan's skin.

He couldn't help shivering as the artificial fear cranked up a notch. Okay, this was definitely spooky, but he'd handled worse...probably.

He shook his head. "No, not just them — if by 'them' you mean the living. I'm here to help you, too."

A scream, starting so low Harlan could barely hear it and quickly rising until it was so high-pitched that Harlan had to clap his hands over his ears in pain, rattled the office's windows.

Michael moaned, taking a step back, and Hamilton covered him. Not that there was anything either of them could do if the ghost — fuck, maybe it really *was* a demon — came after them.

They heard another scream — a *human* scream — from down the hall.

Harlan and Hamilton glanced at each other.

"I'll go check it out," Hamilton offered.

"Okay. Be careful."

He ran.

"Hey!" Harlan shouted at the ghost, wanting to get its attention on *him*. "Stop that! I'm not like the priest or anyone else you might have seen," he insisted. "I'm not just here to get rid of you. I want to talk to you." He didn't. He really, really didn't, but that was the whole reason he'd left the police force and struck out on his own — to *help* spirits, not just...dispose of them like used condoms. *Ew.*

There was a long, heavy, expectant pause. The fear dialed back a little, or maybe that was just wishful thinking on Harlan's part. A red, spectral hand emerged from the wall. Harlan's breath caught in his throat. All right. He'd never seen a *red* ghost before.

Michael screamed.

Harlan gritted his teeth. "Get out of here. Go. I'll distract it so you can get away."

"N-No," Michael insisted. "I'm staying. Do we need to get Charles?"

Harlan sighed, but he didn't have the time or energy or concentration to fight Michael *and* the ghost. He was doing a poor enough job just of the second one, as Michael had so kindly just pointed out. "Fine. But please —" He cut himself off right before telling his...boyfriend? Boyfriend. Before telling his boyfriend to shut up. "Please be quiet. I need to concentrate. And no, we don't need Charles." *Not yet*, he added silently to himself.

Michael nodded. He looked too scared to speak, anyway.

The rest of the ghost-demon followed the sickle-clawed hand out of the wall. All of it was red. Its teeth were as long and black as its claws, and its eyes were yawning black pools of utter nothingness. They seemed to want to draw Harlan in, leading him deeper, making him despair...

He forced himself to look away, staring at a spot on the wall beside the place it had emerged.

Shit. This was a fucked-up ghost — if it *was* a ghost at all, which Harlan was seriously beginning to doubt. Even if they did call Charles, would he be able to help? His talent was for dealing with ghosts, not whatever the fuck this thing was.

Probably. Maybe Charles would be just as good at this as he was at everything else Harlan had thrown at him.

It came closer, trailing a fine red mist behind itself. Harlan felt like it would be a *really* bad idea to breathe it in, but except for turning and running and telling Michael's friend, 'Sorry, we're abandoning the building and letting the spirits have it. Guess you're out of a job', he didn't exactly have a lot of options.

So it was up to him.

He threw up a barrier between him and Michael and the ghost, something he'd only learned to do recently — and only because he'd encountered a kindly spirit who hadn't minded letting him practice. He'd sent xem on, but he was definitely thanking xem now for xyr help.

It wasn't as good as what Charles could do, but it was better than just standing there, and he wouldn't always have Charles around. Unfortunately, he hadn't had a chance to test it on an *angry* ghost. Hopefully he'd be able to keep it up.

The red...thing hit his shield and bounced off, and if he was watching it from the safety of a screen, the completely surprised expression on its face would have been hilarious. With only a thin shield between them, it was...significantly less funny. It was back again for a second pass almost immediately, and now it raked the power Harlan was using to protect them with those deadly looking claws.

Harlan winced. It wasn't the same as them hitting him directly, but he still felt it and it still *hurt*. He didn't think he'd be able to take many more hits like that before the shield broke—or he did. He wasn't honestly sure which would happen first, and he didn't want to find out. But what else could he do? Sure, they were at a stalemate for the moment, but as soon as the barrier broke or he dropped it out of exhaustion, it would be after them again, and it would be even more pissed off.

Fuck. He had to *think*.

"Do we need to get Charles?" Michael asked again.

Not helping, Michael! But Harlan managed not to say it out loud. Just barely. He shook his head, then stopped paying any attention to Michael, because it was too dangerous to lose his concentration.

Normally he would reach out with his power and 'grab' the ghost—or, if it was being extra feisty, he'd do his special *blink* and physically grab it. He couldn't do the latter with the shield in the way, and he didn't think the former would be enough, but he had to do something besides just cowering here in fear with an innocent civilian trapped with him. And who knew how many more people were still in the building, just waiting for its attention to turn on them? *Shit.*

All right. Keeping his barrier firmly in place, he reached around it with his power—which was about as easy as rubbing his stomach and patting his head at the same time with drones instead of his hands—and tried to at least get a feel for the thing.

Terrifyingly, his power just...slid off. It was like ghosts were normally slightly sticky and his power could catch and grab and *stay*, but this thing was Teflon-coated. *Fuck.*

He could feel his body, his mind, straining as he extended his awareness farther and farther, wrapping around the spirit even though he had no assurance that he'd find anything else, anything he could *use*, any weak points, that he wasn't just stretching himself thinner and thinner until he snapped.

He quickly circled it with his power, feeling himself start to shake, sweat beading on his forehead. Nothing. He just kept sliding off.

Okay. What if he didn't try to grab *on*? What if he tried to go *deep* instead? He directed his power into a needle, sharp and thin, and pressed as hard as he could. He felt it start to slide off again, but he pushed even harder somehow, and he was through, his heart beating in his ears. *Fuck.* He was gonna have a stroke or something one of these days if he kept pushing his brain—or whatever organ he was using—like this. But he was through.

And underneath...floating in the red, demonic outline was the figure of a young woman, her eyes closed and limbs drawn up against her spectral 'body', looking like a serene fetus in its protective amniotic sac.

And she was, at heart, just a ghost. A powerful one, but nothing more or less than a human spirit that had gotten trapped on Earth after death and hadn't moved on, for whatever reason. He knew how to deal with —

She opened her eyes and *screamed* at him. He was flattened against the walls of her sanctuary, but he used the slipperiness to his advantage, throwing his power in a thin sheet behind him and bouncing off it, refusing to be pushed out.

"You're not a demon."

She screamed again.

"You're not a demon!" he screamed right back. "You're a *ghost*, and you can't stay here!"

She smiled, and he saw a shadow pass over his head.

He looked up, following it. One of the demonic hands swept past them, swiping at Michael, who was still cowering behind the barrier. *Shit.*

Harlan allowed himself to be swept out of her massive outer form and back into his body. The shield was close to failing. He'd spread himself too thin, tried to do too many things at once.

Michael was kneeling beside him when he opened his eyes. "Harlan? Harlan, say something, please. Where's your phone? I really, really think we need to — "

"No," Harlan grunted. "I've got this." She was still putting up a fight, yeah, but he had things under control. Almost. Sort of. "She's just a ghost."

He dropped the shield, and she rushed him, but he was ready. He *blinked* and grabbed one of her extended claws. Instead of being icy cold, like most ghosts' ectoplasm, it was warm. Hot, even. Harlan didn't care. He hung on, and he poured his power down through their connection. The claw shattered, falling into black crystalline shapes that floated away and immediately disappeared.

She stared down at him in horror, shaking her damaged hand. He had to wonder if it hurt, and he also had to wonder if he was a bad person if he hoped it *did*. Just a little... Just until he'd cut her down to size.

While she was still reeling, he reached past her claws, grabbing her actual hand — well, the demonic form's hand — hoping he could speed things up a little. Another blast of power and the hand disintegrated, crumbling into red dust that blew away on a sudden wind. He could see her actual 'body' inside its cocoon, and he kept going. He wrapped his arms around its middle, ignoring the burn, and poured power through his chest and down to his fingertips. The 'demon' split in half, twisting and shrivelling in on itself until it too cracked apart and turned to dust, leaving her floating there alone.

She flew at him, screaming, and he reacted without thinking, lifting an elbow level with her face, like he could actually break her nose or something. Luckily he'd *blinked* and was able to make contact. It worked, or at least startled her enough that she drifted back a few feet, watching him warily.

"Hey!" he shouted back at her. "You need to leave!"

She growled, and every hair on his body stood on end.

"You killed a priest."

She froze. "He's *dead*?"

"Yeah. He had a heart attack."

"Holy *shit*! I didn't mean to kill him!" She drifted lower until they were eye to eye. Or eye to...ectoplasm. Something. "I just wanted to scare him! He scared *me* with all that *Exorcist* crap, so I told him I was a demon to fuck with him, then I got...stuck. I was just trying to explain why I'm here and why I've been trying to get everyone's attention!"

"You can tell me. I'll listen," Harlan offered. She looked a little lost or unsure where to begin — something he could tell easily with her, but never could with the living — so he asked, "What's your name?"

"Amy."

"Hi, Amy. I'm Harlan. I'm here to help you, to hear your story."

She took a deep breath — not that she needed to, or that she was actually drawing in air or that it had anywhere to go. "Okay. So this guy *totally killed me* and somehow he buried my body in the cement when they were pouring the foundation. I've been trying to tell people where to find me ever since then, but no one would *listen*. I tried to *show* them, but people got scared, and they sent in that *creep* and I just..." Her outline shivered. For a moment her face twisted in rage, her features lengthening and sharpening back into her 'demonic' form. "*Killlll*," she growled, her voice deep enough that Harlan could feel its vibration at the base of his spine.

Harlan held out a hand.

He didn't have to do more than that. Her features smoothed again, and she lowered her head. "Sorry. I'm really sorry. I didn't mean to *kill* anyone. Oh, God. Am I a bad ghost?" She laughed. "Or maybe that makes me a good *ghost*? Am I a bad person? Am I going to Hell?"

"I know you didn't mean to, Amy," he assured her. "You're not going to Hell." Which led nicely into his next point. "But I can't let you stay. You need to move on now." Neither of them needed him to add 'or I'll make you.'

She nodded. "Okay. What do I need to do?"

"First, you need to show us where to find your...remains." That was one of the few Centre-approved words he still used. 'Body' was just so shocking. Almost vulgar.

"This way." She drifted down through the floor.

Harlan sighed, wondering if she'd figure it out or if they should just start heading downstairs and looking for her on every floor they passed.

She popped back up a moment later, looking sheepish. "Oh. Right. Sorry. It's in the basement. I'll meet you there." She disappeared again.

Michael shuddered dramatically. "*Brr*. Of course it's always in the creepy old basement, isn't it?"

"Usually," Harlan agreed. "At least we can take the elevator." It was almost like being a ghost.

He texted Hamilton and told him to meet them downstairs.

Once they got to the lowest level, Amy led them to an empty spot on the concrete floor in the middle of a storage room. "Here."

"You're sure?" Harlan wasn't going to leave without sending her on, but he also didn't want to have to dig up the whole floor.

She frowned at him slightly, but without any of her earlier menace. "Yeah." She shook her head. "You'd think *you'd* know about this shit already. I can feel it. It's tugging at me, all the time. You could *blindfold* me and I—Well, I guess you couldn't. And I guess I'm not *seeing* it, anyway, but... Yeah. It's there."

"All right." Harlan kept himself from apologizing to her—barely. "Are you ready?"

"Yeah. I guess so." She shuddered, wrapping her arms around herself, each hand cupping the opposite elbow. "I can't do it alone. I-I'm lost. I don't know the way."

"I do," Harlan assured her. "I'll help you find it."

Despite his confident words, he worried that opening the veil for her might be more difficult because she specifically thought she was 'lost', but it practically fell open as soon as he focused on it. She was ready to leave this world behind, and the next world was waiting to welcome her.

"Wow. That was…" Michael shook his head in wonder, letting out a low whistle. "Just…wow! I've heard of what you could do, but that… Wow!"

Hamilton had an arm across his chest to keep him from getting any closer.

Harlan nodded and Hamilton let him go. Harlan shook his head. "Any medium could have done it."

"Don't sell yourself short. What you just did takes talent. Wow. So, now what?"

"Now we recover her body."

Michael looked at the featureless concrete. "Y'know… She's gone. It's not like she'll —"

"We can't just leave her there!" Harlan told him, a little shocked. "We promised her. We'll know. *I'll* know."

Michael frowned, just for a moment. "Of course. I'm sorry."

"It's okay. I know all this is new and weird for you."

"Yeah. Totally. Okay, what now?" Michael repeated.

Harlan glanced at Hamilton.

"I mean, we could do this through official channels, but because we don't actually know there's someone under there — Harlan, don't frown at me, you know what I mean — it'll probably be a long wait.

But…Charles might know someone with a jackhammer or something."

"Huh. You're probably right," Harlan agreed.

"'Course I am."

"Okay. Let me call Charles."

Charles *did* know a woman with a jackhammer — because, of course he did — and Michael got his friend to agree to let them dig up the basement. It wouldn't be able to happen for a few days, which Harlan didn't like, but there was nothing he could do about it. And, like Michael had said, at least Amy wasn't hanging around waiting anymore.

He borrowed a marker and drew an X on the spot Amy had told them to look.

A few days later, Harlan showed Charles' friend Danielle where to start looking. She slipped on ear, eye and mouth protection and shooed them all out of the storage room. Harlan was disappointed. He'd wanted to be there during the 'unveiling', but he knew she was right. They didn't all need to get covered in dust and possibly injured by flying concrete chips or whatever.

After a few minutes, they heard the hammer stop. Danielle opened the door. Her eyes were red, and Harlan didn't think any of the dust had gotten past her goggles. "She's… I found her. You're the ex-cop, right?" she asked Hamilton.

He nodded.

She handed him a pair of goggles and a face mask, using her arm to bar Harlan and Michael — who'd joined them again — from going in or even taking a look. "It's a crime scene now, yeah?"

"Oh. Right." Harlan stepped back meekly, feeling a little stupid.

Hamilton came out a moment later, grim-faced. "Yeah. That's definitely a body. Good work, Danielle. I'll make the call."

They waited for the police to come and take their statements. While they were being interviewed, crime-scene techs worked to uncover Amy further. A stretcher was waiting in the hallway to set her body free from the building.

"Want to go for a drink?" Michael asked. "Sorry — You know what I mean."

"One sec." Harlan texted Charles.

Are you home?

Sorry. Stuck at the club :(

Harlan was a little peopled-out, honestly, but he didn't feel like just sitting around in the apartment alone waiting for Charles to get home either. "Yeah. A drink sounds great."

Chapter Five

Harlan's office wasn't far from his and Charles' new apartment, and sometimes he walked home if Hamilton left early or if he just needed some time by himself to stretch out his legs. He passed a new ghost, or at least one that hadn't appeared while he was around yet. He'd gotten better at keeping his power in check, so he usually only noticed ghosts who were trying to get his attention in some way, rather than seeing all of them all the time, which was exhausting and overwhelming.

Most ghosts, unless they were really putting in a lot of effort, were easily recognizable as ghosts — their 'bodies' weren't fully formed, just sort of fading out at the edges. They usually had a recognizable mouth and eyes, but their features weren't very distinct — certainly not enough to recognize a ghost from a picture of them when they'd been alive.

This one was different. He probably wouldn't even have realized she was dead if he hadn't stopped while he waited for the light to change. Her face was completely ordinary. She had a bicycle leaning against her — it was *very* rare for ghosts to appear with anything besides the clothing they'd been wearing. She had a helmet tucked under her opposite arm, and she was wearing one of those fancy biking outfits that apparently turned people into the land equivalent of seals slipping through water. Her eyes were narrowed in confusion and frustration, and she kept looking up and down the street.

She turned especially far, and Harlan swallowed hard, looking away. After seeing the back of her head, there was no mistaking her for anything but dead.

He also had a very strong feeling that she didn't *know* she was dead.

He groaned. He hated dealing with that kind of ghost.

Still, he approached her. One of the reasons he'd started Laid to Rest was to help ghosts for their own sake, not just because they were inconvenient for the living.

"Can I help you?" he asked while he was still several feet away, so he wouldn't startle her.

She spun to look at him, hauling her bike in a quarter circle. "Yeah, I'm not interested." She started turning away again, and he had to duck his head so he wouldn't get a second look at the wound that had killed her.

"I'm not —" he began.

She shot him a full-on glare, sighing heavily and rolling her eyes. "*Look*, buddy. Whatever it is you want from me? I don't want it. Fuck off."

Oh, great. Not only did she not realize she was dead, she also hated him. "*Listen,*" he said, adding just a little of his power to the word. He kind of hated doing it, but he was also trying to do her a favour, something he didn't have to do, and he also just wanted to get home.

Her mouth went slightly slack, and her eyes softened. "Yes? Can I help you?" she asked, as though he'd hit a reset button and restarted their conversation—but on a much better foot.

"I'm trying to help *you*, actually," he said softly. He blinked, taking his attention off her for a moment, realizing the other people waiting for the light were staring between him and what was, to them, a blank patch of air.

"Um. Maybe we could go somewhere...?"

"I'm not—!" she began. She started getting onto her bike.

Harlan groaned. It made his skin crawl to do it this way, but he needed to get off the street before someone called the police to report a strange creep talking to himself. He made a fist, turned it knuckles up, and yanked it back towards his body. To any of the bystanders, it would have looked like he had suddenly decided to celebrate a small victory, but he was really using his power to draw her to him.

Her mouth closed and her eyes blurred as she followed him into an alley.

He took a quick glance up and down the lane. He didn't see anyone, and he figured that anyone who was there would probably leave once he started talking to the empty air. Hopefully no one would try to mug him while he was concentrating.

As soon as he was reasonably sure they wouldn't be interrupted, he released his hold on her.

" —going anywhere with you!" she finished. Her eyes widened as she realized she was somewhere completely different than where she'd begun the sentence. "You... W-What? How did...?"

"I'm sorry that I had to do that. I needed to talk to you in private."

"Ugh, get away from me, pervert!" She threw her helmet at him.

It passed through him, completely harmless except for a brief cold feeling. It disappeared before it hit the chipped asphalt behind him.

"What...?" Shaking her head from side to side with horror, she started backing away, taking her bike with her.

Great. Either she'd remembered their earlier conversation, or she'd realized that she hated him all over again.

Her expression cleared, and she threw a leg over her bike.

Shit! All he needed was to chase a bicycle-riding ghost around the city on foot. Theoretically she wouldn't be able to go too far from where she'd died before she reappeared back where he'd originally found her, but she was so lifelike that he had a feeling she'd be able to go farther than usual.

He only had a few milliseconds to decide what to do. He found himself concentrating on her bike, wishing he could make it go away...and it did.

They shot each other equally shocked expressions of disbelief. He'd never tried anything like that before — not that he'd had many ghostly items to practice on.

With one leg in the air, she stumbled and almost fell when the bike disappeared from beneath her, but she managed to catch herself. She backed away from him a step. "How... How did you do that? My bike. My helmet. You just... And now I'm here, and I don't remember..."

Harlan sighed. He was doing a *really* great job of respecting ghosts' rights and not favouring the needs of the living over their own. "I'm really, *really* sorry. I promise I'm not a pervert." *Okay, that definitely sounds like something a pervert would say,* he realized, even as he said it. "I really *am* just trying to help you."

"You made my bike disappear." She thought for a moment, then a smile crossed her face. "Oh, I get it. This is some kind of prank, right? We're being filmed right now?" She put her hands on her hips and looked up at the eaves of the buildings on either side of them. "Ha, ha. Okay, you've played your little joke. I'm done. I have to get back to... I'm trying to find..." All the signs of distress left her face as though they'd been wiped clear. Her bike reappeared against her side, and her helmet was in her hand again. "Can you help me? I think I'm lost."

He sighed again, this time with relief. "Yes. I can help you. You've gotten lost."

She smiled at him for the first time. "Okay, good. I feel like I've been here for a while. Do you think I missed the end of the race?"

He nodded. "I'm afraid so. What's your name?"

"Catherine."

"Catherine, what's the last thing you remember?"

She snorted. "The race." She frowned, shaking her head. "No, that's not right, is it? I was... I was talking to you." She flickered for a moment, leaving her bike and helmet suspended with nothing to support them. "Did you... Is this *your* fault?"

He quickly held up his hands. "No! No, this has nothing to do with me, except that I can help you."

"I'm sorry. I'm just so confused right now." She stared down at her helmet. "Why is my helmet off? Did something happen? Did I... Did I hit my head?" She looked right at him, their eyes meeting. It was unsettling to have such a 'lifelike' ghost's focus on him.

Well. Best to rip the Band-Aid off, right?

"Yes. You did."

She shook her head. "I don't remember." She let out a soft laugh. "No, I guess I wouldn't." She hung her helmet from her bike's handlebars and reached towards her head.

"Don't..." Harlan winced. He hadn't wanted to rip it off *quite* that quickly, but...

She felt up along her forehead and past her hairline. Her hand crossed the crown of her head and her eyes widened. Kept widening as her fingers slid farther. "Oh. Oh, God. Oh no. This feels...bad. Really bad. Shouldn't I be in the hospital or something? Why am I just standing here? This... This should really hurt. Shouldn't it? Am I in shock? Is this what shock is?" If she had still been breathing, she would have been close to hyperventilating.

"You're not in shock," he told her softly. "And there's a reason you're not feeling any pain."

"Well?" she demanded, not taking her hand away from the gaping hole in the back of her head.

"You had an accident, Catherine." He didn't know that for sure, of course, but this definitely seemed like a hoofbeats-equals-horses situation. If he was wrong and she'd been murdered or something... Well, did it really matter as long as he helped her to move on?

She stomped a foot. "*Clearly!*"

Fuck, he hated this part. "You didn't make it."

"Didn't make it...to the end of the race?"

He waited, hoping she'd figure it out on her own.

Her eyes widened. "That… That's not what you meant, is it?"

He shook his head.

"No. Oh, no. What…what are you saying? This is crazy! Are you trying to tell me I *died*?"

"Yeah. I'm sorry—"

"No. No, you're wrong. I'm just in shock. It can make you not feel pain, right?"

"I don't—"

"Because if what you're trying to tell me is true, then I must be a ghost, and I don't *believe* in ghosts!"

It wasn't the first time a ghost had told Harlan that, and it probably wouldn't be the last. "You threw your helmet at me, and it went right through me," he said gently.

"I'm *holding* my helmet," she pointed out, looking down at it. "But I…" She threw it at him again.

He ignored it, doing his best not to react at all, even as it literally sent a shiver down his spine on its way through. He'd sorta been expecting that.

He *hadn't* expected her to pick up her bike and throw that at him, and he instinctively ducked, even though he knew, mentally, that it couldn't actually hurt him.

"Holy fuck. I'm dead."

"Yeah. I'm sorry, Cath—"

"Stop that!"

"Stop what?"

"Stop…using my name like that! Like you know me! You sound like a fucking spam email or something."

Harlan snorted before he could stop himself. "Yeah. I hear it now. Sorry. Yes. You died. You're a ghost."

"I don't believe in..." She went over to the closest wall and stuck her hand through it several times in a row. "Well, fuck me."

No thanks, I'm gay, he thought, but managed to keep himself from saying it.

"Okay. Now what? I have, what, unfinished business? The race..." She looked past Harlan.

He turned. Her bike was gone. He looked back at her. "I don't know. Can you think of anything else?"

She shook her head, digging her gloved fingers into the back of her opposite hand.

"Sometimes it's not that," he said gently, hoping it was the case this time. "Sometimes it's just...if the death is really sudden..." *Let her fill in the blanks.*

She nodded.

"I can help you cross over."

She just stared at him for a long moment, long enough that he worried she'd 'reset' again and her bike would reappear. "What's it like?"

"I don't know," he told her honestly. "I haven't been there, but I've looked through a few times, and it's beautiful."

She sighed. "Fine. Do it. Cast your spell or whatever."

He smiled at her. "It's something we do together." He reached out with his power, feeling the energy keeping her here as well as the tug of where she was *supposed* to be. He followed it down and opened a portal on the wall beside her. He could've put it anywhere, but everyone — him included — seemed to find it less off-putting when they could at least pretend it was a door.

"So that's it. 'The light'." She turned towards it, seeming almost mesmerized.

Harlan couldn't see into it at this angle, but he could see shifting ripples of colour dancing across her form, like dappled sunlight through leaves. "Yep."

"And I just...?" She mimed taking a step.

He nodded.

She took a deep breath—or whatever. "Fine. I'll do it. But!" She turned away from the portal and pointed a finger at him. "If you fucked this up and this sends me to Hell or something, I'm coming back and haunting your ass." But she was smiling as she said it.

Even Harlan could feel the calm serenity coming through the opening. "Deal."

She stepped through, and Harlan could have sworn he heard the little *ding-ding* of a bike bell before it closed behind her.

He took a deep breath—a real one—and let it out. *Not bad for a day's work.*

He couldn't repeat this with every ghost in the GTA—not without an army of mediums and infinite patience—but he could at least start in his new neighbourhood. And he'd go back to his old apartment and help any of the ghosts who 'lived' in that area if they wanted it. It wasn't much, but he'd do what he could.

Chapter Six

Skye was already sitting inside the café when Harlan arrived.

"*Sorry,*" Harlan signed. "*I'm not late, am I?*"

"*No, I'm just early.*"

"*Have you been here before?*"

She grinned at him mysteriously. "*A few times.*"

"*What's good?*"

She passed him a menu.

To his surprise, there were instructions for how to sign different things—coffee, cookies, cake—printed next to each item.

Her grin widened.

He looked up. There were large posters on each wall with hand signs on them. Now that he thought about it, aside from the usual café noises of the espresso machine and things like that, it was pretty quiet in there. Glancing around, he saw that most of the other customers were also signing rather than speaking aloud. Now he understood why Skye had wanted to meet there specifically. *Cool.* He hadn't known there was a deaf café in Toronto.

A waiter came over and Harlan scrambled to figure out what he wanted while Skye ordered for herself.

He signed, *"Hot chocolate and a chocolate-chip cookie, please,"* glancing at the menu to make sure he was doing it right, even though he knew all those signs.

"So," Skye signed, giving him a very pointed look.

Unfortunately, he didn't know what the point *was.* *"So?"*

She reached across the table and smacked his hand. *"So why did you ask me to help you break into the Centre last year?"*

"Oh," he said out loud, partially because he hadn't expected the question and partially because he didn't know how to sign that. He had to stop and think about his answer, and how to sign it. *"I would have thought you'd already heard about all that,"* he signed carefully. Skye had always known what was going on when they went to the Centre together, and he couldn't imagine that had changed much.

She flapped a hand at him. *"Of course I did, but I want you to tell me."*

"Oh." Of course she did. She'd *also* always enjoyed making him squirm. *"Well, my partner — my police partner, Hamilton."* He spelled it out, quickly realizing he'd need to come up with a better solution if he was going to get to the end of the story before the cafe closed. He'd never come up with a name-sign for someone before, and he found it oddly daunting. And weird. He felt like Hamilton should come up with it himself — or at least be there.

Skye rolled her eyes. *"Just call him 'H,' okay? Before you have — "* She finished with a sign he didn't know.

"A what?"

"Never mind, it's not important."

"H," Harlan repeated. "We realized the...ghost problems...were coming from the – " He couldn't remember her sign for the Centre. "C-E-N-T-E-R."

"R-E," she corrected him. "We're in Canada."

"R-E." He knew he was lucky she hadn't made him spell the whole thing again. It would have been very like her.

She made a sign with one fist on top of the other, rotating in opposite directions, and he doubted it was a coincidence that it also looked like strangling someone.

He snorted. He recognized the sign as soon as she made it. "Centre," he repeated, using her sign. He groaned. "Maybe it would be better if I just wrote it – "

She shook her head sharply. "If I wanted you to write it down, I would have written you an email. You're telling me, mister." She looked down her nose at him. "I'll help you if you get really stuck," she offered.

"Thank you," he replied, using his facial expression to show he was being sarcastic.

"You're very welcome," she signed, smiling sweetly. "I'm just looking out for you. It's good for you to practice."

"We went to the Centre – with your help – but we didn't find anything in Mister Addison's office." It felt strange to use the name-sign Skye had created for their former teacher, long before he'd told Harlan to call him Tom. Long before Harlan had killed him. "We went with Morgan." He had to spell that out, too. His fingers were definitely getting a workout. "I think you met them at the party?"

She nodded, grinning.

"Charles was there, too." He thought he might be able to come up with a name-sign for Charles without feeling too weird about it...but he hoped he wouldn't have to, especially on such short notice. *"M"* — he was sure she'd pick it up from context — *"picked the lock on the door of Mister Addison's house."* He wasn't sure how to sign exactly what he wanted, so he settled on, *"It's part of the Centre."*

Skye rolled her eyes. *"Everyone knows the director's house is part of the Centre. Everyone but you, apparently."*

He ignored her and kept going. *"We found the missing mediums in the basement."* There was probably an official ASL sign for 'psychics who work with ghosts,' but he used Skye's sign for it, holding his thumb and forefinger a few inches apart. *"We managed to save...most of them. And... And I killed..."* He couldn't look at her.

She reached across the table and grabbed both his hands in hers, pulling them and his attention back to her. She let go to sign, *"You shouldn't feel bad about that. Not at all."* She paused, giving him a sad smile. *"But you do, don't you?"*

He nodded, still avoiding eye contact. Not that he *usually* made eye contact.

She sighed. *"Of course you do. You're too sensitive, Brand. I've always thought so."* Her expression turned serious. *"Have you talked to anyone about it? You left the police right after, right?"*

He shrugged one shoulder.

"No, not shrug! Have you talked to anyone about it?"

"Yes. My counsellor." He had to spell that out as well. *"And Charles and Hamilton...a little."*

"Why just a little? They were both there. They love you. They would understand better than anyone, right?"

Harlan laughed. *"I wouldn't go so far as saying Hamilton loves me — "*

Skye shook her head. *"Stop it. Stop changing the topic. You should know by now that you can't get rid of me that easily."*

Harlan sighed. He had to stop and think about why he hadn't told them how much killing Tom was actually bothering him, especially the fact that he didn't really remember doing it. It would have been hard enough for him to say it out loud, let alone sign it, but he didn't doubt that Skye would sit there staring at him with that level expression until he'd answered to her satisfaction. *"I don't want to remind Charles of that night,"* he finally signed, simply and honestly.

"But, like you said, he was there. He already remembers it himself. And I'm sure he can tell it's bothering you." She nodded decisively. *"You should try talking to him about it when you're ready. It might help both of you."*

He laughed. *"When did you get so wise?"*

She tapped the side of her head with one finger. *"Silly. I've always been wise. And Hamilton?"*

That answer was more complicated and involved the kind of macho bullshit he'd thought he and Hamilton were above — or at least had moved past with each other, especially since they'd left the police.

"Hamilton... It's complicated. We're not... We don't talk about emotional things," he admitted, almost apologetically. *"Not like that."*

She put up her hands. *"I get it. Guy stuff."* She stuck the tip of her tongue out at him. *"But you should think about it. I've met the new director of the Centre,"* she signed, completely changing tracks, as she often did.

Harlan made a noncommittal sound, then realized she couldn't hear it and nodded. He hadn't been back since his encounter with Tom. He hoped he'd never have to go back, especially not to see the director.

She smiled at him. *"All right, we won't go there. How are things in your personal life?"*

Harlan waved a hand and looked away. *"We've talked a bunch about me already. How are you doing? We should talk about you now."*

"And we will — but I know deflection when I see it. You just moved in with your boyfriend and started your own business. That's stressful, but it should mostly be a good thing, right?"

Harlan sighed, his fingers twitching as he started signing several times, then changed his mind.

"Uh-oh. Trouble in paradise?" she asked.

He sighed again. *"No, nothing like that. It's just…there's this guy…"*

Skye raised an eyebrow.

"And Charles and I are…" He couldn't remember the sign for 'dating', never mind anything more complicated. He settled on finger spelling. *"We're D-A-T-I-N-G him and it's going really well. I love…being with both of them."*

"Okay, that's good," Skye encouraged him. *"Is there a 'but'?"*

Harlan nodded. *"But Charles has been really busy with the club and Michael just seems to be around all the time. It's kind of annoying, actually."* He hadn't really thought it until he said it, but he realized it was true. *"When I'm with him or all three of us are together, it's amazing, but I barely see Charles, and I've kinda been avoiding our apartment. I've been spending a lot of time alone at the office…or with Michael."* He blinked. *"It's funny, but…when I'm with Michael I don't really think about these things. I haven't said anything to either of them."*

Skye steepled her fingers. *"Okay, three things. First — is Michael hot?"*

"Skye!"

She laughed. *"I'm sorry, I'm sorry. I couldn't resist."* She managed to keep a straight face for a second. *"But the question still stands."*

Harlan rolled his eyes. *"Yes. He's hot."*

"Not good enough. I need a picture."

Harlan frowned. *"I don't think I have one, actually."*

Skye raised an eyebrow. *"Weird."*

"It's not weird! I just don't take a lot of pictures."

It was her turn to roll her eyes, but she continued. *"Second — you need to talk to Michael, and especially Charles, about this. You clearly care about them, and if they care about you, they'd want to know."* She held up a hand when Harlan went to protest. *"It doesn't have to be right away. Just, please, think about it."*

He nodded, somewhat reluctantly.

"Third… Have you considered that Michael might have a talent and he might be using it on you?"

"What?" If he'd been a slightly more dramatic person, Harlan would have stood up so quickly that his chair fell over backwards, but he settled for just blinking at Skye in silent disbelief. "Why would you say something like that?" He was so shocked that he accidentally said it out loud and had to repeat himself.

Skye held up her hands. *"Hey, I'm just working with what you told me. You feel good when he's around, but you start doubting your feelings when he's gone, right?"*

Harlan blinked at her again, taking a long moment before replying, *"I guess so…"* He'd never thought of it like that, but…could she be right?

He shook his head. No. It was too farfetched. Why would Michael do that? *"What ability would he even have?"*

She shrugged. *"Could be a number of things. Emotional manipulation isn't all that uncommon."*

Harlan shook his head. *"No. I'm sorry. That's ridiculous."* He stood, looking around for a waiter so he could pay his bill and leave.

"Harlan... I'm just calling it how I see it. Please, don't go yet. I didn't mean to offend you. I'm probably wrong." She gave him a wry grin as he hesitated. *"There are those who call me paranoid."*

He sat down again. *"Like me. Several times."*

"Like you."

They each took a deep breath, and Harlan was relieved when he felt the tension slip away again. At least he hoped so. *"We've talked so much about me!"* he signed, happy to shift the attention away from him — and he suspected she'd let him when she might not have before. *"What's new with you?"*

She grinned. *"I was sort of hoping you would give me your friend Morgan's number?"*

Chapter Seven

The phone rang. Harlan didn't even bother looking up.

It rang a second time and Harlan frowned. He glanced at Hamilton and saw that he was on the other line.

Harlan groaned and picked up the phone on his desk. "Laid to Rest, Harlan speaking."

"Is this Laid to Rest?" a man's voice asked.

Harlan found the question a little odd, since he'd already answered it, but the man sounded anxious — borderline terrified — and Harlan could definitely relate to that.

"Yes. This is Laid to Rest," he repeated. "My name is Harlan. How…how can I help you?"

A sigh filled his ear, then a silence so long that Harlan thought he might have hung up, that Harlan was about to break it *himself*…

"Well. My mother died a few months ago…"

Another silence. Harlan dug around in his desk — accidentally popping open the false bottom Hamilton had insisted on installing, but Hamilton wasn't much of a carpenter — for a notebook and pen. The best he could find — the best he could *ever* find, no matter how many times Hamilton stuffed it with notebooks, pens, and pencils — was a receipt and a...crayon. How had a crayon even gotten in there? He didn't think any children had ever been inside since they'd opened.

Well...not living ones, anyway. If he didn't know better, he'd think the office was haunted.

"Oh. I'm sorry to hear that." He said it because he knew that was what he was supposed to say. He suspected he'd be...ambivalent, at best, when his own mother died.

"Oh, it's okay." The man laughed, the sound rising at the end. "I'm sorry. That makes me sound like a fucking monster. We—I hadn't spoken to her for about...fifteen years?" He stopped, and Harlan suspected he was waiting for Harlan to berate him.

"I haven't spoken to mine in about that long," Harlan admitted. He wasn't sure why he'd said it. It wasn't something he talked about, never mind with strangers, but even though he didn't usually pick up on that kind of thing, he felt like the man needed to hear it.

"Oh." The word was completely flat, with no emotion.

Another silence, and this time Harlan was so sure he'd hung up that he actually started pulling the phone away from his ear.

"Okay. Okay, that's good. I-I think you're exactly who I need to talk to, actually."

"How can I help you?" It wasn't what Harlan usually asked — well, usually he didn't ask anything, because Hamilton answered the phone — but that was what it sounded like the man needed — help.

Another pause, but shorter this time, then all the words came tumbling out in a rush. "She's back. She found me. I-I need you... I need *someone* to get rid of her, or I'm..." He laughed bitterly. "The only reason I haven't done something already is that I'm worried I'd be stuck there with *her*."

Harlan seriously hoped this was a ghost situation, which he was more or less equipped to deal with, and not a mental health situation, which he definitely was not. Well, aside from recommending a good counsellor. He could barely deal with his own, never mind someone else's.

"Your mother's ghost is haunting you, is that right?"

Harlan heard him swallow, almost like he was choking down a sob. "That's right. I — It doesn't... It doesn't make sense! She didn't die here or anything! She didn't even know where I live!"

Harlan drummed the fingers of his free hand on his desk while he thought until Hamilton turned and frowned at him, shaking his head and pointing at the phone he was holding.

Aha. An idea. "Did you go to her funeral, to her grave?" It was rare for a ghost to 'jump' haunting sites, but it was *possible* she'd followed him home.

He tried not to think about how much stronger, more malicious, and difficult to get rid of jumpers tended to be than more standard hauntings.

"No, I didn't." That cracked laughter again. "I'm sorry. You must think I'm a really shitty person, not going to my own mother's funeral."

Harlan couldn't decide if someone — or several someones — had told him this or if it was only his own guilt over going against society's expectations. Either way, Harlan was in no position to judge his potential client, and he didn't want to. "I don't. It sounds like you did what you had to do."

"I like to think so," he said in a very small voice. "So…can you help me?"

"I can at least check out the situation and try."

"My mother was very religious. Do we need a priest?"

Thinking of Michael's friend's ghost, Amy, Harlan replied, "No!" a little too quickly.

"Oh. Sorry."

"It's all right. Sorry." *Wow. Great job, Harlan.* "This is what I do. We won't need a priest. Would you like to come into the office, or would you like me to come to you?"

"Um… I'd rather go there, if that's okay. She can't leave the apartment, right? I've been trying to stay away as much as possible, but I've just been *so tired.*" He yawned.

"Right. Probably not." Harlan felt a little bad lying to his client—a jumper was usually tied to a *person* rather than a place—but he was planning on helping him anyway, and if he could make him feel a little better in the meantime, that was a good thing, right? "What's your name, and when would you like to make an appointment?"

"It's Earl. And are you available…now?"

Harlan opened the shared calendar Hamilton had made them. "Yes, actually, I have an opening—"

"Great. I'll be there in an hour."

Harlan quickly gave him the address and Earl hung up.

* * * *

"Oh holy shit…!" Harlan gasped when Earl walked through the door. It was extremely unprofessional, and he immediately regretted it, but it was too late. Any hope he'd had of peacefully resolving this situation to every party's satisfaction with a sweet reunion between mother and son before Harlan sent her on or they took a little time to get reacquainted, vanished. There was only one way this was going to end, and it was going to be *ugly*.

Earl froze in the doorway, his eyes wide and terrified. "What? What is it?" He stumbled back a step, trying to look everywhere at once.

"Um…" Harlan knew he would have to phrase this delicately—and soon, before the man panicked even more—but he had no fucking idea how. He'd heard of ghosts becoming 'parasites'—latching onto someone and draining their life energy—but he'd never seen one in person. He could have happily gone without *ever* seeing it.

There was a woman perched on Earl's back, her skeletally thin arms locked around his throat and her legs stretched around his middle. Her gnarled fingers ended in wickedly hooked yellowed nails—claws, really—with the tips pressed against her son's throat, ready to pierce it if he struggled at all. Her long black hair fell forward over his shoulders, blocking Harlan's view of her face, for which he was extremely grateful. Even though he knew he'd probably see it eventually, it gave him a moment to deal with what he *could* see before dealing with any further horrors.

She didn't notice Harlan. She either didn't realize what he could do to her—or she was so confident that she didn't care—because even while he watched, she pressed her face tighter to the back of Earl's neck. She closed her eyes, and Harlan could almost *see* her drawing energy out of him in the way Earl stumbled, his skin getting even paler. If Harlan *blinked*, he'd probably be able to literally see it.

Worse, there was a *sound*, a grotesque parody of an infant suckling.

Harlan couldn't hold in a gag, trying to cover the sound with a cough. Before he could stop himself, he blurted, "Doesn't your back hurt?"

Hamilton looked up from his phone call—a different one than when Earl had called—and gave Harlan a sharp look.

"Y-Yeah," Earl agreed. To Harlan's surprise, he was actually smiling a little. "Oh, thank fuck, it's not just me!" He laughed shakily. "I've been to so many doctors. Chiropractors. Massage therapists. I've had X-rays, you name it. But they all say my back is perfectly fine, that it's not even tense, but it *hurts*."

"Harlan."

He'd been so focused on—and creeped out by—the woman's ghost that he hadn't heard Hamilton approach. He startled when Hamilton touched his shoulder.

"Sorry. I need to talk to you for a second. It's about the Marquez case."

Harlan blinked—as far as he knew, there was no 'Marquez' case.

Hamilton cocked his head to the side, giving Harlan a meaningful enough glance for Harlan to finally pick up on it.

"Sorry. I'll just be a moment," Harlan told Earl with the best smile he could manage under the circumstances. "Why don't you have a seat at my desk?" He gestured to it. Even though she wasn't a real *weight*, not in the physical sense, there was a heaviness about her that made Harlan's own back ache.

Earl nodded meekly.

Harlan turned away before he had to see how — or if — the seating arrangements would change the mother's position.

"What?" he signed to Hamilton. He'd been teaching him a few basic signs for moments just like this one.

Hamilton shook his head and, making sure Earl wasn't watching, pointed at the hallway and turned to leave before Harlan could protest or question him further.

Harlan followed him with an annoyed huff. Why was Hamilton interrupting him while he was with a client — well, potential client? "What?" he asked, once they were in the hall with the door closed.

"What's got you so freaked out about this one? It's freaking *me* out not knowing."

"Oh." Yeah, Harlan could see how that would be scary, given the way he'd practically screamed when Earl came in. "It's his mother's ghost. She's a parasite."

Hamilton whistled. Harlan had given him his old Centre textbooks to read up on less-common kinds of ghosts, and he wasn't at all surprised Hamilton had done his homework. "Fuck. Poor guy."

"Yeah. She's latched on to his back, and she's draining him."

"Fuck," Hamilton repeated, with even more feeling. "Do you think you can help him?" he asked, very quietly, his hand cupped around his mouth for extra 'security'.

"Fuck. I hope so. Actually...would you sit with us? Y'know, so you can learn a little more about this kinda ghost in case we run into one again." Not at all because Harlan was scared shitless. *Nope. Not at all.*

Hamilton gave him a funny look, then shrugged. "Yeah. Sure. What's the game plan?"

That was a good question, actually. It was probably smart to stop and take a second to think this through — even talk it through, with Hamilton. "Well, the first step is to get her detached. I don't think we can send her on while she's still...feeding."

"Barf."

"Yeah. Big time."

"How do we do that?"

Harlan liked that Hamilton said 'we', even if it wasn't — strictly speaking — accurate. They were partners, after all. "I'm not totally sure," he whispered, cupping his own mouth. He didn't realize until after he'd spoken that he was doing it on the wrong side, with the opening facing the office door. "Somehow, I don't think *talking* will be enough to persuade her."

"Yeah, no. Not if she's, y'know." Hamilton made a 'kissy' face and sucking noises.

"Gross. Thanks," Harlan said dryly.

"No prob."

"So I'll have to see if I can use my power, and if that doesn't work..." Harlan sighed. "I'll have to actually touch her and *pull* her off."

Hamilton made a face. "Can you get, like, ghost rabies if she bites you? Or an even *smaller* ghost parasite?"

"I..." Harlan had been about to tell him 'no,' but he realized he didn't actually know. Not *completely*. "I don't think so, but thanks for putting that thought into my head."

"You're welcome. Sorry," he added a moment later.

"We don't really have time to research this, unfortunately. Earl doesn't look like he's got much left to drain."

"No, he really doesn't. Okay, so you get her off him. What then?"

"Then it's the same as always — open a portal and get her through. With the added twist that I don't think we'll be able to get her to go through on her own—"

"Uh, no."

"And we'll have to make sure she doesn't reattach."

"Ugh."

"Yeah."

"Well, let's get back in there."

"Yeah. Thanks, Hamilton."

Hamilton frowned at him. "What for?"

"Nothing. Never mind." Harlan opened the door for them and hurried back inside before he had to try to explain himself.

He couldn't see much of Earl or his mother through her long, flowing black hair, covering both her and his back. It probably hadn't been that long in life — and it almost certainly hadn't blown around like that when there wasn't any wind — but darker spirits tended to get…twisted, becoming less and less like their living, human selves as time passed and they got stronger.

Earl was just sitting in front of Harlan's desk. He wasn't on his phone, he wasn't fidgeting or looking at the clock. He was just…perfectly still. It was really unsettling, and Harlan couldn't help a nervous glance in Hamilton's direction — relieved when Hamilton gave him one right back.

"Sorry about that, Earl." Harlan sat behind his desk, and Hamilton pulled up a chair to sit beside him.

He didn't respond in any way, didn't even move. Harlan was about to say something again when he finally looked up, hollow-eyed and looking exhausted.

"It's no problem," he said, his voice utterly flat.

Shit. He sounded even worse than before they'd gone into the hall.

Harlan was torn between wanting to let Earl know what he was going to do and *warning* the spirit.

"Okay, Earl. You were right. Your mother's spirit *is* haunting you." It was so hard to just sit and talk to Earl, concentrating on him, while he could hear that phantom *slurp, slurp* from over his shoulder. It didn't seem like anyone but him could hear it. *Lucky them.*

Earl just kept staring straight ahead, but there was movement over his shoulder.

"She's not haunting a place. She's haunting *you.*"

Earl blinked. "Okay…"

There was a warning rattle from the hunched figure on his back — less like a rattlesnake and more like two dry bones clicking together in the wind. *Yee.*

Two glittering eyes appeared from the darkness beneath her hair, boring into his own. He suppressed a shudder. She didn't need to know how afraid he was. It was bad enough in a reasonably well-lit office in the middle of a sunny day. He couldn't imagine how bad it must have been for Earl, alone in his apartment at three in the morning.

All right. He had her attention. *Great.* Should he keep talking so Earl knew what was going to happen, or try to strike before she did?

No. Even here, informed consent was important. Risk Aware Consensual…Exorcism? He had to tell Earl.

"She's latched on to you—"

That got a reaction out of Earl. He spun in his chair, looking around wildly. "She's here? Now?" He winced as his mother adjusted her grip on his throat. One of her talons was *just* on the edge of piercing his skin.

Hamilton shifted uncomfortably but didn't say anything.

"Yeah. She is. The first thing I'm going to do is remove her, all right?"

"Yes. Please." Fear seemed to have helped break him out of the trance or whatever she'd been holding him in.

"What was your mother's name?" Harlan asked. He didn't think knowing—or not—would make a bit of fucking difference at this point, but it might at least work as a distraction.

"Tanya. Tanya Sinclair."

Harlan nodded as decisively as he could. Forcing himself to look at the darkness over Earl's shoulder, he said, as firmly and evenly as he could, "Tanya, you can't stay here any longer. You have to let your son move on."

Silence. Stillness. Yeah, she wasn't giving up without a fight.

"If you don't let go on your own, I'll be forced to *make* you. This is your last warning."

Weak. Her voice was in his head, wrapping around him. *You're weak, just like him. I can tell. Everyone can. All they have to do is look at you and they know. Just give up. Leave me and my boy alone. He's* mine. *You can't have him. No one can. You're a sissy and a pathetic failure. When I'm done with him, when he's here with me, I'll come for you,* she promised.

He could feel ice creeping through his veins. Yes. He *was* weak. She was right. How had he thought he could —?

"Harlan!" Hamilton's voice was in his ear. His breath was warm, pushing back the chill of the grave that had settled over him. He didn't think it was the first time Hamilton had said his name.

Harlan shivered, wrapping his arms around himself. "Fuck. Sorry. I'm okay. She just... I'm okay now."

Hamilton leaned back slightly, but he didn't look convinced. "You wouldn't answer me for like a minute."

"Sorry. She..." He definitely didn't have a mother-shaped opening in his armour. Nope. Not him. "She got me for a second, but it's fine now." Fuck, it was a good thing he'd brought Hamilton over.

"Okay. Don't scare me like that. What did she *say*?"

"It's not important. It's not true."

It is —

But he was ready for her the second time, and he pushed her words, her presence, away. He was strong. He'd proven it over and over again, with *way* tougher beings than her. In a few minutes, she'd be gone forever, he'd still be there, and her son would be free.

He reached out with his power, going on the offensive while she was still slightly off balance. He felt the borders of her, felt where she'd sunk her mouth — almost like a lamprey's, lined with rows of serrated teeth, nothing remotely human, not anymore — deep into the back of her son's neck, where her claws hovered just above his throat. *Fuck.* He could feel how close she was to reaching in, maybe even possessing him. He'd been through enough — *more* than enough.

He had to stop her before that happened. *Okay, I can do this.*

He could feel where she began and ended, trace her outline with his power, and he began to trickle it into the negative space between her and Earl. He wanted to get that awful sucker off the back of his neck, but he knew that would be the most difficult part, so he left it for last, beginning instead where her grotesquely swollen stomach pressed against Earl's back and forcing his way up, using the slight dip of his spine as a channel to reach higher and higher, flattening out across Earl's back and beginning to separate them, just a hair.

She was still longer than he'd thought she'd be, actually. He'd almost reached her neck before she began to fight back.

Earl screamed as she sank her claws into his throat, spasming in his chair.

"Fuck. Harlan, what is it? What's happening? I can't—" Hamilton shook his head in frustration. "There's *nothing*."

"It's okay," Harlan assured him, not entirely sure that was the truth. "She's fighting me, but that just means I've got her attention."

"Okay, if you say so." Hamilton didn't sound at all convinced. He was leaning forward in his own chair, his elbows braced on his knees as he tried to help fight something he'd lost the ability to perceive at all.

"Tanya, let go," Harlan told her, expanding his power to wrap around her arms, too. He felt a bright line of pain on his cheek. He cried out, clapping his hand over it. It came away wet. The deep scratch was bleeding badly already.

"Harlan!" Hamilton jumped up, looking like he was going to get between Harlan and Earl — or rather, Earl's passenger.

Harlan shook his head. "It's fine. I'm fine. It's just because it's a head wound, you know how much those bleed." He sounded more certain than he felt. *Fuck*. This was bad. She'd been able to hurt him without making contact. She was even stronger than he'd feared.

He motioned for Hamilton to sit again, which he did — reluctantly.

Harlan turned his attention to her hands, trying to at least separate her palms from his neck before he freed her nails.

The sourceless wind that had been blowing her hair picked up, swirling out around Earl and leaving him untouched in the middle.

Harlan felt another cut on his face, but he grimly ignored it. If she was attacking him, she was distracted, and he took advantage of every *millimetre*.

She lifted her head, her mouth still latched on, extending like a proboscis, and he saw her face for the first time. He had to hold back a scream. She didn't look like a ghost, not really. She looked like a *mummy*, withered and leathery, with a *solidity* ghosts didn't have. Her eyes were glittering black pits in her shriveled 'skin'.

"Let. Go," he growled, making a fist and *pushing* against her with his power.

No. Weak. Give in. Pitiful. Sad. Let go. Let me take care of you. Give in.

Harlan hissed, forcing himself to look away, look sideways at Hamilton. Hamilton believed in him. Hamilton was the strongest man he knew, and Hamilton believed in him. He could do it.

She followed his gaze, creaking as she moved.

"Ah!" Hamilton jerked back, cupping his own cheek.

She slashed again, without touching him. Another cut appeared on Hamilton's other cheek.

Fuck. This was spiralling out of control, quickly and badly. Harlan didn't care if she hurt him, but how *dare* she go after Hamilton?

"Hamilton!" he shouted above the rising wind and the fluttering of every loose piece of paper in the office caught in it. "Go! We're just giving her more targets!"

Hamilton shook his head, crossing his arms stubbornly across his chest and ignoring the blood dripping down his chin.

Harlan didn't want to remind him that there was actually nothing he could do to help. "Make sure no one comes in here to see what's happening. Keep the hallway clear."

Was he imagining the way Hamilton's hand lifted, just a fraction, like he was going to salute?

"Fine," Hamilton grunted, or something like that. Harlan couldn't actually hear him. He turned on his heel and left the two of them alone, closing the door behind him.

Well, the *three* of them.

"Sh-shouldn't he stay?" Earl asked. He was in the eye of the storm, and Harlan could hear him perfectly.

Harlan shook his head. "I've got this!" *Wow.* He sounded so confident. Hopefully he wasn't bullshitting both of them.

It *was* a little easier with Hamilton gone. He only had to worry about himself — and Earl.

I'll kill him. You won't have him. I'll kill him, then he'll be mine forever, she hissed in his mind.

"No. You won't. He's going to live a long time without your shadow over him," Harlan shouted back. He *slammed* his power against her, pulling her claws out of Earl's throat and wrapping them in it.

No! She pawed at him, trying to find her grip again, but her hands bounced harmlessly off Earl's skin.

Her glittering eyes turned back to Harlan. A real, physical cut appeared on Earl's neck, just below his ear. A warning.

"All right, bitch. Let's finish this." Harlan *blinked,* even as he stood up. Somehow she looked even worse like this, just a leathery *thing* made of bones pressed against desiccated flesh, nearly breaking through, that should blow away in the wind she'd created except that she was bloated with her son's energy.

"I'm sorry, Earl. This is *really* gonna hurt. If it helps, it's going to hurt me, too. And it's going to hurt *her.*" He'd make sure of that.

He ran behind the chair, gritting his teeth to keep the power he'd already sent out in place.

He grabbed a handful of the hair on the back of her head and *yanked*. It wrapped around his arm, digging in, feeling like a thousand tiny papercuts, but he ignored it. He kept pulling, pouring as much power into his grip as he safely could, and finally there was a horrible wet *pop!* and she was free. Earl was free. Well, she still had her limbs wrapped around him, but Harlan just pulled her head straight back and down and shook her like a dog with a rat — shaking Earl with her, and he moaned — until he managed to get her loose with the help of the power already surrounding her.

He took a stumbling step back, wanting to get some distance between her and Earl. If she latched on again, he honestly didn't think he was strong enough to separate them a second time. He hoped she couldn't feel how drained and exhausted he was. Okay. He'd done part one — the *hard* part. Time for part two, which he'd been doing his whole life. He could probably do it in his sleep. Though ghosts didn't usually fight him that hard so late in the game.

She was *heavy* hanging from his hand, twisting and shrieking, cadaverously thin except for her bloated middle. Luckily she couldn't actually break his wrist — could she? No. Probably not. Still…probably better that he hurry.

She turned enough that he could see her face again, and there was a gaping hole where her mouth had been. Harlan had an uncomfortable feeling he knew where the rest of it was. Hopefully it would fall off or disappear or something once she was gone.

He let her drag him down, because that was the direction he wanted to go at the moment, and let her think she'd won a small victory. He slammed down the palm of his free hand, practically ripping open a portal.

She realized what he was doing and reached up to claw at his arm, her hair digging in tighter until his arm felt like it was about to pop, but he held on grimly, dragging her over the hole.

She screamed, making his ears feel like they were bleeding. The wind picked up. The stupid crayon he'd been writing with bounced harmlessly off his jeans. Well, maybe it was a good thing he hadn't been able to find a pencil.

He got her feet over the opening, and it began to draw her down. It was where she belonged, and the universe wanted to find balance.

She held on, trying to drag him down with her. He couldn't feel his arm, but he'd rather be touching hair than skin. It didn't have the same icy burn that was slowly stealing the sensation in his left hand.

"Get. In!" he shouted, throwing everything he had at her. He looked away when she began to fall. He didn't want to see where she was going.

The wind stopped, all the paper and other debris falling around them.

The portal closed around her writhing hair, severing some of it. It immediately became limp and lifeless, just wrapped around his arm but without digging in. He frantically brushed it off, and it disappeared.

He rocked back onto his heels, panting. Okay, that had been one of the worst ghosts he'd ever dealt with.

Sitting wasn't enough. He flopped onto his back, staring up at the office's ceiling. *His* office, though he probably wouldn't get paid for what he'd just done. That was fine.

"Boss?"

Harlan flopped his head to one side so he could look at Hamilton.

"Oh, good, you're alive. You did it?"

Harlan nodded, just enough for it to be clear what he was doing. Hopefully. He didn't want to have to do it again—and even *more*.

"Fuck, it looks like a tornado went off in here."

Harlan snorted. "That's a mal... A malf..."

"A malphorism?"

"Thaaat's the one."

"Get up." Hamilton offered him a hand.

Harlan took it, allowing Hamilton to pull him up. His legs—his whole *body*—felt completely boneless, and he leaned heavily on Hamilton as he helped him back around to his desk chair. It kept rolling away as

Hamilton tried to put him in it, and he couldn't stop giggling.

"Well, *you're* helpful," Hamilton grumbled, shaking his head, after he finally got Harlan down safely. "How's our client?"

Harlan groaned. He was having a hard enough time worrying about *himself.*

"Yeah, okay, I'll check on him." Hamilton circled the desk again—fuck, how did he have so much energy? And *bones*?

Earl looked up when Hamilton got close. "She... She's gone."

Hamilton glanced at Harlan for confirmation.

Somehow, Harlan managed to nod.

"Yeah. She's gone."

Earl started crying, helplessly, covering his face with his hands.

"Hey," Hamilton said gruffly. "Want me to...?" He held out his arms.

Earl nodded, and Hamilton held him—a little awkwardly, with a lot of back-patting—until he'd cried himself out.

Harlan was just glad the attention was off him for a while so he could recover—and that Earl was all right.

"What's your email so I can send you an e-transfer?" Earl asked a few minutes later, suddenly completely calm like he hadn't just been crying his eyes out. Harlan was impressed.

"Oh, that's, uh..." Harlan felt bad asking for Earl's money. This had been a fucking emergency service.

"And I'll need an invoice," Earl said firmly.

"All right." Harlan printed one and passed it to Earl—with their lowest, most basic rate. "The email's on there."

Earl hunched over his phone for a moment—but it was a light, natural hunch now that nothing was dragging him down—busily typing in the details.

Harlan's phone dinged, letting him know he had a work email. His eyes widened as he opened it. "Earl, uh, I think you hit the wrong number." He'd sent almost double what Harlan had requested.

Shaking his head, Earl straightened. "Uh-uh. That's the right amount." He shrugged one shoulder. "She left me some money. I guess that's why I held on like that for so long, 'cause I felt like I...owed her, or something? Anyway. You really helped me. You saved my fucking life. Please. Take it."

Harlan heard Hamilton clear his throat softly and turned to look at him.

Hamilton nodded, letting Harlan know he should accept.

"All right. Thank you." Harlan accepted the transfer. He'd just give the 'extra' money to Morgan, and he'd be just as insistent as Earl that they take it. *Yeah, right.* Maybe he'd make Hamilton do it.

Usually, at this point, Harlan told clients to come back if they—or a ghost—ever needed his help again, but that didn't seem right this time. "I hope I never see you again," Harlan said very earnestly. His eyes widened. "Oh, fuck, I'm—"

Earl laughed, bright and genuine. "I know what you mean. Me, too. And thanks."

Chapter Eight

There was a young man sitting at Harlan's desk when he got back from lunch. *His* desk, not Hamilton's, which was closer to the door for exactly this reason — blocking people from getting this far without being intercepted by Hamilton.

Worse, Hamilton wasn't there.

The kid — if he was out of high school, it wasn't by much — was clutching either side of a cardboard drink tray like it was the only thing keeping him anchored to the world. The cups were from Starbucks, one coffee and one lemonade. As unsettled as Harlan was by the situation, he couldn't help hoping the coffee was for him, even though that didn't really make sense. Why would a stranger, a client, bring him coffee out of the blue?

There was something so familiar about him, but Harlan couldn't place him. There weren't all that many places Harlan might have met him. He looked too young to be a cop, and even then, he hadn't actually met many cops besides Hamilton.

The Centre? That had to be it.

Harlan gently reached out with his power. No, he wasn't a medium, but that was as much as his ability could tell him. Hopefully he was just a client, and any familiarity would be washed away by the coffee he was holding.

"Can I help you?"

Turning in his chair, the boy shot him a very strange look, one Harlan couldn't begin to interpret.

"Hey, you're back!"

As though Harlan had just stepped out for a minute in the middle of a conversation. As though he knew this guy.

As though this guy knew *him*.

"Yeah. Where's...?" He jerked his head in the direction of Hamilton's desk.

"Oh, Hamilton? He, uh, had to run out. Said it was okay for me to wait for you here." He set the drink tray on Harlan's desk.

"Did he?" Harlan was definitely going to have to talk to Hamilton about that later if that were the case.

He sighed, closed his eyes and pushed his irritation aside. A client was a client, after all. He did his best to smile as he sat behind his desk, facing the boy.

The boy, who wasn't making any attempt at eye contact... He was staring fixedly at the scarred, peeling wooden desk in front of him.

"Can I help you?" Harlan asked again, not sure what else to say.

The boy shook his head. His eyes widened, and he looked directly at Harlan for the first time. "I think so?"

"Are you having a ghost problem?" Harlan asked, trying to move things along.

"No. No, nothing like that." The boy slowly reached out to pick at a splinter on Harlan's desk.

Harlan sighed again. "I'm really not sure how —"

"You're Harlan Brand, right?"

Harlan nodded, getting increasingly uncomfortable. He, Hamilton and Morgan had done their best to keep his name out of the press, but there had still been a few online articles that mentioned him in connection to Samuel Harkness and what had happened at the Centre a year earlier. Maybe the kid was some kind of weird paranormal groupie?

"Okay. That's good. Um. I'm... My name is Aiden. Brand. Aiden Brand." He set the cardboard tray on Harlan's desk and held out his left hand.

Harlan stiffened. Okay. Brand was an unusual name, certainly, but Toronto was a big city. There were bound to be other people with the same last name as him. People who were only distantly related to him, if at all. But the first name...

"Okay. Can I help you?" he asked for a third time, ignoring the outstretched hand and hoping he didn't sound as rattled as he felt.

"Not exactly. I just...kinda...wanted to meet my older brother."

Harlan shot to his feet. His chair rolled away and hit the wall, which was only a few feet behind him. It wasn't a very big office. His foot tangled in the wheels, and he almost fell flat on his face on his own desk.

Aiden stood almost as quickly. "Oh, no, I'm so sorry! I wasn't sure how to say it, but obviously not like that."

"What did you say your name was — your *first* name?" Harlan hardly recognized his own voice.

He probably sounded at least a little unhinged, because the boy just said, "Aiden," in a small voice.

"Wait here." It was brusque, almost rude, but was it his fault if he wasn't at his very best when his brother showed up in his office unannounced? Couldn't he have sent a text or something first? Wasn't that what kids did? Text each other?

All right, it *was* his fault. He was responsible for his actions — but *still*.

Harlan waved a hand in Aiden's direction. He freed himself from the chair and pushed it out of the way. He brushed past Aiden and stumbled over to the office's small closet. The closet was a bit of a point of contention between him and Hamilton. Harlan had partially filled it with a few things he didn't want in his and Charles' apartment when he'd moved, but also wasn't quite willing — or maybe just ready — to get rid of.

Even though the agency didn't really *need* the space, Harlan had noticed Hamilton glancing at it meaningfully several times. Honestly, Harlan wasn't sure why he'd kept a lot of it, but at the moment he was glad he had.

He distantly saw Hamilton stick his head in the door and sign, *"Okay?"*

Harlan frowned at him but returned the sign.

Hamilton nodded and left again. *Traitor.*

It took him a while to find the shoebox holding the letters and cards from his parents, the most recent dated almost fifteen years ago. The box wasn't even half full.

He pulled it out and started pawing through it. It was more or less in chronological order because he'd just thrown things on top as he got them and hadn't really looked at them again.

It didn't take long for him to find the particular letter he was after. He unfolded it, almost tearing the old, creased paper, and scanned it for the word he was looking for.

There.

You have a new baby brother. His name is Aiden.

He hadn't even known his mother was pregnant when he got the letter.

But that wasn't the important thing, not at the moment. He absently refolded it, stuffed it in the box and shoved the box back on the shelf before slowly closing the closet door.

Okay, the name matched. Harlan was pretty bad at both guessing how old people were *and* math, but Aiden seemed about the right age.

The boy in question had turned in his chair and was watching Harlan closely, his hands folded on the back of the chair and his chin resting on them. He didn't seem to mind Harlan staring at him while he tried to see... He wasn't sure what. Some part of himself, of his nearly forgotten parents, in the kid in front of him. His stomach lurched. He wished Hamilton was there and was mad at him for leaving him alone in this situation, but he was also glad Hamilton wasn't here for this. *Fuck.* He didn't even know *what* he was feeling.

"What are my — 'our' — parents' names?" Harlan asked, a little accusatorially. He went back to the safety of his desk and sat down again.

Aiden blinked. "Robert and Sharon...?"

Fuck. "Yeah." Harlan bit his tongue — literally — as he tried to control and sort out the emotion flooding him. "Do...do you have a picture?" At that point it was less because he didn't believe Aiden was who he said, and more because he wanted... What? Confirmation? To torture himself?

Aiden reached into his pocket and pulled out his phone. He must have already had a picture up, because he didn't have to flip through anything for long. He passed it to Harlan silently.

Harlan took it. There was a picture of Aiden with a basketball tucked under one arm and holding a trophy in the other. On one side was his mom, her hands folded in front of her. His dad — *their* dad — was on the other, a hand on Aiden's shoulder in a distantly affectionate way. They both looked older, of course, but they were clearly his parents. *Their* parents.

He wondered who'd taken the picture.

Of course Aiden was the perfect son, the one his parents had always wanted. The one he was *not*, could never be, even if he hadn't been a medium.

"You play basketball," he said woodenly. Fuck, that was a dumb thing to say. Why had he said that?

"Yeah."

Harlan passed Aiden's phone back.

He took it but didn't put it in his pocket. He set it on the desk again. "Oh, yeah, here." He pushed the drink tray closer to Harlan. "I wasn't sure which one you'd like." He pointed to the hot drink. "It's just hot chocolate. Mom says coffee will stunt my growth."

She'd never told Harlan that, but of course why would you say it to a five-year-old? "Thanks." He nodded and took the hot chocolate, taking a sip. It was lukewarm and not caffeinated the way he'd originally hoped, but that was probably a good thing. He was fucking jittery enough already.

"So, um…what made you decide to come find me?" That seemed like the most obvious next question. Hopefully Aiden wouldn't mind.

"Well..." Aiden held up a hand, his eyes squinching with concentration.

Harlan's computer screen shivered for a moment, then a crackling ball of electricity appeared in Aiden's palm.

Harlan leaned back in his chair, hard. "You have an ability."

"Yeah. Technically it's called ergokinesis." Aiden tossed the ball into his other hand, clearly showing off a little for his big brother. Fuck, this was weird.

Harlan nodded. He'd seen the word — and its description, the ability to move and channel electricity — on a list of psychic abilities.

Aiden closed his fist, and his palm was empty when he opened it again. "Mom and Dad don't really talk about you much — sorry."

Harlan shrugged as offhandedly as he could. "It's not your fault."

Holy fuck. Aiden, his parents' replacement son, the one who was supposed to be perfect and untainted by anything paranormal...had an ability as well.

And their parents had kept him. He barely bit back a harsh burst of laughter. Aiden could've ended up at the Centre right beside him while their parents tried a third time.

Aiden was looking at him. It felt like he needed to say something more. "That's a rare one." And it was. He'd never met anyone with that ability at the Centre. It was even rarer than shapeshifting, like Morgan, and that was unusual enough.

Aiden nodded. "And it's pretty strong, but they hired private instructors so they wouldn't have to send me to the — yeah. Sorry," he repeated.

Fuck. That must've been expensive, with ergokinesis being so rare.

Some parents had sent their kids at the Centre money for Christmases or birthdays or whatever. Harlan's never had.

Harlan dredged up a thin smile for Aiden and shook his head. "I'm glad you were able to stay at home." And he meant it. While he'd always been glad he'd gotten away from his parents when they'd made it clear they weren't going to accept that he was a medium, he wouldn't wish growing up in the Centre on anyone else. Not that it had been...bad, necessarily, just that it was better to grow up at home...probably.

"Anyway. I saw a thing about you online and I wanted to... I dunno. Meet you, I guess."

"Well, now you've met me."

Aiden's bright smile disappeared.

Harlan sighed. "Sorry. That was rude." Clearly he had a lot to learn about big brother...ing. *Fuck.* Was Aiden going to be in his life from now on? Was he going to have to introduce him to Charles—maybe even Michael? It was all so weird.

And Aiden's grin was back as if he'd flipped a switch. "That's okay. I know I kinda sprang this on you. Sorry. I probably should have gotten your number from Mom and called or texted or something first."

Probably, Harlan thought, but managed to avoid saying. It was interesting that his mom apparently *had* his number.

On the other hand, if Aiden *had* tried contacting him first, Harlan probably would've kept finding excuses, and they never would have met. He still wasn't sure if that was a good thing or not. In any case, Aiden was there now, sitting right in front of him.

"Well. I should probably get going." Aiden hooked a thumb over his shoulder. "I'm sure you've got lots to do."

Oh, yeah. In my completely empty office. Still, Harlan was exhausted. It was hard enough for him to find the spoons when he *knew* he was going to be doing something social. *This* was just...

He nodded. "It was really nice to meet you," he said softly, surprised to realize he actually meant it.

"You too. Um..." Aiden's cheeks turned a little red. "If you wanted, we could...?"

"Yeah." Harlan smiled at him, even more surprised to realize he meant *that*. "I'd like that. To see you again, I mean."

Aiden nodded eagerly. "What's your number? I'll text you mine."

Harlan told him, and a moment later his phone dinged. He added Aiden as a contact. Holy shit. He had a brother. Well, he had for a long time, but now he really *had a brother*.

"Look... I'm not always great at texting first," Harlan warned him. "...or replying, but I'll...try."

Aiden grinned. "Yeah, Mom said you were...shy."

From the way he'd hesitated, Harlan suspected she'd said something much less kind, but what did he care? "Do you need a ride home or anything?" He hadn't asked how old Aiden was, and it felt too late at this point. "My boyfriend could probably come pick you up." *Maybe. If he's not working. Shit.* Hopefully their parents had told Aiden that Harlan was gay. If he'd intended to come out to his brother, he would've done it a little more carefully.

"Nah." Aiden looked unfazed, but Harlan wasn't sure if that was because he'd known already or kids these days were just cool with it. "I can take the subway."

"If you're sure…"

Aiden shrugged one shoulder, and Harlan couldn't tell if it was familiar, or he was just trying to *find* familiarity in the gesture. "It's how I got here."

"Okay. Be safe. I—love you?" *Fuck.* That had been a totally weird thing to say, and Harlan desperately wished he could take it back or fall in a hole or something.

But Aiden just grinned at him. "Love you too, big bro." He picked up a backpack Harlan hadn't noticed earlier, waved at him and left.

Hamilton finally reappeared a moment later, so he'd clearly been close by.

As soon as Harlan heard the door at the end of the hall click closed behind Aiden, he rounded on Hamilton. "What the hell, Hamilton? Why would you leave a stranger alone in the office? Where were you?"

"He said he was your brother, and he's *clearly* your brother."

Harlan pictured the boy he'd just met. He couldn't see it—certainly not 'clearly'.

"And I had to pee! He was alone for like three seconds."

Harlan sighed. "Sorry. I know you wouldn't do anything to put me or the business in danger."

"Fuckin' A." He looked at Harlan for a long moment before asking gently, "Hey. Are you okay?"

"Yeah. Fine." He didn't quite snap at Hamilton, but it was close.

Hamilton raised an eyebrow.

Harlan let out a shaky sigh. "I'm…a little freaked out," he admitted.

"Of course you are."

Harlan glanced at him, surprised.

Hamilton snorted. "What? You think most people can just walk off meeting their long-lost baby brother? *I'd* be freaked out. Pretty much anyone you'd ever want to meet in a dark alley would be."

"Oh." The tight band of pressure around Harlan's chest loosened just a little.

"Are you convinced that he is who he says he is?"

Harlan grinned despite himself. It was nice to have a paranoid ex-cop on his side. "I'm pretty sure."

"You could call your parents and ask them?"

Harlan shrugged one shoulder, looking down.

"Why don't you take the rest of the day off? Call Charles?"

He nodded. Obviously he didn't *call* Charles, at least not at first, but he did after Charles didn't reply to his text.

Charles didn't pick up.

Harlan sighed. Well, he could go back to annoying Hamilton. Okay, not really. He knew it was just his stupid anxious brain getting in his way — but then he'd feel kinda pathetic, since he'd already left. Or…

He didn't bother texting Michael first. He knew Michael would just call him anyway, so he might as well be the one to start it.

"Hey, Harlan! What's up?"

"I just had something kinda weird happen…"

"Hold on, one sec." He heard Michael talk to someone in the background.

"Oh, shit, I'm sorry. You're at work."

"It's okay. What happened?"

"I just met my brother for the first time."

Michael whistled. "Wow. That sounds like a lot."

"Yeah. Kinda."

"No luck getting a hold of Charles, huh?"

"Yeah. Sorry."

Michael laughed. "It's okay, Harlan. You live with him, after all. Of course he's going to be the first one you call. Tell you what. I haven't had lunch yet. Why don't I take you out and you can tell me all about it?"

Harlan let out a long, shaky breath. "Yeah. Thanks. I'd really like... I'd appreciate that."

"I'll come pick you up."

* * * *

Harlan was back at home by the time Charles called. He had been for a few hours.

"Fuck, Harlan, I am *so sorry*. I just got your text."

Harlan hadn't left a voicemail, both because he *hated* doing that even more than making a regular phone call, and because he'd had no fucking clue what to say. He barely even remembered what he'd texted at this point. Had he mentioned his brother? Yeah. He thought so, especially based on how apologetic Charles was being.

"Harlan?"

Right. Fuck. He hadn't said anything yet. He should say something. "Yeah?"

"Are you okay? Fuck. Of course you're not. I can come home now if—?"

"No, it's fine." And it really was, somewhat to Harlan's surprise. Talking to Michael about it had helped. "I had lunch with Michael. We talked about it."

"About your brother?"

"Yeah."

"Oh. Hey, that's great! I'm glad. Again, I'm so sorry. I'll be a few more hours here."

"No. It really is okay." Harlan smiled, and he hoped that even though Charles couldn't see it—the only thing worse than a phone call was a *video* call—he could at least hear it. "But I *am* really looking forward to seeing you. I'll wait up for you."

"Okay…if you're sure. We'll talk when I get home, okay? Love you."

"Okay. Love you, too."

It was a long wait. Harlan kept trying to distract himself, opening app after app on his phone and closing them again just as quickly. He almost texted Aiden a few times, even getting so far as to start typing something before deleting it and closing Messages.

He rushed over to meet Charles at the door when it finally opened, throwing his arms around him.

"Hey," Charles chuckled, hugging him back just as tightly. "Missed you, too. You okay?"

Harlan nodded. "Sorry. I should've at least let you get in the door…"

"It's okay," Charles assured him. "Want to go sit?" He inclined his head in the direction of the couch.

Harlan nodded again, reluctantly letting go of Charles—just long enough for them to move and resettle.

"So, you met your brother."

"Yeah."

"Want to talk about it, or—"

"Yes! Please," Harlan added, a little embarrassed by his outburst. "Sorry. I'm sure you're really tired…"

Charles shook his head, then laughed. "Well, okay, yeah, I *am* tired, but you're my boyfriend and this is important. How did it go?"

"It was…weird," Harlan began slowly, and that was true, but it wasn't the *whole* truth. "It was good. I liked him. Is that weird?"

"I don't think so." Charles gave Harlan's shoulders an encouraging little squeeze.

"He… He has an ability." He explained what Aiden could do.

"Whoa." Charles' eyes widened. "Holy shit."

"Yeah."

They were both quiet for a while, then Charles asked, "Hey, why don't we have Aiden over for dinner?"

Harlan had to think about that for a moment, but he finally nodded. "Yeah. I'd like that."

"I have another question."

"Okay…" Harlan said, wondering why Charles didn't just ask it.

"Do you want to invite your parents?"

Oh. That would be why.

Harlan's text alert went off, and he laughed.

"What is it?" Charles asked.

"That… That was Aiden. He just texted *me*."

"What did he say? If you don't mind me asking."

Harlan shook his head. "I mean, I don't. I haven't looked yet. I'll wait until I…" He thought about asking Charles what *he* thought, but only one option made his guts clench into a solid mass. "I *don't*. Want them to come." He almost asked if that was okay, but he knew it would be, that Charles would go with whichever option he chose without judgement. The opposite — with *support*. He smiled at his boyfriend.

Charles smiled back. "Then we won't."

"Okay. I'll invite him." Harlan looked at Aiden's message first.

Yeah, I didn't know what to say, but I'm really glad I got to meet you. I don't know if you're a cat or dog person, so here's both.

He'd included a video of a puppy and a kitten eating from the same bowl.

Love you, big bro.

Harlan smiled.

Cat, I guess.

He wasn't really a pet or animal person at all.

Want to come over for dinner?

He hesitated a moment, then quickly added,

Love you, too.

The little dots that meant Aiden was typing appeared almost immediately.

Yeah!

Harlan offered his phone to Charles. "You know when will work for you. I'll let you set it up. If that's okay."

Charles nodded, as Harlan had expected he would. "Should I tell him I'm not you?"

Harlan hesitated a moment, then shook his head.

"All right." Charles took the phone and sent a few texts back and forth with Aiden. "Tuesday at seven, if that works for you?"

Harlan nodded.

"Great! I'll cook," Charles laughed, as if there was any other possibility. "Hmm. Would it be rude for me to ask him about his ability, or would it be ruder *not* to?"

"I honestly have no idea," Harlan laughed, shaking his head.

Harlan didn't want to overwhelm Aiden by introducing him to too many people at once, so he decided to just invite him over for dinner with Charles, without Michael. That, and it felt like more of a family thing, and while he really liked Michael, he wasn't sure if he considered him 'family' yet. He thought about inviting Hamilton—who he *did* consider family—but then he felt like he'd need to invite Morgan—and Skye, probably—and that was just too many people again. Just Charles was enough for the first time.

Anxiety made Harlan think about pushing it back several times. What if Charles and Aiden didn't like each other? What if, once Aiden got to know him better, he didn't like *Harlan* anymore? What if they ran out of things to talk about and just sat at the table and stared at each other, with nothing but the sound of their own chewing?

He knew that if he gave in to his fear, more than likely he'd just never reschedule, and it wouldn't happen. He forced himself to just leave it, even as he got more and more nervous the closer it got.

The night of the dinner, Charles talked with Aiden about high school. It turned out Charles had done a few years of wrestling, which Harlan hadn't known and very much wanted to see pictures of—but later, after Aiden had left.

Aiden brought up his ability on his own, showing it off to a very impressed Charles.

Charles offered him a ride home, but Aiden said he had his own way.

There was a strange feeling in Harlan's chest as he waved goodbye to his brother beside his boyfriend in the doorway of their apartment building—but it was mostly a good one.

Chapter Nine

Charles had asked both Harlan and Michael if they wanted to know his date idea for the three of them ahead of time, and they'd both told him to let it be a surprise.

Harlan hadn't expected that—from either of them. He would've assumed Michael, with his type-A personality, would've wanted to know *exactly* what he was getting himself into, and Harlan, of course, usually got super anxious when he didn't know what was going on. Well, he was only a few seconds from 'super anxious' at any given time, but...

This time he was kinda excited. The last surprise date Charles had set up, a rage room, had been really fun. He trusted Charles. He knew he'd come up with something all three of them would enjoy.

He had no idea what it could possibly be, though. He and Charles were different enough, but Michael was practically a different species of gay man. What possible activity—besides, hopefully, the obvious one again if this date went well—could they have in common?

Part of Harlan found himself wishing it were just him and Charles, but that was really weird. The whole point of this was to have a date *with* Michael. He shook his head and the thought vanished.

After Charles parked, Harlan looked up at the sign above the door. "Axe throwing?"

"Yeah. It's kinda this new thing. Steve, Jim, and Alejandro have done it, but I don't think you were at the game night where they talked about it."

Harlan shrugged.

"But they said it's really fun."

Harlan blinked. "Is there more to it than what I'm thinking, or is it just...?"

"Throwing an axe? Yeah, as far as I can tell, that's all there is to it."

Harlan grinned at the mental image of white-collar, buttoned-up Michael throwing an axe like some kind of Wall-Street Viking. "Okay. This could be fun."

"Looks like Michael's here already. That's his car, right?"

He shrugged. Unless they were very weird-looking or a strange colour, all cars pretty much looked the same to him. "Hopefully our arms won't get as sore from this as they did with the rage room."

"I know, right?" Charles chuckled. "My arms were sore for *days*, and I'm used to hauling around cases of beer. And I didn't break nearly as many things as you. I can't even imagine how it must have been for you."

"It was...pretty bad," Harlan admitted. Hamilton had made fun of how stiff he'd been. "But it'll probably be even worse for Michael." He grinned.

"Heh, yeah. He probably lifts, what? Pencils?"

Harlan groaned. "No. Actually, he probably goes to the gym."

"Ugh, yeah. You're right. He definitely seems like the type." Charles patted his comfortably round stomach and grinned at Harlan. "How did we end up with a guy like that?"

Harlan grinned back for a moment, then frowned and shook his head. "You're kidding, right? You're, like, the most handsome guy I've ever met. Plus, you're way more my type than he is, usually. I don't know how *I* ended up with someone as hot as *you*." He didn't even bother pointing out his obvious flaws — too skinny and pale, for starters.

"Hey, none of that." Charles picked Harlan up a few inches off the ground, big hands cupping Harlan's nonexistent butt. "You're hot and handsome, too. But you're right. It's better not to talk about ourselves like that."

Harlan nodded once, sharply.

"Let's not keep Michael waiting, then." He set Harlan back down and kissed him.

They went inside and Michael bounced up from his seat in the waiting room to hug both of them.

They were given the safety rules and a little basic instruction — though Harlan would have preferred a little more before they just…handed him an axe.

Harlan was really bad at it — he had terrible hand-eye coordination — and rarely even hit the target, but he still had fun. More importantly, the other two cheered like crazy when he *did* hit it and never made fun of him when he didn't — not that he'd expected them to, but after spending most of his life at the Centre, it was still his gut reaction in these situations.

He wondered if it would be something Aiden would enjoy doing together. He and Aiden had texted back and forth a few times since the night he came over for dinner — mostly dumb cat-based memes on both sides.

"I'm like a freakin' lumberjack or something!" Michael crowed as his axe thunked deep into the centre of the target.

"'Or something,'" Charles whispered to Harlan, grinning.

Harlan had to look away to keep himself from giggling, elbowing Charles. "You're bad!"

"Guilty." Charles gave his shoulder a quick kiss before turning back to Michael. "That was a great throw! I thought I'd be better at this, but you're kicking my butt."

Michael grinned at him. "I was thinking we might try that tonight, actually."

Charles glanced at Harlan, who frowned ever so slightly. Charles nodded at him, then turned to Michael. "I think we'll save that for next time. We'll all be tired and sore from this already...but you can definitely come over to our place afterwards."

That sounded reasonable to Harlan, but he could see that Michael was disappointed.

Still, Michael only hesitated a moment before replying, "Of course." He smirked. "I'm sure we can find something to keep ourselves busy."

They took turns throwing. Harlan almost liked watching the other two throw more. Like the rage room, it was surprisingly sexy. He was definitely ready to move on to other activities by the time they were done, though the hour had also flown by.

They took separate cars and reconvened at Charles and Harlan's apartment.

"So, how do we want to do it this time?" Michael asked after they were all naked, eyeing the other two.

Harlan sighed internally with relief that he'd asked so Harlan didn't have to. He *wanted* this, with a pulse-pounding desire, but he had no idea how to…begin, at least. Last time they'd just sort of fallen into something that ended up being sex.

Sure, he'd seen porn with more than two guys, seen at least a few of the possible 'configurations', but those men always just seemed to jump right in like they had a plan—which, obviously, they did, because it was scripted.

Charles laughed—almost a giggle, which was a new one for Harlan, at least outside of subspace. "There's no right or wrong way…" he began.

Harlan sighed. Yeah, there was always more than one way, *blah blah*, but right now he needed answers, needed hands and tongues and skin—and to not be the one directing them. So much for him being a Dom.

Glancing between them, Charles reached out a hand for each of them and gently pulled them closer. "How about this?" He leaned forward to kiss Harlan deeply, putting his other hand on Michael's thigh.

Harlan leaned in eagerly, kissing back, trying to release all the heat building up inside him through Charles' lips. He watched Charles' hand drift sideways and down until his palm brushed Michael's straining erection, Michael's hips rising to meet him while he groaned softly.

Harlan felt a brief, stinging moment of jealousy, quickly dissolved by Charles' tongue sliding into his mouth—and Charles' fingers wrapping around his cock.

"Yessss," Michael sighed, and suddenly it was like a circuit had been completed between the three of them. Harlan felt a wave of pure pleasure — of *ecstasy* — roll through him.

Charles gently pushed the two of them down onto the bed, wrapping his hands around both their lengths, and began slow, even strokes.

Harlan's head fell back. He braced himself with both hands behind him, opening himself up to Charles' hand even more. He slid his shoulder down the length of Michael's upper arm, and he half-swooned against him, leaning more of his weight against Michael than the bed.

Michael was there to brace him, pulling him close with an arm across his shoulders and taking his weight.

Feeling the furious heat of Michael's skin against his own, Harlan melted into him, surrendering himself to Michael's arms and Charles' hand. He didn't have to think, to act, to do anything more than breathe and *be*.

Michael turned to kiss a hot line across Harlan's shoulder and neck. He turned and found Michael's mouth waiting for him.

Harlan hesitated a moment, then pressed his lips against Michael's. It had been a *long* time since anyone but Charles had kissed him, and it was strange for a moment, but he quickly relaxed into it. Michael's lips were softer than Charles', thinner. Harlan kissed him thoroughly, tasting and feeling all the subtle differences between them.

"Mmm," Charles groaned, stroking faster to show his approval and desire.

Encouraged, Michael shifted slightly, then reached across Harlan with his other hand and started playing with Harlan's nipple.

Harlan stiffened for a moment. He didn't have a lot of experience with that—it just wasn't something he and Charles usually did, for whatever reason—even though Charles had a nipple ring. Harlan's few attempts at solo nipple-exploration had never really done it for him.

Michael's clever fingers didn't hesitate, just kept gently pinching, rolling and tugging until Harlan relaxed again, and he began to enjoy it.

"Look at you two," Charles rumbled, his hands strong and sure as he stroked them to the base. "Pretty as a picture." He chuckled. "A very R-rated picture."

Harlan couldn't help blushing, but it just seemed to encourage Michael.

His fingers still deftly teasing Harlan's nipple, he licked a line up Harlan's ear.

Harlan shivered, and not entirely with pleasure. He wasn't sure if he liked the feeling. As soon as Michael pulled away, it left a cool, damp, almost sticky spot, and he had to hold himself back from reaching up and wiping it off.

Michael waited a moment, moaning as Charles did something to his cock that Harlan couldn't see, then he wrapped his lips around Harlan's ear, folding it like a leaf until it was entirely in his mouth.

Harlan started to pull back, but then Charles's hand tightened on him—probably the same thing that had gotten Michael a moment earlier, an oddly distant part of him thought—and he relaxed into it. It was strange and a little gross, but not unpleasant, and really *most* of sex was pretty strange and gross, when he thought about it.

He stiffened again when Michael's tongue began to explore the folds and crevices of his ear. He almost pulled back, but he had to admit that it actually felt pretty good, especially with Michael's fingers on his nipple and Charles still stroking his cock. He looked up at Charles, and they were both grinning at each other.

Beneath their combined efforts, Harlan suddenly felt breathless, and a strange...brightness, like someone was shining a spotlight on him or he'd been singled out by a sunbeam. It was as weird and alarming as it was beautiful.

His ear popped out of Michael's mouth. His hips bucked and he was coming in Charles' hand, arching his chest slightly to move Michael's fingers just right, and everything was so grand and complete and golden that it was almost overwhelming, but he managed to ride it out into one of the most complete, all-consuming orgasms of his life. He distantly felt Michael's nails bite into his shoulder, and while pain — well, receiving it, anyway — didn't usually do anything for him, the sensation added just another level of bliss to the whole thing. He couldn't stop coming. *Might never stop, just keep building higher and higher until...*

He was a gasping, shivering mess in Michael's arms, and Charles was looking down at him with something approaching alarm, though he could feel that Charles was still slowly stroking Michael.

"Wow," Harlan gasped when he couldn't take the weight of their expectation any longer. His voice was rough and hoarse. "That was... Wow." He blushed again when he realized that he was the only one who'd finished so far, but he was so limp he didn't think he'd be of any use to either of them.

Charles pulled away slightly.

Michael groaned, but slowly lowered Harlan to the mattress, supporting him the whole way down.

"Comfy?" Charles asked him, a slightly wild look in his eye.

Harlan nodded. His head felt loose and smooth on his neck, like the connection had been replaced with a ball bearing. He felt a slightly dopey smile spread across his face. "You two keep going," he assured them. He even managed to flop a short distance away so they could have more room on the bed.

"You're su—?" Charles began, before Michael sat up a little, caught his hand and pulled it back down to his groin. "Well, all right, then."

Harlan caught Michael looking in the direction of Charles' round, hairy ass and smiled. Suddenly he *really* wanted to watch him fuck Charles while he was already satisfied, without any pressure on his end. All he'd have to do was watch and enjoy while they put on a little show for him—and each other, obviously.

He nodded in answer to Michael's unspoken question, giving his...permission? Not that Charles needed it. But it was sorta fun to 'give' it, anyway.

Michael grinned wickedly at Harlan over Charles' unsuspecting back. He reached down again and grabbed Charles' wrist, keeping his hand in place on his dick.

Charles gasped, his eyelids fluttering. He tugged back against Michael's grip just a little, but it was clear—at least to Harlan—that he wasn't actually trying to get away. He just wanted to pull and feel that Michael *had* him.

Once Charles had started stroking Michael again, his movements hampered by Michael's grip—not that either of them seemed to mind—Michael purred, "Good," holding out his free hand to Harlan.

Harlan blinked at it stupidly. He didn't want to sit up now that he'd gotten settled in all comfortably to watch the show, but he didn't want to refuse Michael, either. He sat up with a barely suppressed groan, taking Michael's hand.

Michael laughed, shaking his head. He mouthed 'lube', exaggerating each movement so even sex-addled Harlan would understand.

'Oh,' Harlan mouthed back, embarrassed. *Duh.* He hunted around for the lube, then slapped it into Michael's palm a little harder than he'd intended. His whole body still felt loose and boneless from his orgasm, and his hand-eye coordination was never very good to begin with.

Michael winked at him, and Harlan could feel himself blushing as he flopped back down on the bed to watch.

"Hey, Charles," Michael murmured, tightening his grip on Charles' wrist.

Charles moaned, the sound rising to a question at the end.

"Want me to fuck you?"

To Harlan's surprise and delight, Charles turned to him.

Harlan nodded, echoed a moment later as Charles nodded at Michael.

"That's good," Michael purred, "'cause I really wanna fuck you." He let go of Charles' wrist, giving him a little shove. Charles landed neatly on his back and Michael looked very pleased with himself.

Harlan reached out to stroke Charles' fluffy curls, which were suddenly within reach. He was too worn out and relaxed to do much more than that and watch.

Charles butted his hand a little before turning his full attention to Michael—which Harlan thought was more than fair, under the circumstances.

"Do you want it like this or on all fours?" Michael asked.

Charles thought for a moment. "All fours." He flopped onto his front, then raised his ass in the air, keeping his head low.

Harlan shifted slightly so he could keep petting Charles' hair, and was rewarded with a soft, happy sound.

Michael quickly slicked his fingers. "Ready?" he asked Charles.

Charles nodded, then realized Michael might not be able to see the motion and said, "Yes," out loud.

Michael wasted no time sliding his forefinger deep inside Charles. "Fuck, you're tight," he murmured. "Been too long since he was used properly, huh, Harlan?" He laughed.

Charles laughed, too, and Harlan didn't point out to either of them that Charles just hadn't been around enough—or had enough energy—for them to full-on fuck. He forced himself to stay quiet, but he tightened his fingers on Charles' hair for a moment, drawing another moan out of Charles. Harlan smiled. That was all right. He wanted to enjoy this time with Charles— with *both* of them—without thinking about the past or future, to simply drift in the pleasant and pleasurable *now*.

Charles was soon begging for more, and Michael kept giving it to him. Once he had three fingers in him,

Michael leaned forward, running his free hand up Charles' thigh to his hip, farther up to his spine and down to his tailbone, just above where his other hand disappeared into Charles.

Charles pushed back against him just as eagerly, pulling so hard and fast that he almost yanked free of Harlan's hold on his hair.

Harlan held on, making Charles work for it.

Michael took Charles hard and fast and deep, roaming his hands across Charles' hips, ass and back.

"Fuck," Charles moaned, low and earthy. "I *love* being between the two of you."

Harlan mentally stumbled over that for a moment. Charles hadn't said he loved *Michael*, but...

His worry disappeared as Michael said, "Good, because we love having you between us. Don't we, Harlan?"

Harlan nodded, giving Charles' hair a little extra tug.

Michael pounded Charles relentlessly, snapping his hips with every thrust.

Harlan couldn't see the action quite as well as he wanted, but he didn't want to move or let go of Charles' hair.

He could see that Michael was close by the way his head tipped back, with his eyes closed and his face a little flushed. He could tell Charles was close, too, by the familiar pattern of his breathing and the way all his muscles were tight and bunched. Charles was fighting it, trying to hold back until after Michael had come.

He didn't have to wait long.

Michael cried out, his nails biting into Charles' hips as he thrust once more, clearly slamming as deep as he could.

Charles lowered his head as he came, and Harlan had mercy on him and let him move without pulling his hair to keep him in place.

"Wow," Michael gasped once he'd finished, restlessly tracing his thumb on Charles' hip and the red marks he'd left there.

"Wow," Charles huffed, grinning up at Harlan.

Harlan dutifully repeated, "Wow," like the others. He let go of Charles and scrambled to grab tissues so they could clean themselves up.

Wow.

Chapter Ten

"Hello?" called a soft voice, followed by an even softer tap on the wall beside the office door, so quiet that Harlan worried it was a boredom-induced hallucination.

But no—Hamilton, whose desk was closer to the door, was standing.

"Can I help you?" Hamilton asked.

A long pause. Harlan could see Hamilton starting to squirm.

Harlan had a sudden feeling that he was needed. He got up, tapping Hamilton's shoulder to get him to move.

A short, pale white man stood in the hall, shuffling from foot to foot and staring at Harlan's shoes. "Um. Is this Laid to Rest Investigations?"

Harlan nodded. "It is. Please, come in." It was like looking in an awkward mirror, and Harlan found himself immediately hoping he'd be able to help.

Catching Harlan's eyes, Hamilton rolled his eyes and went back to his desk.

"Right this way." Usually Hamilton handled intakes, but Harlan felt like he had to handle this one himself. He guided the man to the chair in front of his own desk. "How can we help you?" Noticing the way the man's eyes kept flicking in Hamilton's direction, Harlan cleared his throat. "Hey, Hamilton? Why don't you take off early? I can handle this."

Hamilton raised a bushy eyebrow but shrugged. "Yeah, all right. I'll see you in the a.m., then." He typed furiously at his computer for a moment, then got up, grabbed his coat and left, shutting the door behind him.

Harlan mentally thanked him. It would get hot in the office, but he suspected that the man in front of him would prefer to keep their conversation as private as possible.

The man visibly relaxed once they were alone. "I'm sorry. I hope I didn't offend him. I've just... I have extreme anxiety, and I've really been struggling since my wife died."

Harlan shook his head. "No, it's fine. I know Curt can be a little intimidating." He wasn't sure why he'd called him 'Curt' rather than his usual 'Hamilton'. Maybe it was less intimidating? "What brings you here today?" he asked gently, not wanting to rush the man, but also not wanting to waste either of their time if he wanted something Harlan couldn't do. Maybe there were mediums who could do seances like in movies — deliberately call up a specific ghost to a specific place that wasn't necessarily associated with its haunting — but Harlan had never met or heard of any.

"She disappeared."

Harlan mentally winced. He really hoped he wouldn't have to bring Morgan in — for psychic work, not accounting. "I'm sorry, but we're not... Have you tried contacting the police?"

The man nodded. "They wouldn't help me. They'd only have sent her on. And now there's nothing..." He wrapped his arms around himself, looking down.

Harlan blinked, trying to read between the man's words. "Wait. Do you mean that your wife's...*ghost* went missing?" he guessed.

More vigorous nodding.

He offered the man the gentlest, most sympathetic smile he could. "Well, it could just have been her time to cross over. She checked on you, saw that you were all right, and so —"

"No. She wouldn't have left. She wouldn't...not without telling me. Not without..." He'd momentarily met Harlan's eyes for the first time, but he lowered his head again. "Not without saying goodbye."

"It's not always their choice when they go," Harlan told him. In fact, the man was lucky. Ghosts who fought against crossing over tended to get...*wrong*. Dangerous. Better for his wife to have left him suddenly than stay and turn into a dark spirit he wouldn't recognize.

"No," the man insisted. "She wasn't ready. She was still helping me."

"Helping you?"

Smiling sadly, the man pulled out his phone, unlocked it and opened his photos. He turned the phone to face Harlan, showing him an image of a laughing Black woman.

Harlan's heart sank. He'd learned already that the photos were always followed by begging for his help, usually with something he couldn't or wouldn't do.

"That's her. That's my Camille." He said it the French way, with an 'ee' sound at the end, rather than an Anglo '-eel'.

"She was very beautiful." He started saying 'mister' but realized the man hadn't actually given his name. Harlan often forgot to introduce himself, so he understood.

"Like I said." The man didn't turn his phone around. Camille's smiling face stared up at Harlan, silently begging on her husband's behalf. "I suffer from extreme anxiety and depression. Camille is — was — an empath. A very special sort of empath."

"I'm sure she was," Harlan assured him, hoping he didn't sound too trite. She must have died recently. Harlan was familiar with the accidental present tense with clients who'd recently lost loved ones.

The man shook his head. "You don't understand. I mean her power was special. Unique, actually, as far as we could tell. She could..." He leaned forward and lowered his voice as though suddenly afraid of being overheard. "She could *change* how people felt."

Harlan felt goosebumps creeping up his spine. He'd automatically leaned forward when the man did, but he found himself leaning away again at that revelation.

The man shook his head wildly. "No, no, no. It wasn't like that! She would never — She didn't use her powers like that! She used them to help me — That's *all*."

Harlan nodded, then straightened in his chair and frowned thoughtfully. "Wait... She continued using her ability to help you after she...passed away?" One of the more annoying things about setting out on his own was a return to the Centre's softened ways of referring to death — though it felt significantly less silly using it with the living than the dead.

The man nodded.

Harlan barely managed to keep himself from saying, 'That's impossible.' Psychic abilities, like most marriages — but not this one, apparently — ended at death. Harlan had never, as far as he knew, encountered the ghost of a fellow psychic — except for Bradley, who'd been killed by Mr. Addison — but that was what he'd been taught, and he hadn't come across anything that made him think any differently.

Well, maybe it was just a placebo effect. That the memory of Camille was helping the man cope with his mental illness, the way having her ghost around probably helped with his grief.

Thinking of him as 'the man' was getting silly. "I'm sorry. I didn't get your name." He realized that, without that social cue, he hadn't offered his own, either. "I'm Harlan."

"Peter."

"Peter, may I ask how Camille passed?" It sounded like he was using their names to sound more caring, but it was more that repeating them made him more likely to remember. *Actually...* He grabbed a notebook. Hamilton was always reminding him to take notes, and it had been helpful with past cases.

The man — Peter — lowered his voice again, leaning so far across the desk that Harlan could feel the puff of his breath on his face as he instinctively leaned forward to meet him.

"She was murdered."

Harlan wasn't sure what he'd been expecting, but not that. "Murdered?" he repeated stupidly.

Peter nodded, not moving away. "She was out of town on a business trip."

Harlan jotted down a note to ask what kind of work she did. It probably didn't matter, but it might. And that way he felt like he was doing something, and he wouldn't have to look at the awful grief etched into Peter's face.

"They found her bo—They found her in her hotel room. They said it was a stroke. Million-to-one odds of it happening to someone so young." He shrugged, and let out a wild laugh. "Just lucky, I guess!" He immediately shook his head. "But even before I saw her again, I wasn't sure. She'd been acting...funny right before she—before she went on this trip."

Harlan mentally groaned again. He really hoped he was misreading the situation. He wasn't *that* kind of private detective.

Peter waved his hands in firm dismissal. "No, no, no, nothing like that! I can see what you're thinking, but you're wrong. She wasn't cheating on me. I was never afraid of that. No, she was *scared*. She was worried that someone was following her. She didn't want to go on the trip, but I"—his voice cracked—"I convinced her to go. Told her it would do her good to get out of the city. Change of scenery, y'know?"

Harlan nodded silently. He would have agreed to anything.

"They let me see her body, and I—" He shook his head. "But she was waiting for me when I got home."

"Her ghost," Harlan clarified.

Peter gave him a puzzled look. "Yes. Her ghost."

"And she continued helping you, using her ability."

"Right."

Harlan took a moment to scribble everything down, turning the pieces over in his mind while he tried to decide what to ask next, what was important and what was merely heartbreaking. "Then her ghost disappeared."

Peter nodded.

"I'm so sorry, but I have to ask, how long ago did Camille pass away?"

"Six—no, seven weeks now."

Longer than Harlan had expected. Probably longer than it was healthy for Peter to have lived with his wife's ghost, but Harlan couldn't judge him.

"And when did she—her spirit—disappear?"

"She was gone when I got home from work yesterday."

"Did you contact the police, either when she first passed or today when she was missing?"

Peter nodded. "Both times. I told them how scared she'd been, that she thought someone was stalking her, that I didn't think she'd died of natural causes. They told me there was no evidence. Made it sound like I was crazy." His voice hardened. "I'm *not* crazy."

Harlan shook his head. Maybe it wasn't a good idea, maybe it was unprofessional, but he found himself saying, "I have anxiety and depression, too. I understand."

Peter slumped forward in his seat, and he was quiet for so long that Harlan started worrying that he'd fainted or something. He had just opened his mouth to ask if he was okay when Peter continued.

"When I called them last night, they made it sound like a good thing that her ghost was gone, like it was one less mess they'd have to clean up."

Harlan winced. He could guess that Peter had spoken to Beth.

"But…they also gave me your information and said you might be able to help." He stared up at Harlan beseechingly. "Can you?"

"I can't promise that I'll find anything, but I will try," Harlan told him.

Peter nodded furiously again. "Thank you. That's all I can ask for. Thank you."

"I'll need a little time to prepare. Can I get your phone number?"

Peter pulled a business card out of a leather messenger bag at his side. "Here. My email address is on there, too. Actually…" He grabbed a pen from his bag and scribbled something on the back before offering it to Harlan. No, not scribbled. Unlike Harlan, his handwriting was actually legible. "Here's my wife's email and password."

"Oh, uh, I won't—"

"I've looked at everything and I didn't see any clues, but maybe *you* will."

Harlan tried to refuse again, but Peter just pressed the card into his hand.

"Please. Just in case. And let me know if you need anything else from me."

Harlan took the card. "Okay. Thank you. I'll get back to you as soon as I can," Harlan told him, stapling the card to his page of notes with their new stapler.

"Thank you." Peter didn't offer his hand, and Harlan didn't either. Not shaking hands suited him just fine.

He walked Peter out of the office and watched him until he reached the end of the hall. He seemed so fragile that Harlan wondered if he should have walked him all the way to his car or maybe called him a cab.

Harlan went back into the office—leaving the door open—and texted Hamilton. He suspected that he hadn't actually gone home but had just retreated to the coffee shop up the street.

How quickly Hamilton got back to the office—and the pair of paper cups and pastry bag—seemed to confirm his theory.

It was a good thing he wasn't that kind of P.I.

"So? Do we have a new case?" Hamilton asked, handing over one of the coffee cups and a muffin.

Harlan gratefully inhaled the coffee smell—his favourite. Mocha with raspberry whipped cream. "I think we might. Unfortunately...I also think this one might need Morgan's help."

Hamilton groaned. "Great. They're not gonna like that."

"I know. But this poor guy—Peter. He's been through a *lot*, and I really want to help him—help them both, him and his wife—if I can."

"All right, but you're making the call."

* * * *

Morgan was busy with their day job for a few days. Harlan understood and respected that, but it was hard because Peter called every day—twice the first day—to ask if they'd made any progress. He didn't tell Morgan that.

They waved to Hamilton as they passed his desk, and he waved back.

Peter was already waiting in the armchair in the 'soft room' they'd set up in a screened-off corner of the office. It had been Morgan's idea, originally just to make themself more comfortable when working with Harlan—rather than just awkwardly trying to hold hands at his desk, like the first time—but it had quickly proven useful for other things, like speaking to grieving family members. Morgan had brought in a Persian rug and a few floor lamps, and they'd taken out the fluorescent lightbulb directly overhead, making it quite cozy.

Morgan and Harlan sat beside each other on the couch.

"Hi, I'm Morgan. My pronouns are they/them," Morgan said before Harlan had to make introductions. "Before we get started, I wanted to talk a little about how this is going to work. I'll need you to imagine your wife as clearly as you can, to think about what you love most about her. Then, I'll take on her form—"

Peter made a soft, strangled sound.

Morgan nodded. "I know. That part can be distressing, which is why I wanted to prepare you for it before we move ahead, even though I know Harlan already explained it to you. Are you all right with this?"

To his credit, Peter hesitated for a long moment, clearly giving their words serious consideration before nodding.

"Okay. After I've made a connection with her, I'll hold hands with Harlan and—if everything goes right—her ghost will appear." They glanced at Harlan. "We haven't dealt with quite this situation before," they warned him.

Harlan nodded. They'd discussed it ahead of time, of course. They didn't need her to lead them to her body, which was presumably still in her grave after her funeral. They needed to find her *ghost*. Hopefully it was just...stuck somewhere, or something, and he and Morgan would be able to call it back.

"But we'll do our best. Is that all right?"

Peter nodded more quickly this time.

Morgan smiled at him. "Okay, then. Whenever you're ready, think about your wife and your love for each other."

"Do...do I need to close my eyes?"

"That's totally up to you. If you think it'll help you concentrate, go for it."

Peter closed his eyes, clenching his hands into fists and hunching over them.

Harlan looked at the spiralling patterns on the rug. He didn't want to watch Peter doing something so...intimate, and he didn't like seeing the actual moment Morgan transformed. It always made his stomach lurch.

"Oh. Wow." The tone of almost-fear in Morgan's voice made Harlan look up at them.

"Oh, *wow*," they repeated.

Peter's eyes snapped open. "What? What is it? Did I do something wrong? Did something *go* wrong?"

Morgan looked like the picture Peter had shown him of Camille...except he could see the couch through them. And they were floating slightly above it.

Morgan held up a hand in front of their face. "I'm a ghost!"

Peter cocked his head. He didn't seem at all surprised, but Harlan guessed that made sense — as much as anything supernatural did. It was a hell of surprise for him, and — going by their reaction — Morgan, too. Fuck, he had *so* many questions, but it wouldn't be appropriate to do a mini scientific experiment in front of Peter. Morgan could always turn into someone again once they'd done it the first time. Maybe later...

"Okay." Morgan's voice was a little higher than usual, but it was back to normal by the time they said, "Peter, is this Camille, exactly as you remember her?"

Peter nodded.

Morgan held out their translucent hand, and Harlan fought back a grimace. He hadn't expected that he'd have to hold hands with a ghost. Would this even work?

"Oh, right." Morgan closed their eyes, appearing to concentrate for a moment, then they were themself again.

Peter wrapped his arms around himself, his eyes enormous, but he stayed still and quiet. *Fuck. Poor guy.* He'd been through *so much* recently, and they were putting him through more. To try and help him, but *still.*

Harlan managed to keep his sigh of relief silent as he took Morgan's hand. Their nails were painted electric blue that day. Their fingers felt slightly cool, as usual.

Nothing happened. It usually happened more quickly than this, didn't it? He glanced over at Morgan, who was looking right back at him. They both squeezed each other's hands a little harder at the same time, as if that would make a difference. They'd never needed to do it before. The ghosts had just...appeared.

Morgan let go and gave their hand a good shake before offering it to Harlan again.

He took it without shaking it first. It couldn't possibly make a difference, could it? Still nothing.

They let go of Harlan's hand again. "Let's try one more thing. I'm so sorry for the wait, Peter," Morgan told him. They *shivered*, and Camille's ghost was floating there beside him again, holding out her hand.

Harlan hesitated a moment but took it. Even though Morgan was hovering — or appeared to be — their hand didn't have the bone-chilling cold of a ghost's. He didn't even have to *blink* in order to take it.

Camille's ghost — the real one — didn't appear.

Harlan wasn't sure which of them let go first. He glanced at Morgan, and they shook their head.

"Peter, I'm so sorry. We're not having any luck connecting to your wife's spirit."

He leaned forward, elbows propped on his knees and a pleading, hopeless expression on his face. "What does that mean?"

Fuck. Harlan looked at Morgan again.

They frowned at him slightly but turned back to Peter. "I'm not sure," they said honestly.

It probably wasn't the best possible business practice, but what else could they say? *Lying would be worse, wouldn't it?* Harlan nodded at Peter.

"So…what now?" He looked at the back of the couch between the two of them.

Morgan glanced at Harlan, who shrugged as discreetly and subtly as he could. They sighed. "We'll keep trying."

Harlan nodded.

"Now that I've made a connection to Camille, Harlan and I can try this again on our own. Maybe there's just some sort of…interference today." They leaned forward, reaching out a hand towards Peter without actually touching him.

Peter took it. "You'll keep trying?"

"We will. If we find *anything*, we'll let you know immediately. And please let us know if you learn anything that might help."

Peter nodded, thanked them and left.

Morgan stretched their back. "Whew. That was rough. What could it mean that she didn't come to us?"

"The most obvious answer would be that she has moved on."

"Without telling him, though? That seems weird."

"I agree. She probably didn't do it on her own. A medium was probably involved. But why?"

Morgan shook their hands vigorously. "Okay. Enough about that for now." They tucked a lock of hair behind their ear. "Your friend Skye is fun."

Harlan blushed slightly, which was ridiculous, but there was nothing he could do about it. "She texted you?"

"Yep."

"And?" Harlan wasn't sure if it was any of his business as Morgan's sort-of boss, but they had been the one to bring it up, after all.

Morgan grinned at him. "Looks like I'll have to start learning sign language."

Chapter Eleven

"Are you really sure about this?" Charles asked, his hand already on the doorknob. "After I open this, there's no turning back." He chuckled. "Well, there is, but it'll be really awkward."

Harlan knew Charles hadn't meant it that way, but it was an effective threat. There wasn't much that Harlan hated more than awkwardness.

Well. Besides things that wanted to kill him and-or someone he loved.

He highly doubted that Michael—plain-Jane I-wear-a-suit-and-tie-every-day Michael—fell into that category.

He *wasn't* sure about this, not at all, but he didn't want to disappoint either of them. He nodded, and Charles opened the door.

"Hey!" A gigantic bouquet of roses squeezed through, quickly followed by Michael's beaming face and the sweet, rich smell of his cologne. Harlan noticed a bottle of wine in his other hand.

"Sorry if this is too much." He glanced between the two of them, letting the flowers droop between his legs. "It's too much. Fuck. I always... I get carried away. I'm just so excited!" he said with a puppy-dog grin. "I'll just put them down here, and we can forget about them." He bent to set the bouquet on the floor.

"Nonsense." Charles touched his arm, gently pulling him to his feet again. "They're lovely. There's nothing wrong with enthusiasm." He winked at Michael, laughing as he took the flowers. "Though I might need two vases to fit all of these."

"That's okay. That way there's one for each of you." Michael gave Charles a light peck on the cheek, stepping closer to do the same with Harlan when he didn't move. "I also brought this. I wasn't sure what you like, but this usually meets with approval." He held up the bottle.

Charles whistled when he saw the label — which meant nothing to Harlan, of course. "Damn, that's..." For a moment Harlan thought he was going to say it was too much, but he said, "You're really spoiling us. I'm usually just a humble beer guy. This is quite a treat." He frowned softly, glancing at Harlan. "Well, spoiling *me*, I guess. Harlan doesn't really drink," he reminded Michael.

"Oh, right. Shit."

"I'll have a little," Harlan interrupted, surprising all three of them.

Charles grinned at him. "If you're going to have a little of anything, it should be this. Not until after we play, of course."

"Oh?" Michael raised a perfectly sculpted eyebrow.

Harlan and Charles glanced at each other. Harlan was surprised by the question. They'd talked about drinking and BDSM when the three of them had first met for coffee.

Michael pouted slightly, gently swaying the bottle in front of them like a hypnotist's pocket watch. "Oh. That. I thought maybe that was just for the club," he said airily. "Couldn't we make an exception just this one time?" He laughed. "I know I'm feeling a little nervous about my first time, and I wouldn't mind a little something to help loosen me up a little," he said suggestively.

Even though he was ninety-nine percent sure what Charles' reaction would be, Harlan couldn't help turning to look at him.

"No," Charles said firmly. "After, or not at all." He even crossed his arms over his broad, muscular chest for emphasis.

Shooting them an aw-shucks grin, Michael nodded. "I'll just put it in the fridge, then." He swept past them into the kitchen.

Even though Michael had been there before, Harlan was surprised he'd just...gotten comfortable. And neither of them had even said the stupid phrase, 'Make yourself at home.'

Charles chuckled, sliding an arm around Harlan's waist. "He's very...forward, huh?"

"You can say that again."

"I guess that's why he's so successful. What does he do, again?"

"Something to do with money?" Harlan shook his head. "No, that's stupid. Everyone does something to do with money. But like...a lot of money? With banks or investments or...something."

"That's okay," Charles laughed. "We can always ask him later if we really want to know." He craned his neck so he could peer into the kitchen. "I see he's found the vases." He shook his head. "Well, the bigger they get, the harder they fall."

"What do you mean?"

Charles' grin was slightly feral. "I mean that I'm going to spank the shit out of him, and he'll like it — unless he's another Secret Top like you, which I doubt. Most of these cut-throat business bros really like being topped in bed. Then the three of us will probably fuck."

Harlan gulped. "Sounds good."

"Let's go get him, then." Charles stalked into the kitchen with Harlan trailing behind.

Michael had already set the roses in two large, matching vases, and he'd done that thing where they looked good and arranged and not just dumped in there the way they always did when Harlan tried to put flowers in a vase — not that he'd done it often.

Should he be getting Charles flowers?

Michael was holding glasses in both hands when he turned around, the stems of two flutes between his fingers in one hand and the other one resting on his opposite palm. The bottle was sitting on the kitchen table, not in the fridge.

Charles glanced at him, raised an eyebrow, and shook his head.

That was all Michael needed. Chastened, he set the glasses down and put the bottle away.

Harlan was puzzled. He had no idea why Michael kept pushing his luck like that, when Charles had clearly told him 'no' several times. Didn't he want to try getting spanked? Wasn't that why he was there? Maybe he was just as nervous about this as Harlan was. No, Harlan decided, he was too certain of himself, too confident. No one was that good an actor.

"Good. Now scoot," Charles told him, giving his bottom a little pat, like a taste of the good things to come.

Even though he hadn't enjoyed Charles spanking him, Harlan knew from experience and witnessing it a few times at the club that Charles was great at it, especially at introducing it to beginners. He was slow and patient and sure, extremely sensitive to his partners' every sound and wiggle.

Practically giggling, Michael scampered off to the bedroom, leaving Harlan and Charles staring at each other.

"He's lucky he's got such a great ass," Charles murmured, making Harlan snort as they followed Michael down the short hallway.

Michael was already naked on the bed by the time they caught up with him, and Harlan couldn't help letting a startled, "*Wow*," drop from his lips. Michael had so much more than a great ass. It was obvious even when he was dressed that he had a great body, but seeing him there, laid out on the bed in front of him, was almost too much.

"Wow," Charles agreed.

Michael's skin was evenly tanned — no lines — and every muscle was defined. His modest cock lay on his thigh, clearly the centre of the little picture he'd created.

Charles shook himself a little, then smirked at Michael. "I don't think that's the part of your anatomy you want facing me — at least not your first time out."

"What?" Michael glanced down, following Charles' gaze. "Ah. How do you want me?"

"Oh, I like that," Charles purred. "You can be on all fours or across my lap, whichever you prefer."

Harlan didn't think he was imagining the shiver that ran down Michael's spine. He certainly wasn't imagining the sudden crop of goosebumps.

"However you want," Michael said very softly, the most subdued Harlan had ever heard him. However, he wasn't running for the hills, and his erection hadn't flagged at all. As far as Harlan could tell, Michael still wanted this.

"Get on all fours, knees at the edge of the bed," Charles ordered, making a shiver roll down *Harlan's* spine. As much as he loved being Charles' Dom, he did enjoy seeing and hearing Charles in 'top' mode.

Michael nodded, a little unsteadily, obediently rolling over and getting into position.

Charles grinned at Harlan. "I'll be right back."

"Wait, what?" Michael spluttered. "You can't just—!"

"Oh, but I can. And I'm about to. Harlan, why don't you get comfortable?" Charles had brought in one of the living-room chairs earlier, and he ushered Harlan into it, giving him a full, deep kiss once he was settled.

Harlan clearly heard Michael moan from behind Charles, and he gave Charles' lip a very gentle nibble. "You're evil, you know that?"

"I know. But now that you've made an honest man out of me, I've got to let my wickedness out *sometimes*, don't I?"

"May God have mercy on him," Harlan intoned, "because I know *you* won't."

"Never." Charles slipped out of the room, walking right past Michael without looking at him.

He was back a few moments later carrying a tray Harlan didn't recognize. Had he bought it especially for this occasion, or had he just never seen Charles use it in his old place?

Of course, it was equally likely that it had come from Harlan's apartment, one of the things the Centre had set him up with that he'd never used or even noticed.

The tray was loaded with bottles of water and chocolate bars — just the thing for post-scene aftercare. Harlan rarely suffered from top-drop anymore, and he knew he could thank chocolate for that.

Michael looked over his shoulder with a pout, his eyes pleading.

Charles groaned, a deep rumble, and stepped in behind Michael with a smirk. "Okay," he said, rolling his shoulders and rubbing his hands together, clearly enjoying tormenting Michael.

Harlan ducked his head to hide a grin, not looking at either of them.

Charles slowly reached out and touched Michael's raised ass.

Michael twitched and jumped like he'd been electrocuted.

Charles waited until Michael calmed down again before he moved his hand, rubbing it in slow circles. Once Michael was completely still, Charles placed his other hand on Michael's other butt cheek.

Harlan could hear Michael take in a deep breath and let it out, his shoulders lowering as he finally relaxed.

"Ready?" Charles asked softly, still petting.

Michael nodded, spreading his knees and lowering his head so he wouldn't be thrown off balance again.

Even though he was expecting it, Charles' spank still startled Michael. He rocked forward, yelping softly.

Harlan could see his fists clench, gathering handfuls of blanket to him. He knew Charles hadn't hit him hard, so he was a little surprised by the intensity of Michael's reaction.

Charles immediately went back to rubbing Michael's ass, smiling down at him. "There," he murmured fondly, "how was that?"

"It was…" Michael let out a long breath again, his head moving from side to side a few times before he finished answering. "Weird?"

"Good weird or bad weird?" Harlan asked before Charles could. He drew up his knees to his chest and wrapped his arms around them, curious about how this little show would play out.

Michael laughed, a little breathily. "I'm not sure?" he said finally.

"Do you want to keep going?" Charles asked, gently kneading the peaks of Michael's hips with his thumbs.

"Yeah. Yeah, I-I think so."

It was strange for Harlan to see brash, confident Michael become so hesitant and insecure so quickly. BDSM really was its own kind of power. He smiled to himself. That meant Charles had *two* abilities. And apparently Charles had been right about Michael.

Charles lifted one hand and let it hang in midair. "Ready?" he asked again. "I'll do the other side this time."

Michael nodded and, when Charles didn't move, said, "Yes. Ready."

Charles spanked him a third time—even more gently, Harlan thought.

Harlan saw Michael's face scrunch up and he shook his head.

Rolling onto his back, Michael shook his head. "No. No, I don't think it's doing anything for me."

"That's okay." Charles smiled at him. "It isn't for everyone. We can try something else if you'd like, or maybe just...do something else?" His gaze slid down Michael's body to his cock, which was mostly soft now.

"Hmm. Maybe" — Michael glanced between the two of them, then nodded in Harlan's direction — "I could spank you."

Charles snorted, and Michael looked at him sharply. "Sorry. It's just... You know Harlan's a top."

"Right." Michael was quiet for a moment, clearly deep in thought. "Okay. What if I spank Charles?"

Harlan froze. He didn't consider himself a jealous person, but he didn't like that idea. On closer reflection — something he'd been working on with his counsellor — he realized that it was more insecurity than jealousy. What if Charles liked the way Michael did it better? Michael was so suave and confident, so...the opposite of Harlan. Harlan had seen Charles spank other people at the club, and it had never bothered him, but he'd never seen anyone else spank Charles. He'd never thought about that possibility before, and he definitely wouldn't have expected himself to react that way.

But it seemed like a shitty reason to keep the two of them from trying something new. A *selfish* reason. So what if Charles did like it better? Didn't he deserve the best?

He opened his mouth to agree just as Charles said, "No."

They both looked at him.

Charles shook his head. "Sorry. I'm not comfortable doing that, at least not yet."

Michael looked disappointed but nodded. "Okay. How about..." His eyes lit up and he actually snapped his fingers. "I could watch you spank Charles?"

Charles glanced at Harlan without speaking.

"That…could work," Harlan agreed slowly. "I don't know how interesting it would be for you, but…"

Michael's cocky smile was back in place. "Oh, I can think of something to keep myself busy while I watch." Once they were both looking at him, he slid his right hand down his shoulder, traced over his nipple and down his firm abs until it came to rest on his inner thigh, where his cock was once again coming to attention.

Once again, Charles turned to Harlan.

Harlan gulped. Well, they had invited Michael here to do *something*. So far it hadn't gone well, but he felt like they should at least give it one more try. He nodded.

"Excellent." Michael stood, giving a little bow and gesturing for Charles to take his place.

Charles did, but he took his own sweet time, making it clear that he was doing it because *he* wanted to.

Michael came and stood in front of Harlan, looking at him pointedly.

Harlan blinked up at him in confusion. "Oh! Right."

As soon as he left the chair, Michael slid into it, after helping himself to the lube from Charles' bedside table.

Harlan stepped in behind Charles, absently rubbing Charles' ass in the same small circles Charles had used on Michael.

He struck the first time without warning Charles, something they did often and enjoyed — though of course neither of them would have tried it with a newbie like Michael. It wasn't a very hard blow. They had plenty of time to work up to that, and Charles liked being at least a little warmed up before they started playing harder.

Harlan gave him two spanks one after the other on opposite cheeks, a little harder.

"Fuck," Charles hissed, his body relaxing into his position.

"Fuck," Michael echoed from the chair.

Harlan spared a glance at him and saw that he'd wrapped a hand around his cock and was stroking himself slowly. It was hard enough for him to be a Dom when it was just him and Charles, never mind with someone watching them. Though it *was* a little hot, having someone get so excited by what they were doing.

He looked away, focusing on Charles again. He gave him a good, hard spank on his right ass cheek, followed by a lighter one that left him gasping.

"Fuck, you just take me apart," Charles murmured, his voice already starting to drift.

Harlan smiled down at him, gently stroking the hot red handprint he'd just left. "I'm glad. I like taking you apart." He glanced up at Michael. Hopefully that hadn't sounded too...cheesy or anything. Well, Michael seemed content enough. And why should Harlan care? This was *his* bedroom, with *his* boyfriends. He could be as cheesy as he wanted.

Charles' ass was nice and red, and Harlan knew he was warmed up enough for him to go harder. He backhanded Charles' left butt cheek, enjoying the sting on his own skin, too. He heard Michael moan, the slapping sound of his hand on his cock speeding up.

After admiring his handiwork for just a moment, Harlan raked the red mark with his nails, making Charles cry out, arching beneath him. Before he had time to catch his breath, Harlan spanked him again, first on his left cheek again, on top of the claw marks he'd just left, then the right.

Harlan spanked Charles harder and faster, making sure to mix it up with a softer one or just stroking him. They built up a rhythm — all three of them — breathing together, one of them moaning, quickly followed by the other two.

He heard Michael cry out and looked up just in time to see him come. When he finished, he quietly got up and grabbed a tissue to wipe himself.

Harlan could tell Charles was close to being done, too. "Ten more good hard ones?"

Charles nodded, groaning.

"Do you want to count, or do you want me to?"

"You."

Harlan alternated the first few, then did three on one side, and the last three on the other. His hand stung by the time he'd finished and just started stroking Charles' hot ass in gentle, soothing circles — but he knew the sting he was feeling was nothing compared to what he'd done to Charles.

"Wow. That was the hottest fucking thing I've ever seen," Michael murmured, grinning at them from the armchair.

Harlan patted the bed, inviting him over.

Michael frowned, looking confused. "But you haven't… You two are still…" He glanced pointedly at Harlan's cock.

Harlan laughed, gently rolling Charles onto his side. He toppled without resisting. "It's not always about getting off," he told Michael. "Sometimes spanking is just" — he glanced at Charles — "enough?"

Charles nodded, throwing his arm awkwardly across the bed to reach out to Michael. "Yeah. C'mere."

"All right, all right, I'm coming." Michael climbed onto the bed, somehow making it look elegant and sexy instead of awkward and clumsy the way Harlan always felt and curled up between the two of them.

"Oh, wait." Harlan grabbed the tray and put it on the bed before the three of them got too comfortable.

Harlan saw Michael look down his nose when Charles passed him a water bottle.

He opened it with a look of distaste. "If you wanted bottled water, I could have brought some. I have cases of Voss lying around. I'd be happy to bring a few over."

Rolling his eyes for Harlan's benefit, Charles tapped the bottom of the bottle, tipping it up towards Michael's mouth. "Drink. It's not about taste or effervescence. It's about getting hydrated. Here." He passed Michael a chocolate bar.

For a moment Michael looked like he might protest. He hadn't really played, so he'd probably be fine without it, but he took the bar with a shrug. "Whatever. It's my cheat day."

Harlan coughed to cover his snort of laughter. He never in a million years would have guessed that he'd have sex with a man who said 'cheat day' in all seriousness.

Chapter Twelve

Harlan didn't look at the call display before answering, even on his personal cell phone. The good old days of ignoring unknown callers were gone since he'd opened Laid to Rest. That number was on his business card, too.

"Harlan."

The woman's voice was vaguely familiar, but Harlan couldn't place it.

He pulled the phone away from his face for a moment and glanced at the screen.

It was a good thing he was already sitting, because otherwise he thought he might have fallen over from the shock.

The display read 'Sharon Brand'.

It was his mother's voice, a voice he hadn't heard in more than ten years.

So long ago that she probably wouldn't recognize *his* voice.

He felt the blood drain from his face and a cold, hard weight dropped into his stomach. He felt at a distance from himself and realized he was dissociating. That was all right. He didn't mind dissociating right now.

His thumb darted towards the red circle that would end the call and restore his world to the way it should be.

He heard her say again, "Harlan?"

She wouldn't have called him if it weren't really important.

He owed her at least a conversation, didn't he?

"Could you please hold for a moment? Thank you."

Or not.

He only heard, "Harlan, is that—?" before muting the call.

In a frighteningly, disturbingly calm voice, he said, "Hamilton?" He'd said it too quietly and had to repeat himself. "Hamilton?"

"Mmm?" From the sound of it, Hamilton might have fallen asleep at his desk. Harlan didn't care. There wasn't anything urgent for him to do.

"I, um, I need to…"

Over his phone's speaker, he could just hear, *"Harlan?"* in that familiar-unfamiliar voice.

"I've gotta go. Out. To do…something. Y-You stay here. I'll be back… Yeah. Then."

He heard Hamilton's desk chair squeak, then Hamilton filled his vision.

Hamilton glanced at the phone in Harlan's hand, which he was holding at arm's length like it was a dead animal or a bag of dog shit. He looked Harlan in the eyes very intently. "Are you in trouble? Do you need help?"

Harlan started nodding, then shook his head. He tried to say, "I'm fine," but only the last word escaped.

"Right. You seem just peachy." Hamilton sighed. "All right, look. You look like shit. You stay here and deal with whatever this is. I'll clear out and take a" — he glanced at the wall clock — "a long lunch break."

Harlan nodded woodenly, counting down the seconds he'd kept his mother on hold. Would she even still be waiting when he unmuted it?

Did he want her to be?

"Text me when my 'break' is over. Promise?"

Harlan nodded again.

"If you're not telling me something and I have to pay a ransom because you've been kidnapped or something, I'm going to be very annoyed," Hamilton told him, "but I'm going to go now and trust that you have whatever this situation is under control. Text me."

Harlan almost told him to wait, to take the phone from him. She wouldn't recognize his voice. Hamilton could pretend to be him.

Hamilton grabbed his phone from his desk and left Harlan alone. He even closed the door.

Harlan glanced at the clock Hamilton had hung on their wall. The seconds were still ticking by — she hadn't hung up.

"Harlan? This is your mother."

Several snappy responses flashed through his head, like, *No shit,* and, *Only fifteen years too late!* but he managed to avoid saying any of them. The problem was that he couldn't think of anything else *to* say.

"Harlan? Are you there?"

He unmuted his phone. "Mother." He could feel her scowl. He didn't care.

"Don't call me *that*. It makes me sound like some sort of…monster."

Harlan allowed a long silence. For once, he wasn't going to get uncomfortable and break it. Let her stew.

No. He couldn't do it. The silence was worse.

"How's *Father*?" he asked, smirking.

"He's fine," his mother said breezily. "Have you spoken to your brother recently?"

"He came over for dinner a few weeks ago, but I thought you knew about that."

A long-suffering sigh that instantly transported Harlan back to a thankfully barely remembered time of footie pyjamas, bath time and all-too-real nightmares that no one had believed.

"Of course I know about *that*. I meant more recently."

"Mmm..." Harlan held his phone away from his face, taking a quick look at his message and call history. He didn't mind making her wait.

He and Aiden still texted each other pretty often, but...there was nothing in the last week or so. Harlan wouldn't have found that strange at all if his mother hadn't brought it up. With the exception of Charles, who he lived with, and Hamilton and Morgan, who he worked with — and now Michael — a week was nothing to go without talking. Sure, he and Aiden were brothers, but they weren't like...*brothers*. Were they?

"Nothing in the last few days," Harlan told her. It was technically true, but he thought it made him sound like a little less of a hot mess for not noticing how long it had been.

"How long *exactly*?" she demanded.

Slightly alarmed, Harlan put her on speakerphone and looked back through their texts again more carefully. "Umm... It looks like three days ago?"

"You're *sure*, Harlan?"

He hated hearing her say his name. He wanted to hear Charles or Hamilton — people who *actually* cared about him — say it right away to cover up the way she'd said it. "Yes, Mother."

"Don't—" Another long-suffering sigh. "Neither have we."

Harlan frowned. "Doesn't he still live at home?"

"Yes."

Did you drop him off somewhere and never go back for him? Harlan had to bite the words back, choke them down. "Okay. You haven't heard from him at all?"

"No. Aren't you supposed to be a detective or something?"

"Or something," he agreed. The more upset she got, the more upset *he* got. Not because she was his mother, or anything like that, or even because they were talking about his brother, but because she was a person who was in pain. Fuck. That sounded so cold, but it was true. *It's just a case. Think of it like a case,* he told himself.

No! His cases were about *ghosts.*

He swallowed hard. "Start from the beginning, okay?" he asked, the gentlest he'd spoken to her so far. He couldn't treat it as a case, exactly, but he could at least treat her like a *client,* if that made any sense at all. "When did you last hear from him?" he asked.

"He left on Friday —"

The day he'd last texted Harlan. Harlan had never replied. *Shit.* He'd accidentally clicked on the text, and he hadn't been up for answering it at the time. Then, because it hadn't had the notification on it, he'd forgotten about it.

"He said he was spending the weekend with a friend. I told him to text me every day, but I wasn't really surprised when he didn't. I know how it is with boys this age."

Harlan made a face at the phone. *Do you? Do you, though?*

"But he has school tomorrow and his laptop is here."

"Okay…"

"He needs it! He wouldn't go without it, and he's a *good* boy! He wouldn't miss school!" she insisted, her voice increasingly frantic now that she'd started to let it out.

Harlan physically recoiled as though she'd slapped him. If she hadn't been so clearly upset, he might've called her on it, but he…didn't care what she thought of him. *Right.*

"And that 'find my phone' app isn't working."

"Have you filed a missing-person report?"

"Tch!" She actually said it. *Tch.* "Of course not! It's not… We're not *that kind* of people."

Of course not. That would fracture their perfect little white-picket-fence, fifties world. The way Harlan had, so they'd dropped him out of it—and that had even been *before* he'd known he was gay. Did they even know their second son had a psychic ability? Harlan hadn't asked, but he doubted it, and he hated that doubt.

"I think it might be time for that," he told her, as gently as he could stomach, trying to keep the sharpness out of his voice.

"Isn't there—oh, I don't know—a waiting period, or something? Your father and I watched a few episodes of *CSI*, and I seem to remember—"

Your father. The words hit him like a punch in the gut. They didn't *apply* to him, hadn't for a very long time.

"No. Not in Ontario. I can file the police report, if you'd like. I still have some connections to the police." Or, rather, *Hamilton* did, but close enough. She didn't need to know the specifics. She didn't need to know anything about his life.

She sniffed, and he wasn't sure if it was disapproval or a sign that she was close to tears. "Yes. We read about…that. You left a perfectly good, well-paying job to…well, whatever it is you're playing at now."

Ah. Disapproval, then. He was eighty-five percent sure his groan was only in his head. What? Had they just…googled him? Too bad they hadn't also looked up *how to talk to your estranged son* while they were at it.

"All right. I'll file the report and look into things on…my end. I'll let you know if I hear anything, okay?" He hated how apologetic he sounded — like he wanted her approval, like he *cared* about it.

He did care, and he hated that.

"I — We'll look into it." Not for her, *never* for her — either of them — but for Aiden.

"Fine. Do whatever you have to."

Harlan filled in the blanks – *to get our good son back.* "Right. Uh…" How the fuck did he *end* this conversation?

"Goodbye. Take care."

"You… You, too." Like that, apparently. He wasn't sure which of them hung up first.

Hamilton was at his side, and Harlan hadn't even seen him come into the office again — and that scared him. Had he lost time? Even if it was just a few seconds, that was seriously frightening. *Did I text him?*

Apparently he hadn't gone very far for 'lunch', like maybe just to the hallway.

"You okay?"

Hamilton being careful with him was even more frightening.

"I'm fine," Harlan snapped automatically. He forced himself to take a deep breath. Then another. This wasn't Hamilton's fault. He didn't deserve to have it taken out on him. "Sorry. I'm...not fine."

Hamilton snorted. "Yeah. I figured. Who was that?"

"My mo—my *mother*."

"Was that the first time you've talked to her since...?"

"Since they stopped visiting me at the Centre when I was like seven? Yeah."

"Holy shit." He set a hand on Harlan's shoulder.

Harlan didn't flinch away, but he wanted to. "Yeah, well, who needs her, right?" he said brightly. He bit his lip. Hamilton had only spoken about his family once, and it had been an anecdote about his childhood. Harlan had no idea what his relationship with his parents or siblings was like as an adult. True, even after all this time, Hamilton was a very private person, but if he'd been cut off from his family, he probably wouldn't be as...indifferent about it as Harlan, whose parents had just drifted away.

"What was she calling about?" Again, Hamilton's voice was so gentle it was almost grating.

"She hasn't heard from Aiden in a few days."

Hamilton raised an eyebrow. "Aiden's *missing*?"

"Seems like it. Fuck, I hope not."

"We're at least marginally a detective agency, right? We'll detect."

"This...isn't exactly our specialty," Harlan reminded him, wording it as carefully as he could.

"Yeah, I know that. We still have connections to the cops, though."

Saying *'we'* was generous of him. "Thank you," he whispered.

"I can't promise we'll find him."

Harlan shook his head. "Of course." Hamilton wasn't that kind of man.

"But we'll do everything we can."

Harlan nodded.

"You call Morgan."

"Right. Fuck."

* * * *

Now that Morgan was using their powers more often, rather than suppressing them the way they had their entire adult life, they'd learned that they could be more nuanced. Rather than only being able to connect through romantic love, they could now take on the appearance of a loved one of any kind.

Harlan had never been 'the loved one' before, and he wasn't sure he could provide the emotional anchor *and* combine his power with Morgan's in the way they needed.

"Relax," Morgan told him. "All I want you to do is think of your brother. Think of Aiden. What colour is his hair?"

"Um...brownish blond?" No, that sounded *so* stupid, and he was already fucking it up. He couldn't even describe his own brother.

"Good."

Were they nuts? He sucked at this! They'd never find Aiden or even know if he was alive or dead, and it would be all Harlan's fault and his parents would hate him even more for getting their *good* son killed, and...

"Harlan? I need you to keep breathing with me. Can you do that?"

He nodded jerkily.

"Innnnn... Ouuuuuut..."

Morgan's breathing pattern was slightly different than his own more familiar one, but that actually seemed to be a good thing, snapping him out of his spiral and making him actually focus on their breath, their words.

"There..." they murmured. "That's it. Now, think of your brother. Don't just try to picture him. *Remember* him. How does he make you feel? What colours do you associate with him?"

This was starting to sound a little woo-woo even for Harlan, but he did his best.

Aiden made him think of cooling rain on a summer's day, of lemonade... "Yellow," he said softly.

Morgan nodded. "You're close. I've almost... There."

A moment later, an exact replica of Harlan's brother was standing in Morgan's place.

"Is this right?"

Harlan nodded.

"All right. I've got a fix on him. Now it's time to make the magic happen." They held out a hand.

Harlan took it. It didn't even *feel* like Morgan, which was unsettling. He'd spent enough time holding their hand to know it intimately—not that he'd spent any time holding Aiden's. Theirs was cool and dry, whereas this one was warmer and softer.

Harlan closed his eyes, even though he'd never needed to concentrate or anything else to make this work before, only contact with Morgan.

He opened them. Morgan was themself again, and there was no ghost—nothing but the two of them.

Morgan squinched one eye open, peering around the room like a bomb was about to go off. "I don't see anything."

"Me neither."

"So, what does that mean?"

Harlan sighed. "I think... I think it means he's alive."

They let out a long breath, sagging slightly with relief. "Yeah. That's what I thought, too. Want to try one more time, just to be sure?"

He nodded.

They held hands again. Aiden's spirit didn't appear.

Morgan laughed. "All right, I know I said *once* more, but..."

Harlan nodded again.

They changed into Aiden again, and Harlan took their hand.

Still nothing.

"He's alive?" Harlan asked softly.

Morgan raised an eyebrow. "I mean, I feel like you're more qualified to answer that kind of—" They glanced at Harlan. "Yeah. He's alive." They sighed. "As far as we know," they added.

"Yeah. As far as we know. Should I tell his...my— *our* mom?" Crap, he'd called her 'mom,' not 'mother'. He was really bad at this whole depersonalization thing.

They shook their head. "I don't think that's a good idea. No point giving her... Well, I mean, we've used this 'technique' before, but it's not an exact science. I'd say it's easier to get a false...negative? Yeah... Than a false positive."

"So we haven't learned anything?"

"Yeah. I guess that's what I'm saying." They reached out and squeezed his upper arm, careful to touch his shirt and not his bare skin. "Sorry, Harlan."

He sighed. "It's not... Thank you for helping me with this. I know doing this kind of thing still freaks you out."

They snorted. "It *should* freak you out."

"I mean, I didn't exactly —"

"Shit, sorry, Harlan. That was a shitty thing for me to say. I didn't mean..."

"I know. If it helps, it *does* freak me out. As far as we know, no one has ever combined their powers this way."

Morgan preened slightly. "Well, mine are pretty unusual, to be fair."

"Unlike mediums."

"I'm not sure how you want me to answer that," they said carefully.

Harlan sighed. "Just tell me my powers are pretty common." It was the one thing that had made him feel like less of a freak as a child. Sure, he stood out compared to 'normal' people, and maybe he was a little more powerful than most mediums out there, but mediumship itself was far from rare.

"Your powers are pretty common," they assured him.

"I was really hoping..." No, that wasn't right. What *had* he been hoping for?

"That we wouldn't see him but you'd somehow know he was alive and exactly where to find him?"

"Yeah. It sounds stupid when you say it out loud like that."

They laughed. "Well, if you're stupid, I'm stupid, too, because I was hoping for the exact same thing." They gave his shoulder another little squeeze. "It's a *good* thing that we didn't see him, Harlan."

"I know. I just…don't know what to do now."

"Well, unfortunately, I think it's up to Hamilton and good old-fashioned policework."

"Yeah, but I suck at that."

They hesitated a moment, then pulled him into a full-on hug. "I know."

"Thanks."

"I know it *sucks*. We'll find him, Harlan."

"Yeah. Of course." He wasn't convinced.

Aiden was, as far as they could tell, alive, but they hadn't learned anything provable or helpful in any way. He hated knowing that he'd have to step back and let Hamilton and his police contacts work the case from there.

And that he didn't have anything to tell their mother.

Chapter Thirteen

Harlan was feeling conflicted at the thought of going on a date when his little brother was missing, but...he didn't want to disappoint Michael or Charles, and maybe it would actually help take his mind off of...everything. He hoped. He knew there was nothing he could do. Hamilton had told him the day before that his police contacts hadn't turned up any leads, and neither had he or Morgan.

Harlan had never thought of himself as a scheduled 'date night' kind of guy, preferring to be loose and spontaneous, but it was really the only way to make it work with Charles and Michael's very different schedules. Since he set his own hours, Harlan was the most flexible of the three of them.

Besides, he realized, he'd actually been doing the date-night thing since he'd first *started* dating Charles, at least when they wanted to do something kinky. Neither of them had wanted to risk dropping at work the next day, so they'd had to carefully plan around days off.

And, of course, after Scheduled Date Night came…scheduled sex. Not all the time, but usually.

Harlan had thought he'd feel even stranger about *that*, but it was oddly exciting. He could spend the whole week — or however long the three of them went without seeing each other — just thinking about it, how sweet the release would be, especially because Charles was usually too busy for them to play by themselves. Harlan knew Charles would change things if he brought it up and told him he was unhappy about it, but he…wasn't. At least he didn't think so. It wasn't uncommon for him and Charles to jerk or suck each other off when they were in bed together, but lately they rarely did more, either sexually or kinkily, unless they were with Michael.

Which was fine.

Plus, it was fun and exciting to introduce someone to the world of BDSM. Everything was new for Michael.

And this night was going to be especially interesting. Charles had told him and Michael that he was finally comfortable letting Michael try spanking him.

Michael had texted back a truly stunning series of excited emojis, and Harlan and Charles had had a good laugh about it — but neither of them could deny they were excited, too.

They did the classic dinner and a movie date, which Harlan had always found silly because there was food at the movie.

Michael chose the restaurant and insisted on paying. He picked them up in a fancy car, but he wasn't driving. "I didn't want to drive because I'd like to have a drink tonight."

Charles raised an eyebrow.

"I know, I know — alcohol and BDSM don't mix. I'm not a complete lightweight. It should be well out of my system before the end of the movie. And, Charles, if you decide I'm too drunk, we won't play tonight. We'll just fuck."

Harlan couldn't help wincing a little at the vulgarity, especially where the driver could hear, which made him feel like an old Victorian man. Why did he have to be so uptight?

"Fine," Charles reluctantly agreed. "But Harlan and I can veto."

"Of course," Michael assured him.

The restaurant was way fancier than what Harlan would have chosen or — from the look on his face, and because he knew him — what Charles would have picked.

And they'd taken Michael *axe throwing*. Though he had seemed to enjoy it, this was clearly more his element — and completely outside Harlan's.

True, Harlan wasn't wearing a suit, but he *was* wearing a button-down shirt with a stiff collar that made him feel like he was at a funeral. Not — ironically, given his familiarity with death and the dead — that he'd ever *been* to a funeral. Maybe once, when he had been really little, before his parents had ditched him — or maybe that wasn't his memory at all. It was probably just from a movie or TV show or something. Not that he knew them well, but his parents didn't seem like the type of people to take a five-year-old to a funeral.

Harlan decided he was just going to get an appetizer, both so he would have room for movie snacks — he wasn't a huge fan of going to movie theatres, but he did love the popcorn — and because he didn't want to get anything too expensive while Michael was paying, even though Michael had insisted that they could order whatever they wanted.

Harlan's resolve lasted until the table next to them got the steaks they'd ordered, and the smell hit his nose. It wasn't something he and Charles had often — Harlan hadn't actually eaten steak all that often in his life — and it was irresistible.

He still ordered the cheapest cut on the menu.

Charles failed, too, opting for surf and turf.

At least they'd gone to the restaurant early, with plenty of time to eat a full meal, so Harlan didn't have to be anxious about getting to the theatre late.

Michael happily watched them enjoying their food. He'd only ordered a salad with light dressing and grilled chicken for 'protein,' along with, as promised, a single drink. He barely glanced at the bill before handing over his glossy credit card.

"Shall we?" Michael said grandly, offering his arm.

Charles took it, laughing, and held out his arm for Harlan.

The space between the tables was too small to keep it up for long — which was fine with Harlan, who felt silly and didn't really like PDA.

Michael called them another Uber, and they went to the theatre.

"I think I'm too full for popcorn or anything," Charles admitted after Michael had scanned the tickets on his phone.

Harlan groaned, the steak churning in his stomach. "Me, too."

Michael shrugged. "I wasn't going to get any for myself, anyway." He led them to their theatre, past the delicious-smelling popcorn Harlan was *way* too full to even consider.

Without any popcorn, the movie just *sucked*.

Harlan squirmed in his seat, glancing between Charles and Michael, trying to decide if they felt the same way he did. He couldn't tell. He tried to focus on the movie, but he kept getting distracted by the smell of popcorn from all the *smart* people who'd gotten some, and the sound of crunching.

Michael leaned forward and whispered, "Do you want to just leave and...?" He slid his forefinger into the ring of his opposite index finger and thumb.

Blushing, Harlan stifled a groan of relief. "*Yes*," he whispered back.

"Whoa, there." Michael laughed, holding up a hand. "Ask Charles."

Charles agreed, but maybe not as enthusiastically as Harlan had.

"Are you sure?" Harlan asked. "If you're enjoying it..."

"Nah. Let's get outta here."

They shuffled their way out of the theatre, and Michael called them yet another Uber.

As Michael and Harlan followed him into their bedroom, Charles laid out some ground rules and reminders specifically for that night, taking care to remind Michael of the stoplight system of safewords.

"'Red' means stop immediately, 'yellow' means pause and 'green' means keep going," Michael repeated.

"Perfect. How do you want me?" Charles asked, sitting on the edge of the bed and grinning up at them.

Harlan could tell Charles was excited, and he felt a little spike of...something. Just for a second. Then Michael smiled at him, and it went away.

If anything, it was a compliment. Charles was so hot that other people wanted him, too. But he'd been Harlan's first. Not that he was possessive—at least, he didn't think so. He didn't want to be.

A low moan drew his attention back to what was happening on the bed.

Michael had given Charles' broad chest a push, gently knocking him flat on his back on the bed. "Roll over," he told Charles.

Grinning up at them, Charles happily obeyed.

"Holy *shit*, he has a nice ass." Michael could barely keep his eyes off it.

Harlan found that he rather liked Michael addressing him rather than Charles—and, from the way Charles squirmed and let out a happy whimper, he did, too.

"He does, doesn't he?" Harlan stepped closer to the bed, his naked body pressed against Michael's, and stroked Charles' ass. "It's so warm already," he told Charles. "And it's only going to get warmer after Michael spanks you." He loved feeling Charles shiver with excitement under his hand.

Michael slid an arm around Harlan's waist, turning him for a kiss. Michael's lips weren't quite as full as Charles', but softer. Charles' always seemed to be slightly chapped. He claimed not to like lip balm, but he had an uncanny way of kissing Harlan right after he'd put some on and 'stealing' it.

Michael was just starting to use his tongue when Charles moaned from the bed.

"Are you two just going to tease me all night?"

Harlan and Michael grinned at each other, Michael still holding Harlan close.

"Up on all fours," Michael told him, tapping him on the foot to emphasize his point.

Charles eagerly snapped into position, his ass raised, offering himself up to them.

He didn't call Michael 'sir', which Harlan appreciated, at least until the three of them had talked about it. That was still just for him and Charles.

"What a lovely sight. Don't you agree?" Michael asked.

Harlan nodded, admiring the muscular curve of Charles' ass, the set of his powerful thighs. From this angle, he could just see Charles' balls, heavy and low. He could easily picture Charles' cock hanging heavy, thick and hot, curving slightly towards his stomach.

Well, he didn't have to imagine, did he?

He slid a hand across Charles' ass, down to his inner thigh then up again, following the thick swell of his shaft from the base to just short of the head.

"Ohhh…" Charles shivered, then laughed. "Hey, now, no fair! If the plan is to spank me before…"

"It is," Michael piped up.

"Right. Sorry. Got carried away," Harlan apologized. He gave Charles a little extra squeeze before releasing him and stepping back again. "Want me to warm him up for you?" he asked Michael.

Michael was staring at Charles' ass almost hungrily. "What? No." He grinned. "I've got this. I've watched the two of you often enough that I think I've got the idea. And it's pretty simple."

Harlan nodded, but he stayed close, his hip pressed against Michael's.

Keeping one arm around Harlan's waist, Michael raised his other and gave Charles' ass a short, sharp spank.

Charles moaned, rolling his hips. He dropped from all fours onto his elbows, raising his ass even higher as he eagerly awaited the next strike.

Michael glanced at Harlan.

Not entirely sure what Michael wanted or was asking, Harlan nodded.

Michael grinned at him before turning back to Charles. He lifted his hand again, making Charles wait for it.

Harlan could see the tension in Charles' thighs, poised to receive a blow he wouldn't be able to see coming. Each breath was practically a whimper of *need*.

Michael brought his hand down.

Charles cried out, rocking his hips for a moment before returning, ready and eager for more.

Michael grinned again, this time not looking at Harlan before spanking Charles. His nails dug into Harlan's hip and Harlan hissed and pulled away. For a moment, Michael tightened his grip, making Harlan feel almost panicky. Michael spanked Charles again, barely seeming to notice Harlan was there.

"Hey," Harlan said, to get his attention. "He's the masochist, not me."

"What?" Michael finally looked up from Charles' ass.

"Everything okay?" Charles asked, lifting his head off the bed and turning to face them.

"Fine," Harlan agreed. "Just…"

Michael followed Harlan's gaze down his arm and to his hand, where his nails were leaving little white impressions on Harlan's hip. "Oh, shit, sorry!" Michael laughed. "Just got excited." He relaxed his hand.

"It's all right. It happens," Harlan assured him, trying not to wince. He waited until Michael was distracted spanking Charles again before flexing his hip.

He had to admit, watching his boyfriend get spanked was surprisingly hot. He circled away from Michael, enjoying the view from several angles. He was half hard already, but he didn't want to touch himself. Not yet. Not until all three of them were ready.

Charles grunted, the sound he made when something was too much, drawing Harlan's attention back to him.

He couldn't see Charles' face, which didn't help.

He hesitated a moment, then made a Dom Decision — and wasn't *that* a laugh, him being a capital-D Dom?

"Yellow," he said softly. He'd never had to use a safeword before, and neither had Charles, at least with him.

Michael swatted Charles again, and Charles grunted again.

"Yellow," Harlan repeated, louder and more firmly.

Charles dropped into a crouch, shuffling ever so slightly forward on the bed, away from Michael.

Michael blinked. "Wha...?"

Harlan set a hand on Charles' back, stroking him in small, reassuring circles. Charles didn't say anything, so Harlan assumed it was up to him to explain, but first he wanted to check in with Charles.

He shuffled around to the far side of the bed so he was in front of Charles, keeping a hand on Charles the whole time. "Charles?" he asked softly. "Can you look at me?"

Charles slowly raised his head, his eyes soft and unfocused, but he was smiling slightly. He nodded.

"Do you know why I paused the scene?"

Charles shook his head, then nodded again. "Too much," he said, and the words sounded like they took a little effort.

"But you're all right now?"

Charles nodded.

Satisfied that Charles was fine for the moment, he continued petting him while he turned his attention to Michael.

"Michael, why didn't you stop the first time I said 'yellow'?"

"I-I didn't hear you. Sorry," he told Charles' back.

"'s okay," Charles assured him.

"It's okay. Charles is fine. You just hit him a little too hard those last few times, without warming him up more." Harlan bit his lip before asking, "You remember the safewords we told you to use?"

Just for a second, Michael looked like he might roll his eyes, but Harlan gave him a quelling look.

"Yes. 'Green' means everything's fine, 'yellow' means pause and 'red' means stop."

Harlan nodded, satisfied. "Just...listen more carefully next time, okay?"

Michael nodded.

Harlan smiled at him. He didn't want him to feel bad about his mistake, but he'd thought it was important to call him on it and make sure he was aware of what had happened.

He rubbed Charles' shoulder. "Are you up for more?" he asked.

Charles was more alert and responsive this time, having come out of subspace slightly. "Yeah. At least a little." He looked over his shoulder to grin reassuringly at Michael. "I don't want your first time to end like that if it doesn't have to. Those last few were just a little sharp, okay?"

Michael nodded.

Harlan realized they'd forgotten an important step. "Michael, do *you* want to keep going?"

Michael grinned at him. "Hell, yeah."

Harlan started shuffling back to his original position, but Michael shook his head. "Why don't you stay there? You can hold his hair if you want. If you guys are into that."

Charles grinned up at Harlan, nodding.

Harlan positioned himself directly in front of Charles, lightly stroking his hair. It was just long enough to start to curl. He waited until Charles' face was nice and relaxed before grabbing a handful and giving it a good, sharp yank.

Charles stiffened, just for a second, then went limp in Harlan's grip, the weight of his head suspended entirely by his hair.

"Apparently you're *really* into it," Michael laughed.

Harlan nodded, settling Charles in a more comfortable position.

After a moment, Charles lifted his head enough to reach Harlan's cock. He also lifted his ass again, presenting it to Michael.

"Hot." Michael nodded. "Ready?"

Harlan wasn't sure if he was asking him or Charles, but he answered for both of them. "Yes."

Michael stroked Charles' ass in little circles, probably imitating what he'd seen Harlan do.

"I'm ready," Charles laughed.

Michael grinned at Harlan over Charles' shoulder, then raised his hand and gave him a good, solid swat.

Charles moaned, rocking forward only to be caught by Harlan's grip on his hair keeping him in place.

It also brought Charles' mouth wonderfully close to Harlan's cock, his breath warm on his sensitive skin.

"Ohhhh..." Harlan moaned, rocking his hips and digging his nails into Charles' scalp.

Catching Harlan's gaze, Michael's grin widened. "Do you think he can...? While I'm spanking him, without accidentally biting your dick off?"

"What?" Charles tried to turn and look at Michael, but Harlan held him fast.

"He's asking..." Harlan could feel himself blushing, but he forced himself to continue. "He's asking if you think you can suck me while he spanks you without you, uh, biting me by accident."

"Please," Charles huffed. "Have *some* faith in me," he laughed. "This ain't my first rodeo."

"Is that a yes?" Harlan asked, hoping very much that it was.

"That was a yes."

Harlan tugged Charles' hair, guiding but not forcing him in the direction of his cock.

Charles eagerly complied.

Harlan closed his eyes

Maybe one day he'd get over it, but for now, every time he had sex with Charles, part of him couldn't believe that someone that hot, that competent, would want to be with *him*, that he would suck his cock. Both Harlan and Charles had very egalitarian views of blow jobs. They didn't see them as automatically submissive. He sucked Charles' cock, too. There was something *very* intimate about it, somehow even more than fucking, at least in Harlan's opinion.

He heard Michael moan and opened his eyes to see him watching him over Charles' shoulder. They exchanged grins.

Michael raised a hand above Charles' ass, asking a silent question.

Harlan nodded, combing his fingers restlessly through Charles' thick hair as he fought to keep his hips still, to let Charles control the speed and depth.

Michael brought his hand down on Charles' ass — more gently and carefully than before they'd paused, Harlan was pleased to note, if distantly.

Charles rocked forward, taking Harlan deep all at once and moaning around his mouthful — being extra careful with his teeth.

Harlan cried out, his hips pitching and jerking a few times to meet Charles, completely overwhelmed with pleasure. *Fuck.* They would definitely *have* to do this again, just take Charles apart between them.

Michael asked the same silent question with his hands raised, and Harlan nodded again, bracing himself for Charles' reaction to the spank. Unfortunately, he thought he might've given away what was coming, because Charles *also* tensed.

Michael shook his head at Harlan, shaking with silent laughter. He ran his hands across Charles' ass, just soothing and gentling him for a moment. He didn't ask before the next spank, probably not wanting Harlan to accidentally warn Charles again, which was fine with Harlan.

Michael rained a sharp series of blows across both cheeks, spreading them out evenly so no one place would be neglected or overused.

Harlan threw his forearm across his mouth to keep himself from crying out as Charles took him to the root each time Michael's hand landed, easing back between blows before Michael drove him deep again. He noticed that Michael's teeth were sunk into his lower lip, as just spanking Charles and watching apparently brought him close to the edge.

Michael gave Charles another quick series of spanks, harder this time, and Harlan could tell from Charles' tensed muscles that it was *close* to the edge for him, but not quite there. Fuck, he'd never had his cock sucked like that before. Charles was forced to pour out all his eagerness, all his energy, all his cries, through Harlan.

Michael rocked back on his heels, staring at Charles' ass, stroking it in slow, thoughtful circles.

Harlan wasn't surprised when he asked, "Hey, Charles? Mind if we…mix things up a bit?"

Charles shook his head, drawing a moan out of Harlan.

As hot as it would be for Michael to just start fucking Charles while he was still sucking him, that wasn't *quite* close enough to consent for Harlan. He reluctantly pulled back, drawing his hips away from Charles until his cock slid out with a wet pop and a disappointed whimper from Charles.

Harlan stroked Charles' cheek and jaw. "I'll be right back," he promised. "If you want. I think Michael wants to fuck you now. Sound good?"

"*Very* good." Charles' eyes were half-lidded and dark with pleasure, a dreamy smile on his damp lips.

"Good." He tipped Charles' head up so he could kiss him, having to do an ungainly shuffle to get his own face low enough to do it. Luckily Michael wasn't paying attention, already grabbing their bottle of lube and spreading it over his fingers, and Harlan was back in position by the time he looked up again.

He licked the taste of himself from his lips, grinning down at Charles.

"Filthy," Charles teased him, laughing.

"You love it," Harlan told him.

"I do."

"Ready?" Michael asked, tracing the fingers of his un-lubed hand up and down Charles' crack and reddened, sensitive cheeks.

"Yesss," Charles gasped, lowering his upper body and eagerly raising his ass.

Harlan watched Michael slide a lubed finger home, felt the shockwave roll through Charles as he was opened. Unfortunately, he couldn't quite see where Michael's finger disappeared inside of Charles, but he'd done it often enough that he could easily imagine it.

"Good," Michael murmured, moving his hand slightly, and Harlan suspected he was curling his finger. He abruptly lifted the hand he was using to stroke Charles' ass, scratching him on his freshly spanked skin.

Charles cried out and jolted forward, bringing his mouth achingly close to Harlan's cock again.

Charles looked up, almost pleadingly.

Harlan shook his head, knowing he was denying himself just as much as Charles — though he doubted Charles would see it that way in the moment. "Not yet. Not until he's in you."

Charles moaned about how unfair it was, but he was grinning, clearly pleased by their little game.

"Ready?" Michael asked again, hardly waiting for Charles' gasped, "Yes," before sliding in a second finger alongside the first.

Charles spread his knees, giving Michael even better access.

Michael barely waited for Charles to relax again before adding a third finger, spreading Charles open quickly now, his goal seemingly within reach.

Harlan had to fight hard not to start stroking himself. *Not yet. Just think how much better it'll be with Charles,* he reminded himself, watching eagerly, hungrily, part of him wishing Michael would just get *on* with it, but the other part just enjoying the show.

"Mmm," Michael purred. "That's it. Nice and relaxed and open for me, hmm?"

Charles nodded. Realizing that might not be enough for either of his lovers, he rasped, "Yes!"

Michael pulled his fingers free, ignoring Charles' needy little cry, so similar to the one he'd made when Harlan pulled out of his mouth.

Harlan heard the crinkle of a condom wrapper being torn. He couldn't quite see Michael's lap from his position, but he could easily imagine the familiar motions of unrolling it into place.

Michael poured a generous amount of lube on his hand, quickly warming it in his palm before slicking his cock, paying special attention to the tip. "Ready?" he asked Charles once again, his free hand braced on Charles' hip.

"Yes. Oh, yes. Yes, please."

Michael and Harlan exchanged grins.

"Are you *sure*?" Michael teased, mock sympathetically. "I wouldn't want to go too quickly and hurt you."

"Oh, fuck you," Charles chuckled.

Michael's smirk got even wider. "*Au contraire. I* am going to fuck *you*. Right now." He used his slick hand to guide himself past Charles' tight ring, still bracing himself with his free one on Charles' hip.

Charles gasped and moaned, rocking slightly as he tried to take Michael deeper, faster.

"Uh-uh," Michael scolded him, dragging him back by the hip. "*I'm* in control here. Isn't that right?"

"Oh, fuck." Charles' voice was almost a squeak.

Harlan could feel Charles' whole body shudder, and he decided to help Michael. He tightened his fist in Charles' curls, keeping him pinned between the two of them while Michael slowly slid deeper.

"Oh fuck, oh fuck," Charles gasped, and Harlan got to watch his eyes roll back in his head as the pleasure overwhelmed him.

"There," Michael murmured to both of them. "I'm all the way in."

Charles shivered, tugging against Harlan's grip on his hair.

Michael nodded at Harlan, and Harlan reached down to tap Charles' chin.

"Wha…?" Charles looked up at him, briefly confused, but his lips quickly spread into a smile of understanding. "Ohhh. Yeah." He shifted himself up, raising his head to the same level as his ass and straightening his spine. He parted his lips eagerly.

Harlan shuffled into a more comfortable position — his left foot had started falling asleep, but he'd been too distracted to notice — and gave himself a few slow strokes to get back to full hardness before rocking his hips forward until his tip just made contact with Charles' plump, flushed, slightly swollen lips.

Charles hummed happily, rocking forward to take Harlan's cockhead into his mouth.

Harlan loosened his grip on Charles' hair to let him move more freely, stroking the side of Charles' face with his free hand.

Michael pulled him back by the hip with a laugh, thrusting deep inside him.

Charles cried out, shuddering as Michael filled him, straining forward to reach Harlan.

Harlan rocked closer, making it easier for Charles to reach him.

"Soft," Michael laughed, shaking his head.

Harlan could see him dig his nails into Charles' hip.

Charles cried out again, the sound muffled to a hum around Harlan's cock.

Earlier in his time as a quote-unquote Dom, Michael's remark probably would've made Harlan feel insecure, but now...? He was a little surprised to find it didn't bother him at all. So what if he was a little soft? He liked it, and so did Charles. "Charles makes me soft."

"That's because *Charles* is nice and soft." Michael reached forward to stroke the curve of Charles' well-furred belly. It was a sharp contrast to his own toned midsection, but even though he clearly valued thinness in himself, he'd never said anything negative about the fact that Charles *wasn't*.

Of course, if he had, it would've been a race to see who could throw him out of their bed faster, Harlan or Charles.

Still, Harlan appreciated it, and he was sure Charles did, too.

"He is," Harlan agreed, stroking Charles' cheek.

The corner of Charles' mouth turned up ever so slightly around Harlan's cock.

"Enough talk," Michael declared, his hand reclaiming its spot on Charles' hip. "Let's fuck."

"Cheers," Harlan said, immediately wanting to facepalm. Fuck, that was a weird thing to say!

Luckily, Michael just repeated, "Cheers," and even raised a hand before driving deep inside Charles, pushing him forward, farther onto Harlan's cock.

Harlan moaned, and he could feel Charles' answering hum around his shaft. He closed his eyes with pleasure, just letting himself be in the moment and relish the feeling of Charles' hot, wet mouth wrapped around him and the sound of Michael's breath speeding up as he fucked Charles.

He let Michael take charge and set the pace, pushing Charles' mouth to the base of Harlan's shaft with each thrust, pulling him back until his head *almost* but not quite popped out before driving deep again.

"Fuck," Michael growled, "I'm close."

Harlan nodded jerkily. He was close, too, but he didn't want to be the first one to spill.

Charles groaned beneath him, the sound translating into vibrations so intense they made Harlan's head fall back. While Michael thrust, he shuffled himself so he could get one hand between his legs and stroke himself in short, sharp jerks.

"Oh, fuck," Michael moaned. He dug his nails into Charles' hip, making Charles cry out, muffled, as Michael came deep inside of him.

Harlan could feel Charles' hand speed up, feel how close he was. Before Michael had finished, Charles went completely stiff, his spine arching between the two of them as his body shook.

Harlan let out a long breath. He loved watching Charles come. It was too bad he couldn't see his face.

Charles sucked him to the root, his mouth wonderfully tight and wet.

With one hand still fisted in Charles' hair, his knuckles white, Harlan's other fell to Charles' shoulder. "Charles," he warned him, "I'm..."

Charles nodded slightly, barely distinguishable from the bobbing motions as he sucked, but Harlan could tell the difference.

He came down Charles' throat, having to restrain himself from thrusting too hard before finally going still.

When he came back to himself enough to take in what was going on around him, he saw that Michael had just pulled out and was starting to take the condom off and clean himself and Charles up.

Harlan sank back on his heels, gently pulling free of Charles' hot, welcoming mouth—which, since he'd come, was getting a little overwhelming for his over-sensitive dick. "Fuck," he groaned, slowly coming down from his peak.

"Fuck," Michael agreed, laughing a little shakily. He sprawled on one side of the bed, leaving plenty of room for the other two.

Charles smiled dreamily up at Harlan, his lips damp and kissable looking. He wiped his mouth with the back of his hand, panting a little, before he too went limp, curling up with his back against Michael's front.

Michael reached out and idly stroked Charles' black hair.

Harlan smiled down at both of them, taking a mental picture. He wanted to remember this moment.

He started flopping down beside Charles, but Charles looked up at him imploringly.

"Oh, no," Harlan groaned.

"I know, I know, I'm sorry," Charles apologized, "but we got a little ahead of ourselves."

"Oh?" Michael asked.

"We forgot to set up for aftercare."

"Do we *really* need it?"

Harlan sighed. "Yeah. We do." He really just wanted to snuggle, but this was more important, and the other two had already settled in. Besides, he'd probably done the least 'work.' "All right, I'll get it."

"You're the best," Charles told him, his voice slightly raspy.

"You are!" Michael agreed, holding Charles close.

Harlan stumbled out of the bedroom and into the kitchen, where he grabbed a few bottles of water from the fridge and a handful of chocolate bars from their little aftercare basket, then shuffled back to the others and distributed his loot.

Charles managed to prop himself up on one elbow to eat and drink.

Michael made a face at the chocolate, but he ate it in just a few bites.

Harlan lay down beside them, drinking a little more slowly and taking the occasional bite of chocolate after tucking the three of them in.

"Holy shit, that was amazing," Charles murmured once they'd all finished and settled in together comfortably.

"It *really* was," Michael agreed. "I don't know if the spanking makes the sex better, or the other way around."

"Both," Charles laughed, patting Michael's arm.

"Both," Harlan agreed with a happy sigh.

"Well, either way, it was amazing. Wow. And *you*," he jostled Charles, "getting to be the lucky Pierre."

Harlan frowned. "The *what*?"

Charles tipped his head back and exchanged grins with Michael.

"You've never heard that before?" Michael asked.

Harlan shook his head.

"It's the person who gets to be in the middle," Charles explained.

"Oh. Oh!" To his shame, Harlan could feel himself blushing, but luckily he didn't think the others could see.

"How's your ass?" Michael asked.

Charles snorted. "Which part?"

"Well, I meant your cheeks, asshole," Michael laughed.

"My asshole is fine. My cheeks are a little sore, but I've had worse."

Michael whistled. "Damn! Way to tell me to step up my game!"

Harlan froze, even though this wasn't about him.

Charles just took it in stride, chuckling and shaking his head. "Not what I was saying...but you're welcome to try harder next time."

"You bet I will!" Michael groaned. "Turn off the light."

This meant Harlan had to be the one to move *again*, but the switch was closest to him, and fortunately he didn't have to get up — the bedroom light had a switch by the door and one above Harlan's side of the bed. He reached up, fumbling blindly a few times, before finally managing to hit it. "'Night," he murmured.

"'Night," Michael replied, reaching across Charles to stroke Harlan's thigh.

Harlan felt like he was at a sleepover. Well, not that he'd ever been to one, at least not that he remembered before being sent to the Centre. But he'd seen them in movies and read about them, and this seemed pretty close — except for the sex and spanking.

Charles mumbled something vaguely affirmative, clearly almost asleep already.

Harlan was exhausted — pleasantly — but he was the last to fall asleep. He listened to Michael's breathing shift. But every time Harlan closed his eyes, he kept thinking, *Aiden, where are you?*

Chapter Fourteen

Harlan woke after only a few hours from a nightmare about looking for Aiden.

Charles was fast asleep, but Michael looked up when he got out of bed.

"I'm going to the...corner store." Harlan hadn't been to the one closest to their apartment yet, and he couldn't remember what chain it was part of, only that he'd seen one nearby.

"It's late. Early? Want me—either of us—to come with you?" Michael offered after glancing at his phone.

"Nah, that's okay." Somehow he was restless *and* he wanted to just be a lump, but he knew from experience that if he indulged his lumpishness he'd regret it the next day. It sometimes happened, even if he'd done proper aftercare the night before and had something sweet. *Huh.* Could he get top drop by proxy? He hadn't really played the night before, but it *had* been some pretty intense sex—apparently intense enough that his body had interpreted it as play. Or maybe it was just his dream and his worry about his brother. He just knew he had to get up and moving, even if he didn't go far.

"Make sure you take your phone with you," Charles mumbled from where his face was pressed against Michael's back.

"Okay." Harlan appreciated that Charles hadn't mentioned *why* he needed to take his phone in front of Michael. He had a tendency to get lost, even somewhere he was familiar, and he hadn't spent nearly enough time out in their new neighbourhood to feel comfortable going out without a map.

He got dressed as quickly and quietly as possible, grabbed his phone and headed downstairs.

Both to prove to Charles — and himself — that he could find it on his own, and because he wasn't in any particular hurry, he set off in the direction he thought he'd seen the corner store. The street kept getting busier and busier, which seemed promising, but then he found himself in a strip mall. He turned around and tried the opposite direction. He considered just packing it in and going home as he passed their apartment, but that would mean admitting defeat. No. He was determined to find it, and without using his phone if at all possible. It was a good way to get to know the neighbourhood, even if it was the middle of the night and he was starting to get slightly anxious.

Fuck. Okay, more than slightly. He really hadn't thought it was that far away. He'd turned down several promising-looking streets and gotten completely turned around.

Sighing, he got out his phone. Well, he hadn't found the store, but he'd at least accomplished his secondary goals of getting out of the apartment to stretch his legs and see some of the neighbourhood. He was definitely taking Charles with him next time.

Double fuck. When he opened the map app, there were pins dropped at Rattling Chains and both his and Charles' old apartments…but not their new one. And, of course, he couldn't remember the name of the street their shared apartment was on.

"Shit," he said softly, and he saw someone across the street lift their head. He waved his hand in a way he hoped meant, 'Sorry… I'm fine.'

He couldn't have gotten *that* far away, could he?

He didn't want to call Charles, not yet, not until he'd at least *tried* on his own.

Ignoring the sharp spike of rising panic in his gut, he turned around and started back the way he'd come. Nothing looked familiar. He realized that the person on the other side of the street was keeping pace with him, *directly* across. He put his head down and sped up. The person hadn't done anything, not really, but they were starting to give him the creeps.

He decided to turn off onto a side street and see if they'd follow him. If they did, he'd call Charles or maybe even the police.

Just before he turned, he felt the hairs on the back of his neck stand on end, and he couldn't help trying to smooth them down. It didn't work.

He turned, almost in slow motion, like he was in a horror movie, half expecting to find the stranger standing right behind him. His heart was pounding, and he felt more afraid than he thought he should, but what did that mean?

The person was still on the other side of the street, but they were *looking* at him now.

He blinked. No. It wasn't a person at all, at least not anymore. He'd thought that the way they just seemed kind of blurry and indistinct was because of his nervousness and not looking at them very closely — that they were maybe wearing a trench coat or something — but it was because they were *dead*. Some ghosts could look very much alive, at least briefly, but this one either couldn't or wasn't bothering. Its eyes were black pits in the rough shape of its face, and its mouth was a yawning chasm.

It started moving towards him, passing through the occasional cars between them without hesitation.

He closed his eyes, just for an instant, just long enough to pull himself together.

Okay. It didn't matter if he went the wrong way right now. The only important thing was getting away from the ghost. It wouldn't be able to follow him far. It was bound to its spot, and he wasn't. By extending his senses just a little — not enough to piss it off or draw even more of its attention — he could feel the edge of its territory. It wasn't far. He just had to make it there, and he'd be safe. Just a few more steps.

Unfortunately, he knew he couldn't run. That would only attract its notice. He had to walk, slowly and calmly. He couldn't bring himself to turn his back on it. Hopefully he wouldn't trip on anything and break his neck and join it there for eternity. Charles wouldn't even be able to visit him. He let out a strained laugh, quickly closing his mouth when the ghost perked up.

He could also trip over something, then land on his ass and it would catch up to him, or...

Okay, Harlan, not helpful.

One step back. Then another.

The world shimmered for a moment, then disappeared. Harlan was floating in an endless void full of the same black nothingness as the ghost's eyes, alone, despairing, formless and adrift.

He opened his mouth to scream, only he didn't have a mouth — *just a gaping black hole* — didn't have *anything* —

Everything went white, and Harlan could scream, then he couldn't *stop* screaming, couldn't cover his eyes or whatever he was using to see. There was nothing but whiteness.

Everything got quiet, not just Harlan's screaming, but a roaring, rushing noise he hadn't been aware of until it stopped.

He opened his eyes — yes, eyes, he had them now for sure, and wasn't *that* a fucked-up thought?

There was a horse on the street. Not, like, *loose* or anything. It was pulling a wagon, but it didn't look like the kind that tourists rode in, and he didn't *think* they were near any of the places that offered them.

None of the people around him so much as gave the horse a second glance, and he didn't see any film cameras or anything, so it didn't seem like a publicity stunt or whatever, either.

Actually, now that he looked around, everyone was dressed really weird. The women were all wearing full-length dresses, and the men were wearing suits. Had he stumbled onto a movie set somehow?

It was *day*.

Even with all the film-set lights, they couldn't turn night into day for someone who was there, live. Could they?

Oh, fuck. He knew what was happening. It was another thing he'd read about ghosts being able to do but had never encountered in person, and holy *fuck,* did he wish he never had! It had dragged him into its memory, a little bubble of almost time-travel. Part of Harlan expected everything to be sepia-toned, but it was in full, vivid colour.

The whole thing was pretty rare and special, and Harlan got to experience it. Great. Wasn't he lucky? He hated it and wanted out immediately.

But where was 'out'? There was only the world surrounding him, as far as he could see, in every direction—including *up*. Not the same world he'd just left, the one he'd spent his entire linear life in, true, but the *world*. There were no obvious exit signs, no subtle doorways set against the backdrop for employees of this whacky amusement park to come and go.

No sign of the ghost that had dragged him there, for that matter.

Apparently it had been saving the energy from not appearing human to do *this* for a long, long time. Was there something it wanted to show him, something left undone that it thought he, as a medium, could help it with? Something that was keeping it from crossing over? Well, he'd made it his life's work to help spirits like this one. He'd have to figure it out.

He sighed. That seemed like the obvious starting place—which, with his luck, probably meant it was exactly the wrong thing and he should do the opposite, but...he couldn't think of any other options. Not good ones, anyway, ones that made sense, aside from just standing in the middle of the street and screaming until one of the...ghosts? No, that wasn't right. Shades? What did that even mean?

Until one of the *memories* surrounding him noticed — and probably took him to the loony bin, or whatever they'd called it back in the day.

On that note, he realized he probably shouldn't call too much attention to himself. Even if nothing around him was real — or, rather, had once been real but wasn't currently, except to him and probably everyone around him, if they were even self-aware and weren't just...recordings of some kind...

Fuck, this was confusing. He'd always hated time-travel stories. Not that this was true time travel, at least he didn't think so. It was just a memory. '*A kind of engraving on the world, pulled collaboratively from the environment and the consciousness of the spirit who conjured it.*' At least, that was how he'd heard it described once. He wished that the author had spent less time describing it and more time explaining how to *escape* from it.

At least he couldn't change anything in the past and fuck up the future. *Probably. Shit.* How far did this bubble reach? Could he just keep walking until he found his own great-to-the-whatever grandparents and tell them, *Holy shit, tell your kids to accept* their *kids no matter how they turn out or what completely hypothetical powers they have*? Psychics were probably still underground at this point, right? Not that Harlan had paid much attention in Tom — Mr. Addison's — history class, not enough to have any real idea where he was. *When.* He was pretty sure he was still in Toronto. Holy fuck, he hoped so.

He shook himself. No, he had to focus. It didn't matter when or even where he was. *Find the ghost. Shake the shit out of the ghost. Make the ghost take you back. Yeah.*

So far no one had noticed him — not in a *Christmas Carol* 'literally no one can see you' kind of way, just in a 'people are too busy doing their own thing to notice one weirdo' way.

Actually, that *was* weird. He should stick out, right? He liked to think that, if a time traveler was dropped in the middle of twenty-first century Toronto, he'd at least *notice*, right? That the clothes would give them away?

Though maybe that wasn't the best example. Toronto definitely had more than its fair share of weirdos.

Still…

He looked down. He was wearing little leather shoes with leather laces. And above that, suit pants. He could feel a hat on his head, just like the men walking around him and not looking at him. It was definitely not what he'd put on when he'd left the apartment. Well, no wonder no one was looking at him funny. *He fit right in.*

He shuddered. Somehow, out of everything, *including* suddenly finding himself in the past, the fact that a ghost had changed his clothing was the creepiest part. He wasn't sure what, if anything, that said about him, but…

Luckily he was standing on the sidewalk, so he'd had time to freak out a little as he figured out what had happened and he hadn't been hit by one of the funny little cars on the road — though, now that he thought about it, several of the pedestrians had bumped into him. Apparently Toronto didn't change.

Hadn't changed? Wouldn't change? *Ugh.*

He walked for a while, hoping he was following some sort of subtle ghostly trail his kidnapper had left for him, but more realistically, he knew he was probably just blindly wandering. If nothing else, hopefully he'd hit the 'edge' of this ghost's little world, and maybe that would help him find a way out. It had to end eventually. Didn't it?

He stumbled over nothing and had to throw out a hand to catch himself on the nearest building, scraping his palm. He checked to make sure it wasn't bleeding.

It wasn't his hand. It was too broad and hairy, and... He poked his left hand with the right. *No nerve damage.*

He looked at his reflection in one of the store windows. He wasn't *himself*. His hair was too dark, and he was older, with heavy lines around his eyes and mouth.

I am the ghost. That was why he couldn't find it. It had been him all along. This was all from his — the ghost's — perspective. *His* memory.

Great. Where did *that* leave him? He couldn't really threaten *himself* into taking him back when he belonged... Could he?

While he was still trying to decide what to do, 'his' body — hopefully temporarily — suddenly started walking, this time with direction and purpose. *Fuck.* It had just been toying with him before, letting him wander its little world before taking over.

The ghost stopped a man on his own. Oh, fuck. Harlan could *feel* what the ghost was about to do, what was going to happen. What *had* happened. He was there, looking out through the ghost's eyes, speaking through his mouth, but they weren't his words. He was moving, but he wasn't in control.

They persuaded him to come into a nearby alley with them. They pulled out a knife and stabbed him, over and over, covering his mouth and holding him up in a horrible parody of affection until he stopped moving. Then they let him drop onto the bare dirt of the alley.

That was what the ghost had brought him there for, what it had wanted to show him? He could feel it laughing as it bent over the body, mocking him.

It started going through the man's pockets.

Harlan wasn't in control of their breath, which was a good thing or they'd probably be hyperventilating.

The world jerked and Harlan was whipped back to the entrance of the alley, the man still beside him. Still alive. The sick fuck was just, what, replaying it over and over? Had it even brought Harlan here on purpose or had he just gotten swept up in its memory?

Fuck. He couldn't just stay trapped there forever, watching a decades-old murder over and over again.

He watched — no, it was more than watching. It was *him* doing it, his hands on the knife… He was helpless as they stabbed the man again, and right at the moment the body went limp, he realized it was distracted, enjoying the thrill of the kill.

Okay. I'm going to reach into my pocket – the pocket of these dumb little pants that come up to my nipples – and my phone is gonna be in there. There is no try.

Except that he was terrible at convincing anyone of anything, *especially* himself.

No.

Pocket. Phone. Home. That simple.

His pocket suddenly felt heavier. *Yes.* This world was of the ghost's creation, but Harlan was a medium, and that trumped anything a *ghost* could do. He reached down, slowly and carefully, slipping the bloody knife into his jacket pocket. He reached into the pants, and there it was. His phone. He pulled it out, grimacing. Hopefully it wouldn't still be covered in blood when he got back to the real world. He knew he only had a few more seconds before he attracted the spirit's attention. He tapped the Messages icon. It was still open to his conversation with Charles, and he typed 'sos' with one hand, not taking the time to capitalize it, then hit send. Hopefully it wouldn't autocorrect to something crazy, and Charles would understand.

And, most importantly, hopefully his *text* from a fucking *ghostly realm* would actually reach Charles.

He heard a thud, and his left hand wrapped around his right wrist and *twisted*. Harlan could feel the bones grind together, and he dropped the phone with a cry.

"No!"

"Harlan?" Warm, gentle hands on his shoulders.

He opened his eyes. "Charles," he breathed with relief.

"Yeah." Charles held him close, stroking his back. "You okay?"

"I-I think so. Fuck."

"We tracked your phone, and there was this crazy bubble where everything looked all old-timey, and you were right in the middle of it, then Charles got closer and it just disappeared!" Michael crowed.

Harlan had been so focused on Charles that he hadn't noticed Michael. "You could see it?" Harlan asked him, after several long moments of just letting Charles hold him, reassure him with his warmth and strong arms and *realness*.

"Yeah...?"

"Me, too," Charles agreed.

Fuck, that wasn't good. It was a good thing it was the middle of the night and no cars had driven through.

He didn't know what would've happened to them and their drivers.

Harlan bent to press his face against Charles' shoulder, just burying it there for a moment while Charles rubbed his back in small circles and made soft soothing noises.

Michael was keeping his distance, and even though Harlan wasn't sure why, he couldn't blame him...for any of the reasons he could think of.

Fuck. He didn't want to do this, but he didn't think he had a choice. Well, he could call Benjamin, but he was trying to make *less* work for the two remaining police mediums, not more. And, while his experience had been terrifying, it hadn't *exactly* been dangerous, and the crime scene was more than half a century old, not exactly high priority. Who knew when Benjamin or Beth would be able to get around to dealing with this place?

Maybe it had drawn energy from him to create its illusion, or maybe it was something it did all the time. Maybe it would *use* the energy it had stolen in order to make it happen more often. What if he left, safely tucked in Charles' bubble, and there was an incident he could've stopped? He couldn't risk that. It had to be stopped, and Harlan was right there already. So *he* had to be the one to stop it.

All right. At least he knew it was there now, and what kinds of tricks it might try. He gave Charles one last squeeze before letting go and looking him directly in the eye. "Okay. Back up," he said grimly. There was no way he could reason with this ghost. He had to get rid of it, plain and simple.

Charles nodded, keeping one hand on each of Harlan's shoulders for a moment. "Ready?"

"Ready for what? What are you doing?" Michael asked, his voice a little shrill. Of course, between getting possessed the first time they'd met and the nearly disastrous 'exorcism' he'd done in Michael's friend's office building, Michael's experiences with ghosts and Harlan had been...far from good.

Michael shook his head, his eyes wide. "Let's get the fuck outta here!"

"I have to deal with this," Harlan told him, his voice surprisingly calm. He *felt* surprisingly calm, actually. He had a job to do, and he was going to do it. "You can leave now, before I start, if you want."

Michael shook his head again, a hint of genuine terror in his eyes. "Uh-uh. The second I get too far away from Charles, that thing can get me. Let's just wait here until someone can come and help us. Someone —"

Harlan raised an eyebrow. "Competent?"

Michael's shoulders slumped. "Harlan, I —"

"It's okay. I know I've gotten myself in a bit of a pickle tonight." *A bit of a pickle?* Why the fuck had he said *that*? "And dealing with Amy's ghost wasn't...quite as smooth as we might have wanted, but I can do this." He wasn't sure if Michael would believe him. Fuck, he wasn't totally sure he believed himself.

He quickly squashed that thought. "I *am* the someone." He wasn't really sure if that sentence made grammatical sense, but that wasn't important. "Stay close to Charles and you'll be safe." Unfortunately, he couldn't do the same.

He let go of Charles, pointing in the direction he wanted him to go. He wished he could have a portal already open when Charles moved out of range, but whatever Charles' power did to block ghosts, it also blocked Harlan's abilities. He'd just have to be quicker on the draw than the ghost.

He *also* wished he knew if it was frozen in place, so he'd know approximately where it was when Charles' shield went down, or if it could move freely and could be anywhere in its territory. They hadn't been able to experiment enough with that to really find out.

Again, he imagined the ghost right in his face when he turned around. He suppressed a shudder. He didn't want Charles or Michael to see how afraid he was, after he'd declared that he'd take care of the situation.

Well, Charles, at least, could probably tell he was frightened, but there was only so much he could do.

"Okay. I'm ready."

Charles gave him one last look and nodded. He put an arm around Michael's shoulders and started backing away slowly.

As soon as Charles was out of range, there was a kind of *pop* that Harlan was pretty sure was only in his head. The ghost *was* practically in his face, and he had to hold in a scream. Had it been there the whole time, separated from him only by the thin—but, so far, impenetrable—barrier of Charles' power? Harlan shuddered at the thought.

He almost lost the advantage of surprise, but he was still the first to react. He *blinked*, then reached out and grabbed the closest trailing part of the ghost's form, sinking his left hand deep into its chest. It would be painful, and he'd have to work quickly, but he didn't want to risk letting it get away. He gritted his teeth as the icy, bone-numbing cold immediately sank into his fingertips, quickly spreading up his hand, racing towards his heart. This ghost knew what he was planning, and it intended to kill him before he could do it.

Harlan threw himself onto the sidewalk with all his weight—not that there was much of that—and his *will* behind it. His knees cracked hard on the cement, and he flinched but didn't let go.

The second his free hand made contact with the pavement, bits of gravel and probably less pleasant things digging into his palm, he forced power down his right arm, *slamming* open a portal to the other side.

The ghost wailed and screamed, somehow making the hollow cavity inside it even *colder* as it first tried to attack him, then, when that didn't work, fought desperately to get away.

He clung to it grimly as it struggled, slowly but inexorably winning the fight and dragging it closer and closer to the portal. He could feel it trying to close the opening, which only a few ghosts had ever attempted with him. Most of them were distracted by him and didn't seem to notice the openings until it was too late, which he appreciated—and that meant he was fighting on two fronts when he'd already been struggling with one.

He was surprised that he hadn't noticed a ghost this powerful and practically right around the corner from him—unless he'd wandered farther than he'd thought. Obviously, he'd scanned the area carefully when they first moved in, mostly for his own protection, and out of curiosity, but he hadn't noticed this one. Well, sometimes older ghosts—which this one clearly was, to have accumulated that kind of power and based on the 'old-timey bubble' it had put around them—almost went into hibernation, just resting and saving their energy until something interesting enough to get their attention came along.

Lucky me.

Harlan gave a good yank, making up for the distance it had managed to pull away from him, and dragged it closer. While it was off balance—if that applied to something floating and completely disconnected from the physical world—he pulled again. Part of its 'back' made contact with the portal and it started drawing the ghost in.

Grinning wickedly, showing blackened, razor-sharp teeth, it grabbed at his arm. Realizing it had lost and it couldn't kill him, it had decided that if it was going down, it was taking him with it.

Harlan rolled his eyes. "Predictable." He let go, and before it realized there was nothing holding it in place but the pull of its own afterlife trying to correct its mistake and take it where it should have gone at death, it was drawn under and disappeared.

He fell back from the portal and *kicked* it shut with one foot, which he'd never done before and hadn't actually known he *could* do, especially with shoes on.

A car honked at him, narrowly swerving around him.

Harlan hadn't realized he was in the road. He flipped off the driver, which he didn't normally do because it could easily lead to a dangerous confrontation, and he just wasn't usually that kind of person, but he was frightened and exhausted. *That* was the thanks he got for saving the city from a powerful, dangerous ghost?

On the other hand, he was lying flat on his back in the middle of the road, and he hadn't been paying attention to anything happening in the 'real' world around him for…at least a minute. He was probably lucky the car had seen him, and he hadn't died right after sending the spirit on—and wouldn't *that* have been ironic? Or something.

Luckily, the car kept driving.

He forced himself to sit up.

"Harlan!" Charles called out, jogging over with Michael in tow. "Are you all right?"

"Fine," he groaned. He *blinked*. Even though he wasn't actually using his physical muscles—at least, he didn't think so—he always ached after doing a hardcore 'exorcism' like that. Maybe it was just because he held himself really tense or something.

"Let's get you out of the road, then."

Over Charles' shoulder, Michael nodded.

Charles offered Harlan a hand up. "You're done, right? It's gone?"

Harlan took it gratefully. "Yeah. Thanks."

Charles got him back to the safety of the sidewalk before letting go of him.

Harlan pretended he didn't see him make a face and wipe his hand on his jeans. "Sorry." He always seemed to land in something nasty when he had to take on a ghost like that one. At least a regular street was probably cleaner than an alley, like the one where he'd rescued Michael.

Speaking of whom…

Michael laughed. "Ew. I can't believe you touched him!"

Harlan looked down. He *was* pretty gross. But Michael was already looking away from him.

"Charles, that was amazing! I've been wanting to see your power in action for a while now."

Charles and Harlan exchanged glances.

"You just stepped in there and *poof!*" Michael clapped once. "Gone. No more ghost."

"Harlan was the one who got rid of it," Charles pointed out gently, offering Harlan his arm when he stumbled.

"Yeah! You were great too, Harlan!"

Harlan shrugged. "Thanks." It had probably just looked like him playing tug-o-war while flat on his ass, which was basically what had happened. "Wait, you could *see* the ghost?"

Charles and Michael both nodded.

"Is that unusual?" Michael asked. "I saw What's-Her-Face. Amy, the ghost from my friend's office."

"Pretty unusual." Fuck. It must've been powerful, and *really* pissed off, to appear as a full-blown apparition.

"Harlan, you're shivering," Charles told him.

Harlan realized it was true, and he was a little freaked out that he hadn't noticed. Or noticed that he was wet. Had it rained earlier or had the street been even nastier than he'd realized?

"Let's get you cleaned up." Charles very kindly put an arm around him and started walking him back to the apartment without any hesitation. He clearly knew exactly where they were.

And no wonder. They were barely three blocks away—which was good, because Harlan felt like he was about to collapse. He'd almost been tempted to ask Charles to go get the car and pick him up, except that he didn't want to let him out of his sight—not even with Michael there—and he didn't want to get the inside of Charles' car as filthy as him. *He* was a lot easier to clean.

But he knew Charles would do it for him. *Aw.*

Yeah, he was definitely feeling a little loopy.

Michael excused himself when they got back to the apartment. "I hope you don't mind. You guys seem like you could use some alone time."

Harlan felt like he *should* have been disappointed, but he just...wasn't. He just wanted Michael to go away so he could go upstairs with Charles and shower—preferably *also* with Charles.

"Yeah. It's fine," he assured Michael, a little more bluntly than he'd intended.

Charles shot him a funny look but nodded. "Yeah. See you later?"

"Of course." Michael blew them both kisses—well, they were *both* pretty gross at that point, so Harlan wouldn't have wanted to actually kiss either of them—and left.

Harlan had a strange feeling of relief.

As Harlan had hoped, they showered together. It was Harlan's firm opinion that what was even the point of having a boyfriend or a shower if you had to do it alone?

Afterwards, they curled up naked.

Harlan's thoughts started drifting toward Aiden again. Maybe he was being disloyal, but he didn't want to think about that right now. He was already freaked out enough about what he'd just gone through. To distract himself, he said, "Michael was really impressed by you." Harlan felt like he was on the edge of realizing something, but he couldn't quite grasp it. He always felt so different when Michael was around. Things were so much easier. Simpler.

Charles stroked his hair. "He was impressed by you, too," he assured him.

Harlan laughed. "Mediumship is pretty common—"

"But you're *really* good at it!"

"Charles..." Harlan shook his head in fond exasperation. "But what you do is...really special."

Charles kissed the top of his head. "*You're* really special."

Harlan laughed again. "It's okay. You don't need to make me feel better. But, jeez, you're usually better at it than this!"

"Yeah, not my best work," Charles admitted. "I'm *tired*. I've never had a ghost fight me like that before."

Immediately serious, Harlan propped himself up on one elbow so he could see Charles' face. "It *fought* you?"

"Yeah." Charles shrugged. "Michael made it sound so simple, but when I walked closer to the bubble, it didn't...pop right away. I had to *force* my way through."

"Fuck. That can't be good!"

"Maybe I was just tired already."

"Maybe. Sorry for waking you up." Harlan shook his head. He didn't like that, not one bit. He yawned. "Let me know if you feel it again, 'kay? Even if you're not sure?"

"'Course," Charles assured him. "Are you ready to sleep? Can I turn off the lamp?"

Harlan yawned again. "*Very.*"

Once it was dark and they'd been quiet and still for a while, him warm and safe in Charles' arms, he murmured, "Sorry I fucked things up with Michael today."

Charles started stroking his hair again. "What do you mean?"

"Well, we were all supposed to spend the night together. He left."

"I kinda don't mind it just being the two of us."

Charles' voice sounded a little weird. Harlan wished he could see his face so he could get a better idea of what he was thinking — but not enough to turn on the light or ask Charles to do it. "Me neither," he admitted.

"I'm sorry I've been so busy lately."

Ah. That must've been why Charles sounded weird. Now Harlan was *glad* it was dark, and he could take a minute to think of how he wanted to respond without worrying about Charles seeing his expression. "Don't be," he said finally. "Your business is growing and expanding. That's a good thing. I can't be jealous of that." Shit, that just made him sound jealous AF, didn't it? "And...and Michael's been around a lot lately. It's not like I've been on my own," he quickly added.

"Mm. If you're sure."

"I am."

"Because you know you come first with me. I'd cut back on my hours if — "

"I know." Harlan sighed. "Hopefully things will pick up at the agency soon, and I'll be busy, too."

"Yeah. You know I'm serious, right?"

"Yeah, I know. Softie," Harlan teased him.

"I am. I freely admit it. I'm not ashamed of it."

"Good. Love you." It wasn't something they said often, at least compared to other couples and polycules he knew, but that moment seemed to call for it.

Charles kissed his ear. Harlan wasn't sure if that was what he'd been aiming for or if he'd missed his real target in the dark. "Love you, too."

He listened to Charles' breathing get slow and even. *Fuck.* He still hadn't actually found that corner store. Or Aiden.

Chapter Fifteen

Harlan was looking forward to just spending the day with Charles. It felt like it had been a long time since they'd gotten to do that. He didn't have any appointments booked or anything, and Hamilton had offered to cover for him at the office. Michael was busy and Rattling Chains was closed, so it would just be the two of them.

Charles wasn't in bed when Harlan woke up. That wasn't unusual, but for some reason that morning Harlan felt a strange jolt of dread. Charles' side of the bed was cold, and while that *also* wasn't unusual, Harlan didn't hear him moving around in the kitchen or living room. It was Tuesday, one of their days off together. Charles sometimes got up earlier than him to make breakfast, but Harlan was used to waking up before nine a.m., while Charles preferred to wake up closer to noon, even when he hadn't spent the small hours of the morning closing down a nightclub. Harlan usually woke first, but Charles was usually the first one to get out of bed while Harlan just fucked around on his phone. And on their days off, they didn't tend to get out of bed right away when they woke up.

Well, maybe Charles had been hungry or something had woken him.

Forcing a smile onto his lips, Harlan rolled out of bed. Usually he would have just walked out of the bedroom naked, as he was, but a cold shiver ran up his spine. That nebulous, sourceless anxiety — a feeling he'd had less and less since meeting Charles — still hadn't gone away completely. He grabbed his light bathrobe off the back of the bathroom door and pulled it on. It didn't help with the coldness — that was coming from his core — but if there *was* something wrong, at least he wouldn't be facing it with his balls out.

If there was nothing wrong — and of course there *wasn't* — his smile would brighten when he saw Charles, and Charles would just think he was a little chilly, maybe even trying to flirt a little, not preparing for an imminent invasion or...something.

Charles wasn't in the living room and there were no breakfast smells. Harlan's already-lifeless smile was beginning to flatline. He peered around the exposed-brick arch leading into the kitchen like he was afraid he might get shot if he made himself too large a target.

No Charles, at least not on his cautious first glance. He forced himself to step fully into the doorway so he could see the whole room properly. It was still empty. The fridge door was closed, killing Harlan's brief hope that maybe Charles was behind it.

Harlan could feel panic starting to creep up from his hindbrain, and he forced himself to stop, slow down and take some deep breaths.

In...

Out...

In, slow.
Out, slower.

Sometimes Charles just forgot cell phones were a thing — so did Harlan, apparently, because he hadn't checked his phone yet to see if Charles had needed to leave and texted him about it — or left a note. He'd told Harlan exactly where to look for them, but what place had he *said*? Harlan's useless brain could remember jingles from when he was a kid but not something that fucking important!

He checked the fridge door first, since he was there already. Just the usual — some pictures of the two of them alone and with Hamilton and Morgan, pictures of Charles at different places in the world he'd been to and Harlan had not, and a scattering of fridge magnets that Charles had brought into the relationship. Harlan was distracted from his growing dread by two new, smaller anxieties — would Charles want to travel with him? Did he *want* to travel? His last venture out of Toronto — just to small-town Ontario, nowhere exotic — had been a *nightmare* and had made him never want to leave the comforts of his city again. But maybe he'd enjoy somewhere more cosmopolitan, more like Toronto — New York or Paris, even Vancouver. Or maybe they'd be *too* 'cosmopolitan' and he'd just feel like a little lost country bumpkin. He'd have to make sure he could get his medication, and that Hamilton and Morgan would be able to take care of Laid to Rest while he was gone, and...

No, that was ridiculous. It wasn't like Charles had stuck plane tickets to the fridge, and even if he had, Harlan had to *find* Charles before they could go anywhere together.

Secondly, Harlan had never seen fridge magnets before he'd met Charles. Maybe those alphabet ones in movies and TV shows. True, the fridges in the Centre were in the industrial kitchen, where students were forbidden from going, but the one in his apartment had been bare the whole time he'd lived there. That was a little surprising, now that he thought about it. The rest of the apartment had been decorated, including shelves of books he'd never touched and artwork he'd hated.

No, no, this isn't important! He slammed his fist on the marble countertop to refocus on the thing he *should* be worried about.

Not *worried*. Not yet.

Where else would someone leave a note? The front door seemed like an obvious choice, but there was nothing there, either. Not on either of the end tables or either bedside table or...

Harlan made himself do his calm breathing again.

His phone. He *still* hadn't checked his fucking phone!

He grabbed it off his nightstand, almost knocking it onto the floor. The screen just showed his current lockscreen picture—a potential logo for Laid to Rest that Morgan had quickly drawn on their computer. No notifications of any kind. He unlocked it anyway and tapped the Messages icon, even though it didn't have any little red numbers in the corner. He accidentally clicked the top text, which was spam, before remembering that texts from Charles were in their own little bubble at the very top of the screen. He tapped Charles' profile picture. The last text was something Harlan had sent—*Love you, too.* It was timestamped from Sunday night.

Groaning, he threw his phone down on the bed, then followed it, letting his arms and legs sprawl and taking up as much room as he wanted. He would have given anything for Charles to be there instead.

He just closed his eyes for a few minutes, barely managing to keep tears from pouring out.

This is useless. I'm useless. He sat up and grabbed his phone. *What next? Hamilton.* That was the obvious choice.

He started typing a text, then changed his mind and made it a voice call. Texting was too slow for the terror he was feeling.

Always-Answers-On-The-First-Ring Hamilton didn't answer until the *third* ring, which was not helping Harlan's anxiety.

"Hey, boss. What's up? It's not like you to *call*, especially on a day off."

"Charles isn't here, and he didn't leave me a note and he hasn't texted or anything." It all slipped out in a rush before he could stop himself.

"Whoa, whoa. Slow down. Okay. Charles isn't in the apartment?"

"No."

"And, as far as you know, he hasn't told you where he's going?"

"Right." Somehow, even though Hamilton was just getting him to repeat things he'd already said, it *was* starting to make him feel better.

"Is his car there?"

"Is his...? Oh! That's a really good idea!"

He could *hear* Hamilton grinning, even over the phone. "Yeah, I have 'em sometimes."

"I'll check." Harlan scrambled off the bed — probably treating Hamilton to several seconds of just his heavy breathing — and half-ran into the living room. He mashed his face against the front window until he could just barely see the sidewalk in front of their building. The place where Charles usually parked had an unfamiliar car in it. "I guess he could have parked somewhere else," he told Hamilton, thunking his phone against the glass and not really believing what he'd said. "The spots aren't assigned or anything. He just usually…"

"Yeah. Totally." Hamilton sighed. "Look. I know I'm probably barking up the wrong tree, but I have to ask. Did you guys have a fight or anything?"

"What? No! Why would you — ?"

"Hey, kid. It happens, even to the best of couples. I gotta check."

Harlan forced himself to take a deep breath so he wouldn't snap at Hamilton to stop wasting their time. "Right. No, you're right. You have to check. You're just doing your j — Well, your *old* job." His shoulders slumped. "No, we didn't have a fight. We" — his face burned — "we, uh, went to bed normally last night. When I woke up, he wasn't here."

"Uh-huh."

Harlan could hear the crinkling of paper and knew Hamilton was taking notes on his pad. Some things never changed, and right now that was the most comforting thing in the world. Well, actually the sound of Charles' keys in the lock and him calling out, *'Hey!'* while opening the door would be.

He listened. Nothing.

"And when was that?"

"What?"

Hamilton managed to only sigh a *little*. "When did you wake up?"

"Oh. Uh. I didn't look at my phone." He pulled it away from his face so he could see the clock. "Maybe half an hour ago? No. Probably closer to twenty minutes."

"Okay. Got it." Harlan could hear Hamilton snap his notebook shut decisively. "Who else have you called about this? Let me guess — just me?"

"Yeah."

"Is there anyone else you can think of — that you know how to contact — who might have seen him?"

"Um... Some of his game-night friends, maybe?"

"Good. Call them. We'll check everything we can ourselves before... Well."

"Yeah."

"I'm going to hang up —"

No, no, no! Harlan's brain chanted.

" — and call Morgan. You're going to make your calls, and whoever's done first will text the other. We'll touch base and go from there."

Part of Harlan wished Hamilton would say something like *It'll be okay, I promise* or *Everything's going to be fine*, but he knew that wasn't Hamilton's way. He didn't make promises he couldn't keep, and most of the time Harlan appreciated that about him, but now...

He shook his head, taking a deep, steadying breath. "Okay. I've got it. It's a good plan."

"It is," Hamilton assured him. "I'll be in touch soon."

He hung up, and even though Hamilton had warned him and he'd fully been expecting it — that was more of a goodbye than Hamilton usually gave him — Harlan's stomach lurched sideways and he started breathing too fast, too shallow.

In.
Out.
In, slow.
Out, slower.
Not enough. Again.
In, slowww.
Out, slower...

Okay. He had a job to do. He had to call people. He didn't have the numbers for all of Charles' friends, but he did have the host, Jim's, in case he ever had to get a ride from Hamilton or something. He was part of the email chain with the rest of them, though he'd never sent anything, but email was *much* too slow right now.

His hands were shaking as he touched Jim's icon and prayed he'd answer quickly. It was a Monday morning. Most people — normal people — would be at work, he realized. He couldn't remember what Jim did, but he was pretty sure he worked from home.

Harlan closed his eyes and sighed with relief when he answered right away. "Hi, Jim. It's Harlan. Charles' — "

Jim laughed softly. "I know who you are. Hi, Harlan. What's up?"

He cut right to the chase. "Have you seen or heard from Charles today?"

"Mmm, no. Should I have? I didn't think we had anything planned — "

"N-No, we didn't. I just wanted to see if — "

"Is everything okay?" Jim's voice had turned too sympathetic. It made Harlan nervous and bristly.

"Yeah. Yeah, everything's fine," Harlan told him, assuring himself as much as the other man. "Just...crossed wires, I guess." He hung up before Jim could say anything else. He knew it was rude, but he just couldn't keep talking to him if he didn't know anything. Hopefully he and Charles would be able to make it up to him later.

He realized, too late, that he'd forgotten to ask for any more numbers or ask Jim to contact any of the others, but his instincts told him Jim didn't have the answers he was looking for.

He leaned back on the couch with his head tipped straight up so he was looking at the ceiling. *Why are ceilings always painted white? Was there anyone else I was supposed to call?* He didn't think so. What was he supposed to do next? Text Hamilton.

No luck, he typed, not noticing until it was sent that *luck* had autocorrected to a clover emoji. He wished he could take it back. It was too cutesy for how horrible he felt.

Hamilton called him a moment later. Morgan didn't know where Charles was either. They were back at — had never left? — square one.

"Have you called the club yet?" Hamilton asked. Harlan could tell that he was trying to sound calm, for his sake, but he didn't think he was imagining the worry creeping into his voice.

Fuck. I'm such a fucking idiot! "No. I haven't." He felt a sick, twisting sensation in his stomach as he anticipated Hamilton getting mad at him for not thinking of it sooner, for making them both worry when *obviously* Charles was at Rattling Chains. Harlan realized he hadn't even tried to *text* Charles, for fuck's sake. He didn't tell Hamilton that. The three of them could laugh about it together later, once they'd found Charles, who had never been missing, who'd just forgotten to let Harlan know where he was going. *Yeah. Sure.*

"Call them. I don't know if anyone will be there right now, but it's worth a shot. I'll come to your place. Bye."

Harlan stared at his phone in stunned silence. Hamilton *never* said goodbye before hanging up.

He could feel panic creeping ever closer, threatening to shut him down completely. He dug his nails into his palms, closed his eyes, and forced a few deep, calm breaths in and out. The club. He had to call Rattling Chains. That was the next step.

No. Before that, he should text Charles.

He'd typed *Hey, where are you?* but stopped before hitting send. He made it a voice call instead. He held the phone away from his ear, listening hard. It took him a moment to realize why — part of him expected to hear Charles' ringtone echoing through the apartment.

Silence.

Staring at the little picture of Charles' face, Harlan reluctantly ended the call.

Rattling Chains' number was just a few below Charles' on his favourites list. He just hoped that someone would be there to answer. He didn't have a key to the club. Charles had offered to give him one, but he'd said no. He regretted it. If no one answered, he didn't know what he'd do. Wait for Hamilton to get there, he supposed, and let Hamilton decide. He could barely remember how to breathe between one exhale and the next, never mind come up with any sort of *plan*.

"Hello?" an irritatingly perky voice answered.

Harlan, who'd zoned out, gasped.

"Hello?"

"Hi. It's Harlan."

"Oh, hey! If you're looking for Charles, he's not here."

Fuck. Of course not.

The employee—what was his name? Chad? Brad? Something totally different?—thought for a moment. "Y'know, he did stop by earlier. I'm here cleaning and restocking," he explained when Harlan didn't reply right away.

"But it's Tuesday. His day off."

"It's actually Monday, but yeah, I thought it was weird. He usually lets us know if he's coming in unexpectedly. He told me I could go on my break, and he was gone when I got back. Hey. The door was unlocked. He'd *never* leave the door unlocked with no one inside."

Fuck fuck you fucking idiot *why didn't you let someone know about this hours ago?* "No. He wouldn't," he managed to say without snapping at the dumbfuck.

Another long pause. "Hey. Did you call just now?"

While it was reassuring that there were people even spacier than him out there, it was not the time he wanted to be dealing with one of them. "Yeah. We're still—"

"No, sorry. I mean did you call *Charles'* phone?"

"Yeah. I did, actually. Right before I called you. Why?"

"His phone is here."

A beat where they each thought about what that meant—*might* mean.

"M-Maybe we should look at the surveillance tape."

No shit, Sherlock. "Yeah. That would be great." Harlan found it a little uncanny how calm and steady he sounded when he was just screaming on the inside. "We'll—I'll be there as soon as I can."

"Okay. Do you want me to watch it before you get here?"

Right. There was no need for him to go there in person. Not necessarily. "Yeah. Sure. I'll stay on the line if that's okay."

"Yeah. Of course. Hey…is Charles in trouble?"

Harlan felt his mouth draw up into an awful smile. More of a grimace. He was glad no one was there to see it.

He struggled to think of a response. This was Charles' employee, after all, and he didn't want to fuck up their working relationship. "I don't know," he said finally.

"Okay. Let me just see if I remember how to do this…" There were some shuffling and jostling noises, probably as he tried to balance the phone while he did…whatever he needed to in order to see the security footage. "Okay, here it is. Yeah. Charles sends me on my break, I leave…"

I don't need a fucking play-by-play, Chadley, Harlan thought but didn't say. He didn't interrupt the other man's ramblings, just in case it made either of them miss something important.

"Okay. Here it is," Brad-Chad said again. "Yeah. It looks like someone knocks on the door. Charles goes over and opens it. The angle is really bad. I can only see the back of Charles' head, and the other person is staying too far back to see their face or anything."

Fuck. That meant that the person had checked out the place first and learned where the camera was and the angle it filmed. Right?

"Then Charles goes with them."

Harlan blinked. "He just…goes with them? There's no struggle or anything?"

"Not that I can see."

"So Charles probably knows whoever it is."

"I...I don't know. Sorry."

The apartment's buzzer went off, and Harlan let out a little yelp. "I've gotta go," he told Chadley once he'd swallowed his heart back into place again and hung up before he could answer. He was about to press the 'unlock' button when he realized that, if someone really *had* taken Charles, he might be a target, too. He pressed the intercom button instead. "Hello?"

"Hey. It's me."

"Me who?"

"What the fuck? Let me in, Brand."

Yep. Definitely Hamilton. He unlocked the door and a short time later, Hamilton knocked on the inner door. Harlan opened it.

"What was all that about?"

"Sorry. I called Rattling Chains, and the guy there looked at the security footage. It..." His voice broke and he had to look away from Hamilton until he could get it under control again. "It looks like someone...took Charles."

Hamilton put a hand on his chest and doubled over, looking like someone had knocked the wind out of him. "What? *Fuck!*" he said with feeling. "What the fuck? By who? What happened?"

Harlan shook his head. "I don't know. I figured we'd go there next. See if we can find any...clues." He didn't mention that there was only one clue he'd have any chance of detecting. He didn't want to even think about that possibility.

The same thought seemed to cross Hamilton's mind. He gave Harlan a sidelong look. "So...you haven't seen...?" he asked, clearly trying to be delicate about it.

"No."

"Good. Of course. Charles is fine. Okay. We'll head to Rattling Chains and look at the footage ourselves. See if we can notice something this other guy didn't."

"Right." Harlan didn't think he could force out more than one word at a time.

Hamilton reached out and gave his shoulder a brief squeeze. "C'mon. Let's go."

* * * *

Chadley was pacing outside the club's entrance and smoking when they got there. He gave Harlan a nervous wave and Hamilton an even more nervous glance. Harlan could understand why. Hamilton definitely acted like he was still a cop sometimes.

"Hey. I left it up where he... Yeah." He unlocked the door, led them into Charles' office and gestured at a grainy black-and-white TV monitor.

Hamilton immediately plopped himself down in Charles' desk chair and wheeled it over to the screen. He asked Chadley — his real name, Harlan re-learned from listening to Hamilton introduce himself, was Nathan, so Harlan had been *way* off — a few questions about how to operate it, then shooed him away.

Hamilton took out his notebook, his pen poised. "Okay, here it is. Charles hears something and turns around. Someone must have knocked. He opens the door." He tapped the screen with the back of his pen. "It must be someone he knows if he's grinning like that."

Harlan's heart stopped. *Someone he knows.* It had been bad enough when he'd imagined some nameless, faceless stranger taking Charles, but he knew Hamilton was right. He'd seen Charles' 'customer service' smile, and that wasn't it. Charles looked genuinely happy to see...whoever was on the other side of the door, carefully keeping themselves out of view of the security camera.

The thought seemed to occur to Hamilton at the same time. He turned to Nathan. "Is there an exterior camera?"

"Oh. Yeah. Sorry. I was so nervous I didn't even think of that." He showed Hamilton how to change the view and they rolled it back to the same timestamp as the last—*no, not last, don't think that*—footage of Charles.

"There." Hamilton tapped the screen again. The person Charles was talking to was wearing a dark hooded sweatshirt with the hood pulled up, so they couldn't see their hair or any of their face. Unfortunately, the view was from almost directly above the door, so it was also hard to even tell how tall they were or anything else about them.

"Fuck," Hamilton groaned. "No better angles?"

Nathan shook his head.

"Okay." Hamilton kicked to spin the desk chair so he was facing Harlan. "I know it's not much to go on, but do you recognize this person?"

Harlan leaned so close to the monitor he was practically pressing his nose against it, *willing* the pixels to resolve into something—some*one*—recognizable.

He shook his head.

"Yeah. Didn't think so." Hamilton exhaled, then hit play.

The three of them watched as the top of Charles' head joined the top of No-Name's head and they walked into the alley and disappeared.

They could see slightly more of No-Name's body before he disappeared, and Hamilton took down a few more notes.

Harlan caught himself instinctively craning his neck *around* the TV, as though he could see past the edges of what had been filmed, and he quickly stopped when he realized what he was doing and that he looked like an idiot.

Hamilton snapped his notebook shut decisively. "Not much to go on, not as much as I was hoping for. Still, it's more than we had before," he said brightly. He rewound the footage and recorded it with his phone camera, then switched back to the interior surveillance camera and filmed that, too. "I'll send you the videos on the off-chance they might help."

"Now what?" Harlan asked. Even though neither Charles nor the mystery person were on the screen, he couldn't stop staring at it. It could be the last time he saw Charles. *No!* he mentally shouted at himself. *It's not! You'll see him again, and he'll be alive. Just fine.*

"Now..." Hamilton sighed. "I could try a few contacts from the police department, see if I can convince them to pull security footage for the surrounding buildings. See if we can at least get a car or if they...get on a bus or something." He tapped his capped pen against his front teeth several times, a sound that Harlan found immediately and unreasonably annoying.

He spoke a little too loudly to drown it out, but he couldn't quite bring himself to tell Hamilton to stop. "Let's do it." Like he would play any part in that.

"It'll probably take time — could be a day or longer — *if* I can even get it," Hamilton cautioned him, but he had to stop tapping to speak.

Harlan shook his head. "I don't care. Whatever. Anything we can do."

Hamilton briefly rested a hand on Harlan's shoulder, giving it a gentle squeeze.

Harlan was so high-strung that the touch, rather than comforting him, just felt overwhelming, and he had to fight not to twist away from Hamilton's grip.

"Let's get you back to your apartment."

"Maybe Charles will be there," Harlan said, trying to force himself to sound hopeful.

"Maybe." Hamilton didn't.

When they got back, Hamilton asked, "Before I get started, is there *anyone* else you can think of who might know where Charles is? Anyone at all?"

Harlan hissed, almost a sound of pain, as he closed his eyes and tried to *force* the thoughts out. Nothing came to him. He remembered that he had Charles' phone and he pulled it out, hoping for inspiration, even though he'd already looked at it. He opened the phone app. The last call had been from an unknown number at seven a.m., while Harlan was still sleeping.

He held up the phone for Hamilton and tapped the call record. "This must have been the call that made him come to the club. Can you trace it?" he asked excitedly.

Hamilton shrugged one shoulder. "I dunno. Not really my area of expertise, especially because it doesn't list the phone number. But yeah, I could pass it on to some people, see if they can do anything."

Harlan clutched the phone to his chest, suddenly reluctant to give it up. It felt like his final link to Charles, even though he knew Hamilton was trying to help. Stalling, he tapped on the Messages app to look at his last text to Charles on Charles' phone

He tapped back to the main list of all the texts. His was at the top, as a 'favourite' contact, just like Charles was on Harlan's phone. Below that were a few spam texts Charles hadn't deleted, one from one of his employees, and… "Michael."

"What?"

"Fuck, I'm so fucking stupid!" Harlan had been in such a blind panic that he hadn't even *thought* about Michael.

Hamilton frowned at him. "First of all, boss, you're not stupid. Second, who's Michael?"

Harlan tried to will himself not to blush. "Michael is my… Is *our*…" He sighed. "Michael is a guy Charles and I have been—"

"Ah. Gotcha," Hamilton interrupted, to Harlan's extreme relief. "Yeah, you should definitely give him a call. When was the last time you saw him, or you think Charles saw him?"

"Mmm… It would have been a few days ago. The three of us got together for coffee. As far as I know, Charles hasn't seen or spoken to him since."

"Still, can't hurt. He might know something we don't."

Harlan closed his eyes, fighting back tears for a moment. It felt so good to hear Hamilton say *we* and know he wasn't alone in this. He had backup. "I-I'll call him."

Hamilton had his own phone out and he looked like he was about to make a call until he lowered it from his ear suddenly. "Say. What does Michael look like?"

Harlan's mind flashed back to the grainy black-and-white image of the man Charles had left Rattling Chains with. "No…"

"Shit, really? I was just... Lemme see." He held out his hand for Harlan's phone.

Numbly, Harlan flicked back through his pictures until he found a selfie Michael had taken of the three of them.

Hamilton held it up beside the security feed, paused on the best shot of No-Name.

"What do you think?"

"I mean...I can't tell for sure, not with this video quality and the bulky clothes the person is wearing, but..." Harlan's heart sank. "I don't think we can rule him out?"

Hamilton handed the phone back. "Yeah. I agree."

Harlan juggled his phone and Charles'. "Oh, right. You need this." He pressed it into Hamilton's hand, reluctant to pull away and let go of it completely.

"I'll take good care of it," Hamilton promised.

"I'll call Michael right now." He could only hope that his voice wouldn't give away his suspicions — and that his suspicions weren't right.

No answer. Michael *always* answered his phone right away.

He shook his head.

"Do you know his address?"

Of course he did. Michael was his *boyfriend*. Harlan blinked. "No. No, I don't, actually. We've never gone there. We've never even dropped him off or anything. Oh, fuck, I'm an idiot, aren't I?" Harlan's panic started to spiral upwards again.

"Hey. It's okay. He could just be a really private person—"

"We're *dating*, Hamilton!"

"It still happens. It doesn't automatically mean he's up to anything, that he has anything to do with... Charles."

"O-Okay."

"Still... Let me make a few calls. I'll see if I can find out where he lives. Actually, I need his last name."

Fuck. Harlan was drawing a total blank.

Hamilton didn't say anything or even look irritated, even though Harlan thought he'd earned it.

*Michael...*he prompted himself. It didn't work. He glanced at his phone on the off chance he'd... Nope, the contact just said 'Michael', with no last name. He *knew* Michael had told him it, though. He closed his eyes. Michael had said it when he introduced himself to Charles. "Clark! It's Clark!" he crowed.

"Good job, Brand. I'll look into your Michael Clark. You call Morgan and let them know what's going on. They probably don't know where he is, but maybe they'll have an idea."

Harlan nodded and dialled Morgan.

"Well, well, well. A *phone call* from —"

"Morgan."

"Oh, shit. What's wrong?"

"Charles seems to be...missing."

"Fuck. Sorry. How can I help?"

"You haven't seen him or anything?"

"No, not for like...a week or so?"

Hamilton waved to get his attention. "Ask if they'll come over here."

"Will you come over here?" Harlan repeated.

"Why?"

"Why?" he asked Hamilton.

Hamilton sighed, very gently. "Gimme your phone. Go sit down for a minute." He pointed to Harlan's couch.

Harlan nodded and did as he was told. He just sat with his head in his hands, listening to Morgan and Hamilton talk without really listening or understanding.

"Okay. I've got Michael's home and work addresses. Morgan's going to meet us here, then we'll go check it out. All right?"

Harlan nodded again.

Morgan lived close to Harlan and Charles' apartment, and it wasn't long before the door buzzer went off. Hamilton let them in.

"Hey." Morgan gave Harlan a quick hug. "Skye wanted to come help, but they had to work."

Was Harlan imagining things, or was Morgan actually blushing slightly?

Hamilton frowned slightly. "Wait. Morgan, you said 'they'."

"Yeah. I did. She uses she and they pronouns now."

"Oh. Okay! Skye—she/they," Hamilton said out loud.

Harlan repeated it to himself silently.

Hamilton clapped his hands. "All right. We'll go to Michael's condo first. You and Morgan can...do your thing." He shrugged apologetically. "Then we'll—"

Harlan shook his head. "What? No! We don't have time for that! We have to split up!"

Hamilton sighed. "Okay, I know you didn't have a lot of media options at the Centre, but...c'mon. You must have seen at least *one* horror movie in your life. You know how that goes down."

"Hamilton..." Harlan growled.

"Harlan," Hamilton growled right back.

"Where does Michael work?"

Hamilton glanced at his notes. "Grey Bird Holdings. It's by the port, so it's probably a warehouse or something similar. His job description is listed as 'acquisitions manager'."

"Yeah. It's probably like...an import-export thing, right? It might be a little shady, but I'm sure it has nothing to do with Charles, if Michael is even involved. I can check out his *office* by myself."

"Yeah, because you 'checking out' an office has never gotten us in trouble," Hamilton quipped, but he held up a hand before Harlan could say anything. "All right, all right. You can go check out an office. But you *will* stay in contact with us, and you *will not* get involved in any shit. Deal?"

"Deal," Harlan told him, knowing he wouldn't let anything stop him if he found out that Charles was in trouble. He suspected Hamilton knew that, as well.

Chapter Sixteen

Hamilton offered to give him a ride to the address listed as Michael's workplace before he and Morgan went to Michael's condo, but Harlan didn't want to .waste even that much time. Instead, he splurged on a cab, hoping it would actually be the fastest way to get there. The building *was* a warehouse, but an old one made of bricks instead of metal sheeting.

Harlan paid the cab driver and wandered around as inconspicuously as he could, trying to find a good spot to 'stake out' the place without drawing attention to himself. He remembered a weird old book about spying that he'd found in the Centre's library. It was too bad he didn't have a physical map to unfold as concealment.

The whole building was surrounded by a mesh fence topped with razor wire. The only opening Harlan could find was one of those gates on wheels that opened with a key card or something.

It didn't take long for him to see the first ghost. There was nothing really unusual about that. It was an old building, in an old part of the city. Working in a warehouse was probably a dangerous job, and probably at least one fatal accident had happened in the century or so since it had been built.

Except…this ghost—a young man—wasn't dressed like a twentieth-century dock worker. He was wearing jeans and a logo T.

Harlan spotted another spirit. Then another. All different ages, all wearing modern clothing. *Fuck.* That couldn't be good.

He extended his awareness farther and—hit a wall. Not a physical wall, which wouldn't have stopped him at all, but an impenetrable metaphysical one. A ward. The whole building was completely warded. Why would 'Michael's' office need that protection? He had to fight the urge to rub at his forearms as his hairs stood on end.

Another ghost. Two more. There was *something* bad going on, and if Charles wasn't in there, maybe there'd at least be a clue about where he was. He had to get in.

Wait. Going in alone would be crazy. He had to call Hamilton first.

His phone had no signal. He was pretty sure it *should*, that there was no reason for it not to, but he had zero bars and there was a little gap where it normally said 'LTE'.

Okay. He'd retreat a little ways—and wasn't it funny how quickly he'd started thinking about this as a military operation or something? Not funny ha-ha, just funny as in *stupid*. He was no soldier.

But then a truck rumbled past and the gate rolled open and there was a way *in*, and who knew when he'd get another opportunity?

He ran. Both of the guards at the gate had gone around to the driver's side of the truck as it backed in towards a loading dock, and he ducked past the cab and flattened himself against the passenger side, hoping there *was* no passenger and that no one was watching him on a security camera. He was relying way too much on hope and not enough on planning, but he was making this up as he went along, and he didn't have much choice.

He followed the truck to a door leading into the warehouse, beside the overhead loading-dock door. He tugged the handle, closing his eyes and turning away like it might explode or something.

Unlocked. It opened with a slight creak, and he winced, but the sound was covered by one of the guards or the driver coughing. It was dark and cool inside, and it took his eyes a moment to adjust enough for him to see where it led—a narrow, featureless concrete stairway leading down.

He hesitated a moment. Was he going to do this? Was he *really* going to do this, on his own without any backup whatsoever?

He heard voices coming closer to the back of the truck, and he darted inside, letting the door close behind him. His skin prickled as he passed through the wards. He'd never felt any this strong before.

For a moment he was tempted to call Charles' name, but he quickly put a hand over his mouth. He had no idea who or what might be down there, who he might alert to his presence or if they'd be armed. *Fuck.* What had he gotten himself into?

Feeling a sudden jolt of panic, he pushed against the door. It didn't budge. *Locked.* He was locked in.

He practically ran down the stairs, suddenly desperate to get away from the door and the men on the other side. He found himself in a long hallway with a cement floor. There were regularly spaced drains down the length of it. *Fuck.* That couldn't be a good sign.

Even worse — the hallway was lined with cells. Most of them were empty, but one of them...

"Charles," he breathed. Their fingers met through the bars, drawn to each other like magnets. "I'm going to get you out of here."

"No!" Charles moaned, pulling away, tearing their fingers apart, frantically shaking his head. "No, no, you can't be here. They can't... You can't let them find you." Charles' voice was...wrong. Where it had always been warm and steady with an edge of laughter, it was broken and hoarse. Harlan wouldn't have recognized it if he'd just heard a recording.

"It's all right," Harlan whispered, trying to take Charles' hand again.

Charles stayed out of reach. "No. You have to get out of here."

"I will, just as soon as I get *you* out of here."

"No. There's no time. Harlan. This is serious shit. The guards have guns."

"I saw. And this whole place is ghost-warded." Harlan could *feel* the hungry, eager ghosts pressing against the wards, against Charles' power, which he'd never felt before — or maybe he'd just always ignored it. "Why is it so heavily warded? What *is* this place? There were a *lot* of ghosts outside..."

"Harlan..."

"Tell me. Please."

Charles sighed. "As far as I can tell—the guards wouldn't talk to me, but there was another prisoner here before they took her away—they're kidnapping psychics and selling them for their powers."

"Fuck."

"Yeah."

"The ghosts...?"

Charles smiled grimly. "Some of them fight back. Some of them..." He shrugged and looked away, gripping the bars tighter.

"I'm glad you didn't," Harlan said fiercely.

"Knew you'd come for me." Charles looked up at him again and they exchanged grins, even in this awful place.

"Have you seen, I don't know, an armory or something?" Harlan looked around for anything they could use for weapons—not that anything just lying around was going to do them much good against a *gun*, especially without the element of surprise, which was lacking in the featureless hallway. Why couldn't it be a good villain lair and have some *pillars* or something, at least? And mirrors so they could look around corners, but only in the direction they were going so they couldn't be used against them.

"Harlan," Charles hissed urgently, "I think I hear someone coming."

Harlan froze. Now that he was listening to something besides his own frantic heartbeat, he could hear footsteps approaching. Any second the person would appear around the corner and see him standing there outside the cell.

He and Charles exchanged horrified glances. The only thing Harlan could do was run farther down the hall and hope he made it around the far corner before the person appeared, but running was also loud and would draw attention to him.

A booted foot appeared around the corner, quickly followed by the rest of the person, while he and Charles were still gaping at each other. Clearly they weren't cut out to be mercenaries.

"Hey!" the guard yelled, recovering from his surprise far more quickly, even though he'd had less warning. He drew his pistol.

Training, Harlan supposed, distantly. *Maybe I should talk to Hamilton about that if I'm going to keep getting into these situations. If we live through this, that is.* His thoughts were oddly calm, considering he was looking down the barrel of a gun.

"Who are you?"

"Hey, now, there's no need for any of that," Charles said in his calmest, de-escalating, I-used-to-be-a-bouncer voice. He pressed himself against the bars, hands raised. "Let's just—"

The gun was pointed right at Charles' chest.

"Harlan. Harlan!"

Charles was kneeling, reaching through the bars to shake him. But that didn't make sense. Harlan was *standing.* Wasn't he?

"Oh thank fuck," Charles breathed, rocking back onto his heels, hands braced on his thighs as he looked straight up at the ceiling. "You're awake. You're…"

Harlan sat up. No, he'd definitely been standing a moment ago, but now he was flat on his back. The back of his head throbbed. "Did I…? What *happened*?"

Charles' face was so round, so pale, like the moon, floating above him. A *frightened* moon. He wanted to reach up and touch it, call down the moon for Charles. Only the moon *was* Charles. He giggled a little to himself, even though he was pretty sure it wasn't actually funny.

"You..." Charles' gaze cut sideways, and Harlan followed it.

"No—" Charles started saying, but it was too late.

The guard's body lay on the floor, exactly where Harlan remembered him. Except...like Harlan, he'd been standing, and now they were both on the ground. There wasn't a mark on the man. He was just...dead. Harlan wanted to ask, wanted to be small and weak and pathetic and ask Charles, but he knew the man was dead.

No. That wasn't true. There *was* a mark. His right arm was shriveled and brown, and there was something horribly familiar about it, but—

He leaned forward, scrabbling at Charles' forearm. "What *happened*?" he repeated, even more urgently.

"You... He..."

Harlan hoped he was imagining the way Charles pulled away from him. Was Charles scared *of* him now, not just *for* him?

Charles gestured with both hands, starting with them palm to palm before ripping them in opposite directions.

What had he done?

"I-I don't understand."

"Harlan, we have to get going. We can't just stand here. We don't know when another guard will come."

"What. Happened?" Harlan repeated.

"You, um... I think you did what Sam—what Harkness did."

"*What*?"

"I think you ripped his ghost out."

"I... What? No. That's not possible. I couldn't..."

Charles shrugged, his shoulders barely moving. He didn't look away, though, and Harlan was grateful.

Harlan managed to haul himself to his feet, ignoring Charles' slightly too late offer of a hand to help him up. He had to do this on his own.

He staggered over to the guard. He was dead, and Harlan could feel that his ghost — his soul? — was gone from his body.

He remembered...something. A flash. Stepping in front of Charles, his hands raised, then...darkness.

"He-he *threatened* you." Harlan stumbled away from the body, back to Charles' side, close but not quite touching. "He would've killed — "

"I know." Charles stepped close to the bars and wrapped Harlan in his arms as best he could.

Harlan had never wished Charles was taller than him before, but he did now. He wanted to feel small and safe. At least he was facing away from the body — the man he'd *killed*. He shuddered.

"Hey. You did the right thing."

"What?"

Charles laughed, feebly. "Well, maybe not the *right* thing, but the *only* thing. They kidnapped me and, like you said, he would've killed me, then he would have killed you, so then who would've gotten out and stopped them?" Charles was clearly trying to make it a joke, but he just sounded close to panicking. Charles, his rock, was crumbling. Strangely, it made his own panic retreat. Just a little. "You did the only thing you could have done in that moment."

Still, Harlan couldn't help confirming, "You mean it?"

"Look at me." Charles' face was grim, his mouth a perfectly straight line. "I mean it."

Harlan believed him. He looked down. "Love you."

"Love you, too. Come on. Let's get the fuck out of here."

"Right."

For a moment they both just stood there, equally lost.

Charles scuffed one foot on the concrete floor. As though the movement had physically broken him out of his immobility, he said, "He probably has keys, right?"

"No…"

"I'm sorry, Harlan, but it's the only way."

Harlan nodded. He could do it. He *had* to do it to save Charles.

He knelt beside the guard's body and started feeling through his pockets. There was a keyring hanging from his belt loop.

For an awful moment Harlan was certain that the broken-off half of the horrible Taz keychain from his old apartment — which he'd kept for some reason, even after turning his keys in — would be swinging from it, but of course it wasn't.

It took him a second to figure out how to unfasten it, then he fumbled with the keys, trying them one by one and getting increasingly frantic when none of them would turn in the lock on Charles' cell.

For once it wasn't the last one that worked, but close enough that he had been starting to panic. He opened the door and fell into Charles' arms — or maybe Charles fell into his.

Charles leaned against him for a moment while they drew comfort from each other. "We should get going. Actually…" He grimaced.

"What?"

"Let's drag his body into the cell. If we put him on the bed and tuck him in, they'll see him and might not realize it's not me right away."

Harlan realized he was taking too long to respond, and Charles was starting to look worried, so he reluctantly nodded. "It's a good idea." He didn't move. "Let's do it," he said out loud, hoping the words would get him going, but he was still frozen. Oh, fuck, he didn't want to touch the body, didn't want to get anywhere *near* it.

Charles nodded and gently let Harlan go.

Harlan still didn't move. He heard Charles make a soft sound of distress, then a grunt. Then the horrible sound of something heavy being dragged across concrete. Harlan shut his eyes tight, but of course that did nothing to block out the *sound*. He wasn't quite enough of a coward to reach up to cover his ears. Not *quite*.

He opened his eyes as he heard Charles pass him. One of the man's legs had folded up under him at an unnatural angle, and a wild, desperate — or maybe just deeply human — part of Harlan wanted to fix it for him, even though he knew the guard was long past caring.

"I'll need your help getting him onto the bed," Charles said carefully.

"Right." Harlan's legs moved him forward and his arms reached out, but he was far, far away. He felt like he was hovering somewhere close to his own shoulder, next to but not inside himself. It was a relief, especially when he grabbed the body's ankles and its skin slid and rolled beneath his hands. He had to close his eyes for a moment and take several quick breaths through his nose. They didn't have time for him to lose it.

The man's pants rucked up and Harlan's fingers brushed his bare skin.

He barely had time to drop the body before turning away to throw up.

They really didn't have time for this, but he couldn't stop himself.

When he was done, Charles gently patted him on the back and handed him a few squares of toilet paper. He silently filled and refilled a water bottle that had been sitting on the cell's floor from the prison-style sink and poured it over the mess until it was gone. There was a drain in the middle of the cell floor, and Harlan did *not* want to think about what that was for.

Harlan caught the flat, glittering eyes of the dead man, his mouth wide in a silent scream.

He quickly looked away, breathing deeply through his nose to keep himself from retching or throwing up again.

He didn't want to touch the body again, he didn't, but together, they managed to get it up onto the bed. Charles was the one who tucked him in, rolling him to face the wall.

"Wait." Charles pulled back the blanket and grabbed the man's gun and radio—tentatively, with only two fingers, as if afraid of contamination.

Harlan couldn't blame him. He eyed the gun nervously. "You ever used one of those?" Hamilton had tried to convince him to go to the range when they were still cops so he could get his firearm license, but he'd never done it.

"A few times. When I was a kid."

"A *handgun*? Not a rifle? I thought they were illegal."

Charles' only response was, "Redneck cousins."

"Why are you taking the radio? It could" — even in this state, he couldn't help smiling, a little ghoulishly, at the ridiculousness of it all — "give away our position." A real action-hero line there.

"True. But it'll also let us know if they're onto us. And *their* positions. You're right, though. I'll turn it way down, just to be safe."

"Okay."

"Okay."

Harlan's mouth twitched in something that might have been a grin. "It's almost like we have a plan."

"Almost." Charles tucked the gun into the back of his jeans after looking at it for a moment — Harlan assumed he was checking the safety, but he really had no idea. "Harlan?"

"Yeah?"

"The gun is going to be loud."

"Yeah...?"

"So we can't use it unless we absolutely have to."

"Right. But it's not like we have a...machete lying around." Harlan's stomach roiled again. Even if there *was* one, he knew he wouldn't be able to use it. He'd barely been able to deal with the perfectly intact — except for that *arm*, oh *fuck* he'd drained him! — corpse, never mind hacking someone to pieces. He hoped Charles wouldn't be able to, either. He didn't think so.

"Harlan." Charles was looking at him like he was missing something important.

"...Yeah?"

"We have another weapon."

Harlan spun in a slow circle. Nothing. "We do?"

Charles reached out and gently touched his forearm. *"You."*

"Me? I don't— No. Charles, no. I can't. Not again. I *can't.*"

Charles just kept looking at him levelly.

"Even if I wanted to do it again—which I don't—I don't know if I *can.* That was an emergency. And I passed out after!"

Charles laughed, a little brokenly. "Harlan, I don't know if you've noticed, but we're kinda still in an emergency situation. Sorry. That was... It's just, like you said. We don't exactly have a lot of options."

Harlan bit his lip. "We-we could just *leave.* Call the police." Even as he said it, he knew it wasn't an option.

Charles shook his head. "These are some rich, powerful people. If we leave, they'll get rid of all the evidence—including the other prisoners."

Harlan winced. "There are *other* prisoners?"

Charles nodded.

Hopefully Aiden was one of them...or maybe not. "How would they explain the cells?"

"I don't know, but they'd find a way. They'd say it was a themed micro-hotel or something. If they don't just bribe—or kill—whoever shows up."

"Shit. *Fuck.*"

"Yeah."

"It's really up to us, isn't it?"

"'fraid so. If we happen to pass a phone, we can try to call Hamilton."

Harlan nodded. "I tried on my cell, but I couldn't get through. They must have...the signal jammed or something?" Was that a thing? He glanced at Charles.

Charles nodded. "Though, for all we know, that might tip *them* off, too. Where *is* Hamilton, anyway?" He looked around, like Hamilton might have just been standing behind Harlan and he'd missed spotting him.

"He and Morgan are at Michael's condo. We figured, if he'd kidnapped or hurt you, it would probably be at home, not where he works."

"Yeah."

"He's involved, isn't he?"

"Yeah. Big time."

"This...this is too much. Too big. We don't know who else is involved. We can't..." Harlan shook his head.

Charles reached out and took both of his hands. "Hey. We'll do what we can. That's all we can do. We'll get out as many prisoners as we can. And we'll take as many of *them* down with us as possible."

"That makes it sound like we're gonna die, Charles."

"Oh. Right. We'll take as many of them *out* as possible?"

"Better." Harlan shook his head again. "I still don't know if I can—"

"That's fine. We'll figure it out." He gave Harlan's hands a little squeeze before releasing them.

"M-Maybe there's another way."

The ghost wards were carved into the walls—showy, but not all that practical. They'd still have to be painted over regularly—though, Harlan wondered, might the stone act as a kind of sponge for the paint and the power, gather it in the cracks of the carving?

That didn't matter. He just had to break them. Luckily, he didn't have to break the stone itself. He *blinked* and the real wards, not the decorative ones, snapped into his vision. As he'd suspected, there *was* extra power gathered in the crevasses of the stone. Interesting, but still not important.

He'd never intentionally broken a ghost ward before. Did he just have to smear the paint? That seemed difficult, especially on stone. He reached towards it, stopping just before his fingers made contact. *Unravel*, he told the wards. *Let me through. Let me* free *you.*

There was a *snap* he didn't hear with his ears, a spark he didn't feel with his outstretched hand, then several points on the glowing series of symbols lit up even *brighter*, almost blinding him. He touched them one after another in quick succession, then there was a breathless moment of waiting when nothing happened and all he wanted to do was turn around and get back to Charles. He could feel Charles watching him, but he didn't speak. He probably didn't want to break Harlan's concentration.

The glow faded around the bright points, and Harlan sighed. He'd fucked it up somehow. He was just about to *blink* when he saw the *rest* of the ward start fading as well. It finally snapped, the sudden release of energy throwing him halfway across the corridor.

"Harlan!" Charles shouted.

Harlan sat up with a groan — a little sooner than he wanted to, really, but he didn't want to worry Charles. He cradled his head in his hand for a moment, hoping the flashing lights blinking across his vision — with his eyes both open *and* closed — would fade eventually and weren't permanent. Or a sign of brain — rather than psychic — damage.

"Harlan..." Charles repeated, and Harlan could hear how hard he was trying to give Harlan some time, to not let his fear overwhelm him.

Harlan stood and turned to face Charles, dredging up a smile. He doubted it was very comforting, if at all, but it was the best he could manage.

It still wasn't enough—for either of them. He stumbled over to Charles. *The stumbling isn't necessarily a bad sign. I stumble all the time,* he told himself.

Their hands met, and Harlan heard the sound of crumbling rock from behind them.

Charles' eyes were enormous, so Harlan turned, still holding one of Charles' hands.

The carved sections of warding were sloughing off the wall like snakeskin. He grabbed Charles' hand even tighter, closing his eyes. If they were going to be buried when the wall collapsed, they'd be fucking buried together. He wouldn't leave Charles. Not ever again.

After a moment the sound stopped. Harlan's eyes were still closed, and his face was scrunched up as he prepared for impending doom.

"Harlan…" Charles said softly, stroking the back of Harlan's hand with his free one.

Harlan opened his eyes. They weren't buried in rubble. He turned and looked. Actually, almost no stone had fallen, just the narrow band inscribed with the ward. There was a slight dip in the wall, as though someone had run a giant spoon across its surface, but it was almost intact.

He heaved a sigh of relief. It would've been pretty typical if he'd broken the wards only to crush them both, but they seemed safe enough—for now. Hopefully no one would come and check out the noise—or feel the wards' displacement.

"The wards are broken?" Charles asked, clearly trying to get Harlan back on track. He squeezed Harlan's hand too, drawing him back.

"The wards are broken," Harlan confirmed, reaching his senses as far out as he could, trying to get a sense of the whole building. Not an intact ward in the place. *Whoops*. He might've hit it a little harder than he'd meant or needed to.

"What next?" Charles prompted.

"Next we—" Harlan's head snapped back, his eyes wide and unseeing. He was distantly aware of Charles shouting his name and he wanted to tell him to stop before he *really* attracted attention—though these people must be used to a certain amount of screaming and shouting coming from the cells—but it was so far away, so unimportant.

What mattered were the *ghosts*. It was as if, by breaking the wards, he'd set off a beacon and every ghost in the place homed in on his position. He thought it was incredibly sloppy of them to simply rely on the ghost wards rather than sending any of the ghosts on, but it wasn't exactly like they could just call in a random medium without explaining everything that was going on in the building—or the ghosts themselves telling.

And they probably would've been tempted to take the medium prisoner as well.

The ghosts swarmed around him, more and more pouring into the hallway, so many that they nearly overwhelmed Charles' ability, leaving only a narrow void immediately around the two of them.

Harlan's heart sped up and his breath started getting dangerously fast and shallow. It reminded him too much of Samuel Harkness' lair, the only other time he'd seen that many ghosts in one place. He felt thick tears roll down his face, and he wasn't sure if it was his fear—or even *his* emotions at all—affecting him.

"Harlan." Charles was chafing his hand to warm it and get his attention. When had he gotten so cold? He was shivering, and only clenching his jaw was keeping his teeth from chattering.

"Harlan, you're hyperventilating. Your hand is freezing. Come back to me. Focus on my voice, my touch."

Harlan had no idea how Charles could sound so calm. *He'd* been the one being held prisoner for...Harlan couldn't remember how long. Time had gotten distant and swirly. He was there to *save* Charles, but he was the one completely falling apart.

"Right. Right. I'm here. Right," Harlan assured him, not very reassuringly.

"It's okay. Harkness is *gone*. He's not controlling these ghosts," Charles soothed him, accurately guessing at least part of his fear.

Harlan nodded jerkily, taking an unsteady breath in. "No one is."

It came out in a rush, his heart rate climbing back to what it had been before Charles had started talking him down—higher. *No one is.* No one was controlling the ghosts. They'd gathered in such numbers, the most he'd seen that hadn't been intentionally collected by a serial killer, and *no one was in charge of them.*

His teeth started chattering, and he was trembling uncontrollably. He didn't realize that he'd been saying, "Oh fuck, oh fuck," under his breath for...he didn't know how long, until Charles's voice broke through.

"Harlan." He sounded as terrified as Harlan felt.

Harlan didn't want Charles to be afraid—especially when he realized, as he came further back to himself, that he didn't think it was the ghosts Charles was afraid of. He was afraid *for Harlan.*

It took a series of painful clicks, but Harlan finally managed to unclench his jaw enough to force out a single word. "Sorry."

Charles squeezed his hand again. It felt like he was slipping away, even though neither of them had moved. "Are you back with me?"

Harlan nodded. He couldn't stop for a while, but he finally managed to answer using his words. "Yes. I-I will be," he added, more honestly. "I think."

"Harlan, I know this is a lot to ask, and I'm sure you have...mixed feelings about doing this, but... Can *you* control the ghosts?"

Harlan sank his teeth into his lower lip, looking away from Charles. Even though Charles had been the one to suggest it, Charles was pure and good. He shouldn't have to even see Harlan considering doing something so...dirty. "I don't know," he said, the words coming out of him and hanging in the air like they'd simply appeared rather than anyone speaking them.

He very reluctantly let go of Charles' hand and turned to face the horde of ghosts around him. They were pressed as tightly against the thin membrane of Charles' ability as they could get, but only in a semi-circle in front of the cell. They avoided the iron bars.

Charles wrapped both arms around him, filling him with warmth and strength, gently pulling him away from the ghosts until his back hit the bars. The ghosts wheeled and spun around them but couldn't get any closer.

Now that he wasn't quite so overwhelmed, Harlan closed his eyes and reached out to them. There were so many of them, and there wasn't a central source of control the way there had been with Harkness' ghosts, but he could still feel...collective emotions emanating from the horde. Anger was there, yes, but it was a honed, patient anger, waiting for the right time to strike rather than prepared to go off at random the way most ghosts did. They were no longer individuals—or at least no longer *just* individuals. They were bound together, a coalition of their own making, to achieve a single goal—*vengeance.*

Harlan smiled darkly. "That's why I'm here, too." He wouldn't need to control them, and that was a relief, but they were willing to follow him as long as their purposes aligned.

Bright threads of individual emotion shot through the ghost-collective, secondary to the bridled anger—fear, grief, even joy now that they might actually have a chance to succeed, but no malice directed at anyone but the people who had done this to them. Harlan was no longer afraid.

Well, he was pants-shittingly *terrified,* but he wasn't afraid of the ghosts. As long as he didn't try to stop them—and the last thing he wanted to do was stop them. He wanted to *join* them—they wouldn't harm them and might, in fact, even try and keep them safe.

But first...

"Harlan, what're you doing?" Charles whispered. "We've gotta keep moving."

"I know, I know, I know," Harlan babbled, "but I have to... I can't..." He took one step away from Charles, then another, and they were on him. There were so many ghosts flickering around them that he thought it might be hard to single out the one he wanted, but their monstrous connection drew the man he wanted out of the crowd. The guard's right arm—the place Harlan had touched, the place he'd begun draining him—was shriveled and brown, even as a ghost.

Steve, my name is Steve, I went to Saint Philip's Community Preschool —

Harlan shuddered. Yeah. He needed to get this guy—Steve—gone. No time, no energy for anything fancy, for dignity, for explanation. He grabbed Ste—no, *the ghost*, that was easier—by his withered arm. He knelt and opened a portal, so quickly it almost hurt. It snapped open as if the very laws of the universe detested what he'd done and wanted to hide the shameful evidence as quickly as possible. He slammed it shut almost on top of the ghost's head.

He stumbled back, open-mouthed panting. Luckily all the other ghosts swirling around him gave him some space, even though he was still outside of Charles' protective bubble. He hit the stone wall behind him, and he could feel the missing section where the wards had been carved, even as his sneaker slipped on a piece of rubble. He had to catch himself on the wall. He cried out as the rough stone scraped his right hand. It was *good*, though. He was pretty sure he would've thrown up again if the pain hadn't distracted him.

"Harlan?" He heard Charles take several steps closer, but he didn't touch him.

"I'm f-fine. We should k-keep going," he assured Charles, sounding totally fine.

"Right." Charles gave him a long, searching look, then sighed. "Let's go."

"You don't know where the other prisoners are or the best way to get everyone out, huh?"

"Nope."

"I guess we'll just—wait." Harlan held up a finger as the hair on the back of his neck suddenly stood on end.

"What is it?"

"Listen." Hopefully Charles would be able to hear it, too. Hopefully it wasn't just in his head.

Charles froze. "Holy fuck."

"You hear it?"

"*Yeah.*"

All around them, the ghosts had stopped, all looking in the same direction — away from the two of them. And they were all whispering, "*Harlan, Harlan, Harlan,*" over and over again, overlapping with each other in a twisted chorus.

"What the fuck?" Charles hissed.

"I-I have no idea."

The ghosts parted and Harlan threw himself in front of Charles, prepared to defend him to the death. When they'd probably just get stuck there with the rest of the spirits. He had no idea what they were going to reveal, but it couldn't be *good*.

It was so much worse than anything he could have imagined.

"Hi, big bro," Aiden's ghost told him with a sad smile.

Chapter Seventeen

"Aiden," Harlan breathed.

"Yeah."

"*They* took you. Mother — our mom called me and told me you were missing. Aiden, I'm so — "

"Please don't. It happened, and it's not your fault."

Fuck. How was he going to tell her? Selfishly, he hoped he wouldn't have to be the one to do it.

Aiden got too close and vanished.

"Back up," Harlan told the empty air where he had been, hoping he could hear and understand. "You're too close to Charles. His power isn't letting you appear. Back up again."

It took a moment, but Aiden appeared again. "Cool power, Charles."

"Thanks, Aiden."

"What happened?" Harlan asked softly. Not that he *wanted* his brother to have been sold off to the highest bidder for his ability, but at least then he'd be *alive*. Right? Wasn't that better?

Lightning crackled across Aiden's surface for a moment before sinking into him again. Harlan had never seen a ghost with an ability before.

"I didn't let them sell me," Aiden said simply. "Hey. I know where the other prisoners are. Um. The other *living* ones."

The ghosts surged around them, and Harlan could feel their rage, their *fury*. "Please," he told them, pressing a hand against his head and closing his eyes.

"Don't hurt him! He's my brother. He's trying— He's *going* to help us!" he heard Aiden tell the crowd.

The awful pressure eased, and Harlan could think again, breathe again. "Thank you," he gasped.

"Sorry. It's not their fault. They're just…"

"I know."

"What now?" Charles asked Harlan.

Harlan sighed. As much as he hated the thought, he knew what they had to do. "We can't just leave. We have to stop this."

"How?"

"We need…proof?"

"The auction house," Aiden said, silently snapping his ghostly fingers.

"What?" Charles asked before Harlan could.

"There's an auction house upstairs. Where they…"

"Holy fuck."

"If you can get pictures of that and a few other things, it might be enough to take them down, right?"

Charles nodded slowly. "Yeah. Maybe. It's the best idea we've got, anyway."

"You killed the guard," Aiden said. It wasn't a question, and Harlan hated that his younger brother knew this about him.

"Harlan had to," Charles said, a little defensively.

Aiden flickered, his mouth melting into a pool of black nothingness for a moment, curving into a wicked smile. "I know," he growled, his voice almost unrecognizable.

He flickered again. "Sorry. Sorry. You did what you had to do. The other guards will be in the security room. If we take them all out, you'll be able to go wherever you want. There's no auction today, so it should be pretty much empty upstairs."

"There aren't any security cameras?" Charles asked.

Aiden shook his head. "No. They get some... exclusive clients who wouldn't want to be caught on film in a place like this."

"Careless of them."

Aiden shrugged. "It's this way."

Harlan glanced at Charles. Were they *really* going to do this? Kill the other guards—or let the ghosts do it, which basically amounted to the same thing?

Charles was looking right back at him, clearly waiting for him to decide.

Fuck. Harlan didn't have the time or energy for a complex ethical problem. Maybe for some of them it was just a job, but they *had* to have known that the job involved keeping people against their will and selling them, right?

"Let's go," he said as firmly as he could.

Charles nodded.

Harlan wasn't sure if that meant he thought he was making the right decision or just that he'd go along with it. Maybe both. Maybe they were the same thing.

He turned and followed Aiden down the corridor, the other ghosts racing around them like eager dogs.

Aiden reached out a spectral hand and touched Harlan's shoulder, and even through his shirt he could feel the icy chill. "*It's the next door,*" he whispered in Harlan's mind for only him to hear.

It took Harlan a moment, but he had done this before. "*What will you do?*"

Aiden flickered but didn't change. "*We'll...take care of them.*"

Harlan shook his head violently. "*Wait here!*" he thought urgently, almost saying it out loud—but he didn't want to warn the guards.

Already the ghosts were swirling faster, with more purpose. Harlan could feel their control slipping. They *wanted* to hunt. To kill.

"*Please, Aiden, stay here. Don't do this.*"

Flicker. Aiden darkened, his form growing long and thin and twisted. "*You're willing to let them do your dirty work, but you don't want your little bro involved?*"

Yes, Harlan thought, but only in the silence of his mind, not directing it at Aiden. Hopefully he wouldn't 'hear' it. "*Aiden, it's not...*"

"*I'm already dead, Harlan. There's nothing left to protect me from.*" Aiden turned, rejoining the mass of ghosts. They poured down the hallway. A few moments later, the screaming began. Then it abruptly stopped.

Harlan, coward that he was, pressed his face against Charles' shoulder, letting Charles' strong arms wrap around him so he could pretend that everything was okay. The feeling slowly returned to his frozen arm.

"It's done," Aiden said over his shoulder, startling him into letting go of Charles.

He whirled, his eyes wide. There was a spatter of blood on Aiden's arm, and as Harlan watched, it slowly faded, melting into his ectoplasm and disappearing.

Harlan swallowed hard.

"We... We should probably go have a look," Charles said, the shakiest Harlan had ever heard him, even after everything they'd been through together. After he'd been taken prisoner and held against his will.

"What? No! We don't need —"

"There might be evidence in there," Charles said, calmer and gentler now, and Harlan hated that he'd forced Charles to pull himself together again that quickly.

Harlan sighed. "All right. I know you're right." He glanced at his brother's ghost, then back at Charles. "You could... You could just wait here," he told Charles, so quietly he could barely hear himself over the humming of the fluorescent lights above them.

"No. I'm going with you. We're going together." He reached out a hand.

Harlan took it, giving it a squeeze.

The security room wasn't as bad as he'd feared. There were four bodies inside, and they were mostly intact. One of them had a massive scorch mark on its chest, which Harlan assumed was Aiden's handiwork. There was a long smear of blood on one of the walls that Harlan didn't look at too closely. That must have been the source of the blood on Aiden's arm.

Charles looked around, somehow seeming to just take in the background while ignoring the corpses. "Hey, look."

Harlan carefully followed his pointing finger. There was a whiteboard hanging on another wall with a list of names divided by thick black lines and several columns with checkmarks or Xs beside them.

He swallowed hard. *Charles'* name was on that list. He stretched out his sleeve and erased it.

"Harlan..."

"What?" He hadn't snapped at Charles, not *quite*, but it had been close. "Sorry. What?" he repeated, more gently.

"We should get a picture of that."

"Oh. Right. Should I...write your name in again?"

"Nah. This is fine," Charles assured him. "Pass me your phone?"

Harlan frowned at him, but of course they would've taken Charles' when they locked him up. He opened the camera app and passed it to Charles. *Actually...* Trying to ignore the bodies the way Charles had, he spotted a clear plastic box partially full of cell phones. He shuddered. Did they keep them and sell them for a little extra profit? He was about to grab the one on top when Charles stopped him.

"Wait. Let's get a picture of that, too."

Harlan nodded, yanking his arm back like he'd been burned. "Oh, wait. I have your phone. Here."

Charles took a picture, then cautiously reached into the bin, pulled out a phone and turned it on. "The battery's low, but it still works." He shook it. "No signal."

Harlan put an arm around his waist and gave him a good squeeze.

"We should, um... We should take these with us. They might be evidence, right?"

"Yeah," Harlan agreed.

Move move *move*, the ghosts whispered around them.

Harlan waved an arm, sending out just a little of his power with the gesture. "You'll get your revenge," he told them. "But we want to make sure this ends here and now."

Their frantic swirling around the room — pressing oh so tight against the edge of Charles' power, and how long could he keep it up? — slowed again.

"Here." Charles passed him a plastic bag and filled it with the phones.

One of them caught Harlan's eye, and he fished it out again. There was an honest-to-God cell phone charm hanging from one corner of the case, swirling letters that spelled *Camille*. He tried to turn it on, but the screen stayed black. How long ago had Peter said his wife had disappeared? Longer than a cell-phone battery, probably.

Harlan held it against his chest. It wasn't a common name in Ontario, but in a city the size of Toronto, there were probably hundreds if not thousands of Camilles. The odds of the phone belonging to the *specific* Camille he'd been hired to look for were probably pretty small. Right?

He tucked it into his pocket.

If Aiden's phone was one of them, he didn't say it, and Harlan didn't ask.

"Wait," Charles said after he'd grabbed the last phone, taken the bag from Harlan and decisively tied it shut.

Harlan cringed, doubling over as the ghosts' impatience hit him in a wave again.

"I'm going to call Hamilton." Charles pointed at a landline sitting on a desk in the corner.

"Good idea." Harlan motioned again, and the ghosts settled, just a little. Harlan knew they wouldn't wait much longer, but his phone still said *no signal* and they could really use the backup.

Charles frowned. "No dial tone."

Harlan almost burst into involuntary laughter when one of the ghosts murmured, *"Try dialing nine first."*

"Oh. Right." Charles shook his head. "Still nothing. Maybe there's a code or something, or maybe it's just not connected." He followed the cable on the back of the phone to where it was plugged into the wall, jiggling the cord a little. He shrugged.

"Well, it was worth a try." Harlan smiled at him as he put the phone down.

"Let's *go*." Aiden's voice rose above the constant background hum and murmur of the other ghosts.

Go, go, go, go, the others repeated.

Harlan glanced at Charles, who nodded.

"Lead us to the other prisoners," Charles told Aiden.

Chapter Eighteen

None of the other captive psychics seemed to know each other, aside from a few of them having spent days or weeks in side-by-side cells. A few of them spoke only a few words of English, or none at all, but they were willing to follow a group who let them out of their cells and seemed to be leading the way *out*.

Once they'd collected everyone, Aiden led them up a flight of concrete steps to an unmarked metal door. "The auction house is just through there."

Harlan turned. At least a dozen pairs of frightened eyes looked back at him. There was no need to traumatize them more than they had been already. And…he hadn't been able to stop Aiden earlier, but maybe he could now.

"Get them out of here. Take them somewhere safe," he said grimly, without leaving an opening for protest. Harlan smiled. "I don't know if I have the right to do this, but please, listen to your big brother. Just this once. This isn't just me trying to protect you. This is me asking you for a favour. Get them out of here and don't come back." Aiden opened his mouth again, but Harlan just shook his head. "You can scout ahead of them without being seen. Only you can keep them safe."

Aiden sighed, an icy-cold exhalation that felt straight from the grave and made Harlan shiver, but he nodded. "I'll go."

Barely hesitating, Harlan *blinked* and held out his left hand.

Aiden took it.

"If we succeed here...I don't know if I'll see you again." The ghosts were shifting restlessly, but Aiden's focus seemed to be keeping them more or less steady, at least for the moment.

Aiden flickered, just for an instant, with what Harlan imagined was disappointment that he wouldn't actually be part of the vengeance, but he nodded.

"I know we didn't know each other all that well, but..."

Aiden smiled at him. "I love you, too, big bro." He turned away and wrangled the prisoners into a ragged line before leading them away.

Harlan watched until they disappeared around a corner.

The auction house was dark and empty, lit only by a bare bulb on a stand in the middle of the raised platform — stage? — the door had opened onto. The front of the door was painted to match the back wall.

"We should — " Charles began, but Harlan had already let the door go and it closed behind them with a sharp click. Charles tried the discreet handle. "Locked."

Harlan gave him an apologetic smile. "Sorry."

Charles gave his shoulder a squeeze. "It's okay."

The ghosts immediately spread out, filling the large, luxurious space, but they quickly began to swirl and flicker again when they realized there was no one there for them to punish.

Before Harlan could do or say anything to stop them, the first ghost slid through the wall and disappeared into the rest of the building.

Harlan and Charles glanced at each other. While they were still trying to decide how to react, the rest of the ghosts began to follow, first just one or two at a time, then a trickle, then a flood. Within a few seconds, Charles and Harlan were alone in the auction house.

"Can you bring them back?" Charles asked.

Harlan reached out with his power, then shook his head. "There are too many of them, and they're too spread out. And they're *pissed*."

His head snapped around when he heard a distant scream, and he turned to Charles, wide-eyed. "Should we...?"

Charles shook his head. "No. We're going to take pictures of this and get out of here. Then we're going to call the police and give them all the evidence we have against these fucks."

Another scream.

Charles had been kidnapped by these people. It was up to him. Harlan nodded, took out his phone and started snapping pictures. There was an open book on the podium with pictures of people's faces with numbers beside them and a short description of their powers. Harlan felt sick, but he flipped through a few pages and took photos of each one. At least he didn't see Aiden listed with a number next to his image.

There was another scream. That one was even easier to ignore, though Harlan hated himself for it. He looked at the book again. These people were *monsters*. They deserved…

Hopefully there was no one innocent in the building. Harlan didn't think the ghosts would stop until everyone but the two of them was dead.

They both froze when a door on the far side of the auditorium opened, letting a rectangle of light spill inside. A man came inside and silently closed the door behind him, leaning against it.

He looked vaguely familiar, but Harlan couldn't place him, especially once the door shut and he was in darkness again.

Charles' eyes widened and he grabbed Harlan's sleeve, trying to pull him away from the light they were standing next to.

But not before… "Harlan." A voice he knew all too well, but cold, no longer even pretending to care about him. "I should have known this was *your* fault."

"Michael."

"Charlie."

"Don't fucking call me that." Charles had the gun out and aimed faster than Harlan would've believed possible.

"Whoa!" Michael held up his hands. "You wouldn't shoot an unarmed man, would you?"

"But you're not unarmed, are you?" Charles asked, slowly and steadily.

Michael smiled. "No. I'm not." His face tensed with concentration.

Harlan felt a brush of…something against his mind, just for a moment.

"Fuck! Fucking wards!" Michael swore.

That didn't make sense. Harlan had *broken* the wards. "You're…a medium?" Harlan asked.

"What?" Michael laughed. "No, Harlan, I'm not a medium. You really think ghosts — mediums — are the only thing that can be warded against? This place is protected against psychic powers you've never even heard of, which, unfortunately, includes mine. I think you can at least guess what that is by now, can't — ?"

Charles cut him off. "What *is* your power, exactly?"

Harlan was pretty sure he was stalling, but he didn't know for *what reason.*

"Well, I'd love to show you, but..." Michael sighed dramatically. "Not to put too fine a point on it, but I can manipulate emotions." His voice was still a rich purr, but it was only that — a voice. Like he'd said, whatever power had lain behind it was gone.

Charles shook his head sharply, his finger visibly shifting on the trigger.

"Hey, now," Michael said, the first hint of genuine fear appearing in his eyes.

Good, Harlan thought fiercely.

"You were using us. The whole time, you were using us," Charles confirmed.

"Yep." Michael shrugged.

"Why?" Harlan demanded, trying to keep the anguish out of his voice.

Michael shrugged. "I heard that Charles here had a real special ability, but my bosses demanded that I see it in action, personally, first."

"Why are you *doing* this?"

"Obviously I'm doing it for the money." He laughed at whatever he saw on their faces. "What? You wanted some big, long-winded 'I'm evil because Mommy didn't give me enough attention' speech? Don't be naïve." He smirked at Harlan. "Well, more naïve than you can help. Grow up. I do it because otherwise I'd be right there on the auction block with you."

"Why are you helping them… Helping them betray other psychics?"

"Puh-leeze. Don't act like there's some noble connection between all of us. There's no honour amongst thieves, and there's *definitely* no loyalty amongst psychics. Trust me — well, don't. We're just a group of people who have something wrong with us. There's nothing holding us together. And not all of us are mediums, *Harlan*. No one ever wanted me around when they found out what I could do." His hands balled into tight, angry fists. "I tried being 'good', keeping my power under control. It didn't go well." He grinned. "And I realized it was so much easier, so much better, to just *make* them like me."

Camille had the same power, and she used it to help her husband, Harlan spat back silently.

His skin crawled. Somehow it seemed so much worse that Michael had tried to sell a psychic with *the same power* as his own.

Harlan shook his head in complete disbelief at Michael's bullshit. "You took my *brother*."

"Yeah, that was a stupid mistake on our acquisitions team's part."

Harlan shuddered, his own hands clenching into fists. He'd said it so *casually*, like he was talking about sourcing…paper or some other office supply instead of human lives.

How could he not have seen any sign of this side of Michael? Well, aside from the fact that he'd literally been using his power so he and Charles *wouldn't*, but still. It felt like he should have sensed *something* off about him.

Michael shrugged. "We don't like to shit where we eat, so we don't usually take people from Toronto, but I knew you were estranged from your family, so I figured we'd be all right."

"Harlan," Charles said calmly, "if I shoot him, it'll be hard to cover up, and there's a chance they won't find a connection between him and this place."

Harlan risked looking away from Michael. "*What?* Shoot him? What are you talking about? W-We just have to keep him here until the police come. The other prisoners…they'll call for help." He didn't hear sirens. At least he didn't hear any more screams, either.

Michael smirked. "He's right. I'm a rich white man with no criminal history. This won't go well for you. Even *if* the police take me into custody, I'll get out on bail, and then…" He snapped his fingers.

Harlan turned back to him, shocked. "Are you *trying* to get him to kill you?"

"Maybe." Michael shrugged again, looking completely relaxed as he stood there in the near-darkness. He lunged for the door with one hand.

Charles fired, missing his fingers by a few inches. "Don't test me," he growled. "I'd rather go to jail than let you live."

"All right, noted!" Michael laughed, holding up his hands again.

"Harlan." Charles didn't look away from his target. "No one knows you can do this. If *you* finish him —"

Harlan shook his head, hard. "No. Charles! I can't. Not again. Please."

Charles sighed, letting his breath out in a slow, steady stream, his whole *body* centring on Michael.

Fuck. Was *this* his choice? Either let his boyfriend become a murderer or use a power he'd learned from a fucking *serial killer*?

It wasn't a choice.

He leapt off the stage, and for once he didn't stumble. He didn't think he could do this without physical contact. He remembered touching the guard's arm now. For one sick, slippery instant as he ran at Michael, Harkness' horrible words echoed in his head — *"Their ghosts, I can see them, on the surface. They want to be free."* He could *see* the connection between Michael's body and his...soul, for lack of a better word — for Harlan's purposes, his ghost. This time, his eyes open and fully aware of what he was doing, he wrapped his left hand around Michael's wrist beneath the cuff of his white button-down shirt and *yanked* at that connection.

Michael screamed briefly, his whole body stiffening, then going completely limp. He stopped moving, and Harlan could see the exact moment his muscles gave out and gravity took over, pulling him straight down. His right arm was shrivelled, just like the guard's, his eyes wide and staring, his mouth open.

Harlan looked away.

"Harlan..."

He heard Charles start climbing down from the stage, too, and he held up a hand. "Wait. Don't get any closer."

"What?" Charles demanded.

"Sorry. That came out wrong. I want you here — so much — but we have to wait a second. To make sure his ghost..."

"Ah." Charles sat on the edge of the platform, but it clearly took a great deal of effort.

Harlan carefully didn't look down at the corpse of the man who'd shared their bed.

Michael's ghost didn't appear, and Harlan didn't feel it. After a few minutes, just to be certain, he said, "I...I think he's gone."

He stared down at Michael's body, the body he knew so intimately. The *corpse* of someone he'd thought he...loved? Cared for, anyway. Had *any* of it been real?

He was tempted to kick it, spit on it, but a wave of dizziness made him turn away and stumble into Charles' arms. Charles who, as always, was right there when he needed him.

"Whoa. Hey, careful now. I've got you," Charles murmured.

"You always do," Harlan told him, a little dreamily.

Charles hugged him tight. "Always." He shot Michael's body a dismissive glance. "I think we should keep our relationship closed."

"Agreed. I love you."

"I love you, too." Harlan closed his eyes with relief. He could feel that the mass of ghosts had crossed over on its own. Apparently they'd gotten their revenge, and it had been enough for them.

Epilogue

"I've never been to a graveyard before." Harlan signed it as he spoke, for Skye's benefit—they were there with Morgan and *for* Harlan.

Even though they were slightly behind him, Harlan could see Charles and Hamilton exchange glances. Normally Charles would have been at work at this time, but he'd cut back on his hours and delegated a lot so he could spend more time with Harlan.

"Yeah, I know. Irony or whatever." Harlan sighed, his shoulders hunching so far they were almost close enough to meet in front of him. "What do I do?" he whispered.

After a long moment of silence, Charles stepped forward and put a hand on Harlan's shoulder. "Are you asking him?" He angled his head towards the grave.

Harlan shook his head. "No. I mean, I've never done this before. What am I supposed to do? What am I supposed to say?" He'd already set down the flowers they'd brought with them, but nothing had happened.

Nothing had changed. He'd done what he was supposed to do, but he didn't feel any better.

He wiped his eyes with the back of his hand.

"Ah. I think I understand." Charles unexpectedly let go and—even more unexpectedly—sat down. He avoided the strip of fresh, raw earth over top of the grave, settling on the grass beside it. He patted a space next to him.

Harlan's eyes widened. "I-I don't think we're..."

Hamilton sat on the opposite side of the grave, facing them, and smiled softly at Harlan. "Ah-ah. You did say you'd never done this before, and you asked us for advice."

"That's...true."

"Well, we're giving it. Sit."

"Why are they sitting?" Skye asked.

"I'm...honestly not sure," Harlan told them.

Morgan sat close to Hamilton, shielding their eyes from the sun as they smiled up at Skye, holding out their hand.

Skye took it, then shrugged and sat beside them. *"Sit,"* she commanded.

Harlan groaned but plopped down beside Charles. Harlan had never even been to a funeral before, never mind a graveyard, but he'd seen them in movies. They didn't look like this. Still, looking across at Hamilton, he could see a *weight* in his eyes. He'd done this before...more than once. He turned to Charles and saw that same heaviness.

Not that Harlan had been *invited* to Aiden's funeral and not that he would've gone even if he had been. Probably. He hadn't spoken to his parents since his mother's phone call, and he was all right with that. He had a life without them, and clearly they felt the same.

Why dig up the past if you didn't have to? At least he hadn't had to be the one to tell them Aiden was dead.

"Okay. Now what?" he murmured. He looked down, but that meant he was looking at the grave. He looked up at the skyline and a nearby tree instead. *Yeah.* That was better.

Charles wrapped an arm around him and pulled him close, and Hamilton gave him a gentle smile. Which, coming from him, was honestly just more unsettling than comforting or whatever he'd been going for, but it was the thought that counted...maybe.

"Now...it's up to you," Charles said.

Harlan shook his head, a little wildly. "No, that doesn't work for me."

"Right. Sorry. Well, you could tell him that you miss him."

"I do." Harlan frowned. No, that wasn't right. "I...miss you?" he told the spot where a gravestone would eventually be. That was another thing that was different than the movies. He'd been told that the stone might not be ready for six months or more. It felt like it would have been more of a focal point than the gaping brown rectangle of dirt.

He glanced at Charles, who nodded.

"I miss you," he repeated, more confidently. "I miss you a-and...I wish we had gotten to spend more time together." Then he didn't need to look away for approval, he just kept going. "I wish we could have gotten to know each other better." He hiccoughed, wiping his eyes — but unselfconsciously. Everyone here knew and cared about him. "I wish I could've helped you, not just with your death, but with your life. I wish I hadn't been such a fucking idiot and a coward. If I had just reached out to you, I could've helped you with your ability and you wouldn't have been all alone. With *them*.

"I wish you hadn't..."

"This isn't your fault," Charles said just as Hamilton cleared his throat and said, "Harlan—"

"Shut up. Can't you see I'm talking to my brother?" Harlan told them, very softly. He kept his head bowed. He was restless and fidgety. Would it be all right to...? Well, they could tell him if he was doing this wrong. He picked up a handful of dirt from his brother's grave. It was still a little damp, even though the days had been hot. That was how fresh it was.

He let it trickle through his fingers, imagining and also trying not to imagine Aiden's body beneath it. The police had found it buried in a shallow grave behind the warehouse, along with several others—including that of Camille, Peter's wife.

He lifted his head, physically pulling his attention back to the land of the living. "This isn't *right*. He... He was supposed to be the good one."

Charles grabbed Harlan's shoulder and gently turned him to face him. "Hey. Is that what you think? That you're *not* good?"

"What? No! I just..." Harlan shook his head. "He wasn't supposed to have this life. I didn't mind everything I went through as much, knowing it meant he didn't have to." He'd never told anyone that before and barely admitted it to himself in his thoughts. "He was just supposed to be happy and normal. It's the only thing I agree with my parents about. They were right. This is my fault. I never should have answered his text. He would've been better off if he'd never heard of me. I would have done anything to keep him out of my world, to keep him safe."

Hamilton grimaced, shooting Charles a not-so-subtle glance.

"He knows," Charles said confidently.

"What?"

Charles let out a soft laugh, and Harlan frowned at him.

"Sorry. It's just... If anyone knows that he can hear you, it's you, right?"

Harlan nodded shakily.

"He's moved on, right? He's in a better place."

"I'm not sure." He picked up some more dirt, crumbled it, dropped it, then did it again.

Hamilton suddenly stiffened slightly, as though he thought Aiden's ghost would pop up through the ground at any second. "Do you... *Have* you seen him?" he asked quickly.

"Not since...the warehouse." He could see a few ghosts lingering around the graveyard, pointedly ignoring him the same way he was pointedly ignoring them, but Aiden wasn't there.

He threw down his latest handful a little harder than he'd intended, showering the cuffs of his jeans. He brushed it off, focusing his entire mind on that small, stupid task.

Aiden's ghost shimmered into existence, and Harlan yelped.

"Sorry. Hey, big bro."

Hamilton was the first to recover, even before Harlan. "Holy fuck, don't *scare* me like that! What was that about?"

"S-Sorry. He's here now."

"Aiden?" Charles asked softly.

Harlan nodded. "You can't see him?"

Hamilton glanced at the others, then shook his head.

"I don't think he has much energy."

"Do you want us to...?" Morgan offered.

Harlan shook his head. "No. You can stay. *Hey, Aiden. You didn't move on.*"

"*Nah. Wanted to see you again.*"

Harlan doubted that was the reason, but he was willing to let it be. Hopefully Aiden wasn't there because he was still out for revenge.

As if reading his mind, Aiden asked, "*They got all of 'em?*"

Everyone they could link to the auction house with solid evidence, but Harlan wasn't going to mention that. "*Yeah. They did.*"

"*You killed Michael?*"

Harlan closed his eyes, then nodded.

"*You won't get in trouble for it?*"

"*No. No one knows it was me. That I can...do that.*"

"*Good,*" Aiden said, a little fiercely. He flickered for a moment.

Harlan sighed. "*You know I can't...*"

"*I know. I'm ready.*" Aiden spread his arms, closing his eyes and wincing. After a moment he opened one eye. "*What do I have to do?*"

"*Nothing,*" Harlan assured him. "*Well, that's not quite true. I'll open a portal. You just have to pass through it.*"

"*Will it hurt?*"

Harlan remembered the blood sinking into Aiden's arm, and he veered away from that thought before Aiden could see it on his face. "*No.*" Before Aiden could ask, he added, "*I don't know where you'll go, exactly, but it's where you belong.*"

Aiden nodded.

It was really literal, but Harlan just leaned forward over Aiden's grave to open a portal. His hands were trembling a little, but he didn't stop. Warm, glowing light and the scent of lemons poured out of it, and Harlan smiled. Yeah. Aiden was going somewhere good.

Aiden smiled at him, his expression unreadable. At least to Harlan. "*'Bye, big bro.*"

Harlan smiled back, hesitating only a moment before replying, "*'Bye, little bro.*"

Closing his eyes, Aiden drifted closer to the portal, and it gently drew him in, closing behind him.

He was gone.

Harlan wiped his eyes with the back of his hand, a little surprised to realize he was smiling.

Charles took his hand, startling him a little. "Sorry. He's gone?"

"Yeah."

"You okay?"

"Yeah. Yeah, I am, actually." That was a bit of a surprise, too, but it was true.

Charles gave his hand a squeeze. "We can stay here as long as you'd like," he assured him.

Harlan squeezed back, smiling at his family. "No. I think I'm ready to go."

Want to see more like this?
Here's a taster for you to enjoy!

Demon Mates: Demon's Dance
Xenia Melzer

Excerpt

Alerion, King of all Demons, the Mighty Warrior, Defeater of the Unruly, was flat on his back somewhere in a clearing in Canada, trying to comprehend what had just happened. There had been two growls, the nuance less threatening and more possessive, then a dual *"Ours"*, followed by two muscular bodies barreling into him. As he had just been talking to his favorite son Sammy — although he had a feeling Jon would soon join Sammy on that pedestal — the attack had taken him by surprise.

It was hard to hear anything over the excessive sniffing taking place on both sides of his neck, but from what he could discern, people were rather more amused than worried. From somewhere, a *"Well, fuck me sideways!"* drifted to his ears, of no real consequence because the scent enveloping him — raspberries and cream with an undertone of cinnamon and clove — was way too pleasant to be thinking about anything else. The declarations of *"Mate!"*, *"Ours!"* and *"Claim!"* left him in no doubt as to what was happening.

I'm so lucky my mates are shifters! Otherwise, it would be the same back and forth that his sons Dre and Barion had had with their mates, and Alerion knew he could do without that drama in his life. In fact, ruling all demonkind was a drama in and of itself, which was why he tried to avoid it in all other aspects of his life — not that there was so much going on aside from cowing unruly demons and patiently explaining for the three-millionth time how nobody was as sturdy as a demon and, therefore, playing with other species — humans in particular — was forbidden. Nobody could accuse demons of being quick on the uptake.

"Uhm, Declan? Troy? Could you perhaps let Dad up?" Of course it was Sammy, the best son-in-law a demon king could wish for, who tried to end the spectacle. Alerion was of two minds about the sniffing ending because yes, getting to see his mates would be nice, no doubt, but on the other hand, it was also *very* nice to be so close to them.

"I'm not sure they can hear you, Sammy dear." *One of the witches...Mavis or Maribell.* Alerion didn't know them well enough to identify them by voice alone.

"Why do I have the sudden urge to bare my neck?" Jon, on the other hand, was easy to pick out.

"You're not baring your neck to anybody but me." *Barion, growling like a lion defending a fresh kill.*

"I didn't say I would do it — just that I have the feeling I should." Jon sounded part wounded, part soothing.

"What are we baring and why? Is this some custom nobody has told me about?" *Amber, the banshee,* Alerion thought. Her voice was quite distinctive, the screech to warn heroes of their impending death always present as an undertone. Most people couldn't discern it and just found Banshees' voices a bit unnerving, but Alerion wasn't most people.

"Well, I'm always up for a little baring of body parts." That voice sounded adventurous. It had to be

Corrywin's mate, Jon's Grann, the Voodoo priestess. Interesting woman and a perfect fit for his restless uncle.

"As much as I love all your body parts, *ma chere*, I think we should be helping Alerion first." *Corrywin, helpful as always...not.*

"I thought we had to get naked?" Amber again.

"Nobody is baring anything!" Dre, his second oldest son, the lucky bastard who'd snatched Sammy.

"Can somebody explain to me what's going on?" Judging from the harmonious sound, it had to be Emilia, the vampire. Alerion liked her because she was very down-to-earth, despite her royal ancestry.

"It's simple, dear," one of the witches said. "Declan and Troy have finally found their third, and in their exuberance, they have forgotten not only their manners but also to shield their auras, which can be overwhelming, since they are uber alphas — hence the urge to show submission. Declan! Troy! Stop with the sniffing and get up. Your mate must be uncomfortable with both of you pinning him down."

The last sentences were said with a scolding undertone of 'bad boys!', which caused the sniffing to stop. Alerion bemoaned this for about half a second before he realized he was now free to admire his mates.

"What's an uber alpha?" Sammy again, always eager to learn. What a smart son he had gained!

Once more, it was one of the witches answering. "Uber alphas are very rare. The last one was born some two hundred and fifty years ago. They are so powerful all shifters immediately unite under them, which inevitably leads to bloody war. One prime example is Napoleon Bonaparte, the French emperor. He was the last uber alpha we knew of until Declan and Troy came along."

"Wow. Are you planning to do that any time soon? It's just that war is such a waste of lives and time." Sammy was addressing Alerion's mates, who had lifted their heads enough to stare at Sammy, which in turn gave Alerion a wonderful view of their breathtaking profiles. One of them was blond, the other's hair a rich dark brown. Their noses were sharp, their jaws like carved marble and their skin flawless perfection.

"Sammy, we're having a moment here!" the blond whined, his hands still resting on Alerion's chest, which he didn't mind at all.

"I can see that, Declan, but you have to admit that impending war is kind of a serious topic."

So, his blond mate was Declan—which meant the dark-haired one had to be Troy, who was the next to speak. "Sammy, how long do you know us? Three years? Four? Have you ever gotten the impression we would strive for world domination?"

Through the space between his mates' faces, Alerion could see Sammy furrowing his brows. *My son is a such a thinker! And my mates are so gorgeous!*

"Well, you're certainly rich enough to buy large parts of it," Emilia said matter-of-factly.

"Says the vampire with the *very* old money," Amber said, winking.

"So you don't want to wage bloody war?" Sammy sounded so happy.

"No." Declan sighed. "We don't like messes, remember?"

"Uh, almost forgot that. Well, a battlefield certainly isn't the place for somebody who dusts the *undersides* of their windowsills." Emilia grinned. "A trait I deeply admire."

"Because you completely lack it?" Troy raised the brow Alerion could see from his place on the ground. It almost made him swoon. *So beautiful.*

"I guess a battlefield is kind of messy — and unsanitary." Jon seemed to be deep in thought.

"If you wanted to conquer the world, you would tell us, wouldn't you?" Amber sounded suspicious.

"Nobody is conquering anything — or waging bloody war or buying the world! All Declan and I want is to get our mate somewhere quiet with a nice big bed — emphasis on quiet. If you would excuse us?" Troy gracefully got up, offering Alerion his hand. Declan was on his feet as well, staring at Alerion as if he were a bloody steak and Declan was starved. It was nice to be looked at with such hunger. Alerion felt his cock, which had been hard since the moment his mates had tackled him to the ground, twitching.

"Yes, I think a quiet place would be nice. How about we visit my little cabin in Whitewater where we can...proceed." Alerion had tried for subtlety and obviously failed spectacularly, given how everybody gathered around them was snickering. The two witches, Mavis and Maribell, seemed to have their own little film going on in their heads while Grann was shamelessly making out with Corrywin. Sammy stared at them with big eyes — he was still so innocent, bless his sweetness — while Jon smiled at them encouragingly.

"Yes, let's proceed." Troy winked.

Both alphas were still holding Alerion's hands, and he tried to decide which one he should let go of to slice space and time when Dre stepped forward with a long-suffering sigh and solved this terrible conundrum by doing the slicing for him — he, too, was a good son and had brought Sammy into the family after all — and nodded at him. "Have fun, Dad. And congratulations. Declan, Troy, congratulations to you as well. If you hurt my dad —"

"Yeah, yeah, you will do to us what we will do to you and Barion if you hurt Sammy or Jon." Declan was already stepping toward the slice.

"I just wanted to have it out in the open."

"It is. Bye. Enjoy the party." Troy was following his mate, tugging Alerion along. He knew his smile had to be showing all his teeth, but he was on his way to mate with the two most gorgeous creatures that had ever lived!

"Dre, thank you. Barion, Jon, I'm sorry I'm leaving so soon. I'm going to invite you to dinner. Promise. Sammy, don't worry."

They all waved, Jon saying something along the lines of "Finding your mate is the most important thing!" while Sammy was furiously wiping away his tears and simultaneously smiling so hard that his cheeks had to hurt.

"Congratulations, Dad, and have fun! You too, Declan, Troy."

"See you next Wednesday!"

Alerion stepped into the slice in space still holding the hands of both his mates. This day was certainly one to be remembered.

About the Author

T. Strange didn't want to learn how to read, but literacy prevailed and she hasn't stopped reading—or writing—since. She's been published since 2013, and she writes M/M romance in multiple genres, including paranormal and BDSM. T.'s other interests include cross stitching, gardening, watching terrible horror movies, playing video games, and finding injured pigeons to rescue. Originally from White Rock, BC, she lives on the Canadian prairies, where she shares her home with her wife, cats, guinea pigs and other creatures of all shapes and sizes. She's very easy to bribe with free food and drinks—especially wine.

T. Strange loves to hear from readers. You can find her contact information, website details and author profile page at https://www.pride-publishing.com

PUBLISHING

Sign up for our newsletter and find out about all our
romance book releases, eBook sales and promotions,
sneak peeks and FREE romance books!

www.ingramcontent.com/pod-product-compliance
Lightning Source LLC
Chambersburg PA
CBHW020553260626
47157CB00003B/681